10.99

D0293079

Burial Ground

John Richards lives on the south coast of England with his
_____ ovel, following
_____ and *The Darkness Inside*.

Burial Ground

JOHN RICKARDS

PENGUIN BOOKS

PENGUIN BOOKS

Published by the Penguin Group

Penguin Books Ltd, 80 Strand, London WC2R ORL, England

Penguin Group (USA) Inc., 375 Hudson Street, New York, New York 10014, USA

Penguin Group (Canada), 90 Eglinton Avenue East, Suite 700, Toronto, Ontario, Canada M4P 2Y3
(a division of Pearson Penguin Canada Inc.)

Penguin Ireland, 25 St Stephen's Green, Dublin 2, Ireland (a division of Penguin Books Ltd)

Penguin Group (Australia), 250 Camberwell Road, Camberwell, Victoria 3124, Australia
(a division of Pearson Australia Group Pty Ltd)

Penguin Books India Pvt Ltd, 11 Community Centre, Panchsheel Park,
New Delhi – 110 017, India

Penguin Group (NZ), 67 Apollo Drive, Rosedale, North Shore 0632, New Zealand
(a division of Pearson New Zealand Ltd)

Penguin Books (South Africa) (Pty) Ltd, 24 Sturdee Avenue, Rosebank,
Johannesburg 2196, South Africa

Penguin Books Ltd, Registered Offices: 80 Strand, London WC2R ORL, England

www.penguin.com

Published in Penguin Books 2008

1

Typeset in Garamond MT by
Palimpsest Book Production Limited, Grangemouth, Stirlingshire
Printed in England by Clays Ltd, St Ives plc

A CIP catalogue record for this book is available from the British Library

978-0-141-02117-1

To Aidan, my little fire.
To Rachel, my whole heart.

I

The sudden gust of wind booms against the windows like a hammer blow. The people in the bar jump at the noise, eyes running across the painfully fragile glass as if it's about to shatter completely. As if at any moment now the air will be full of flying shards, then masonry, as the storm takes the rest of the building with it. It's that kind of night. The parking lot outside is momentarily painted stark white, the glare from a big rig's lights turning the driving rain into a luminescent fog, an impenetrable blanket of flickering neon around the front of the roadhouse. Then the glow dies and the world outside the glass goes black again, and all the bar's patrons are left with for company is the noise of the elements pounding to be let in. Like massive phantom beasts scrabbling at the walls, their angry scratching all but drowns the faint, crackling country music playing on the radio in the corner. The static-shredded warbling does nothing to make the atmosphere more convivial.

The old man perched at one end of the counter with a steaming mug of coffee shakes his head and says to the world in general, 'It's a bad one all right.'

The barman looks up from the quiet conversation he's been having with a young guy in a slick black leather jacket. The expression on his face says that this sort of opening gambit is familiar ritual territory and his response is an automatic one. On a night like this, well, why not? 'Yeah,' he says. 'Real bad.'

'That shack Banks built to keep his tools in is gone. Totally gone. There were pieces of it blown all over when I left the house. Imagine how far it would've had to blow to make it here. That's a real storm for sure.'

'Banks never was any good with his hands,' the barman says. He's large, somewhere well past forty, built like a leather sack stuffed with rocks, and there's steel mixed with the boredom in his gaze. The lazy arrogance of a big man in a small place. Brown hair worn long in a ponytail, full beard. Lines forming at the corners of his eyes give him a permanent look of distrust. 'That's what his wife said at his funeral, anyways.'

The old man gives the obligatory snort. 'I hear she's remarried down in Florida. Some feller who sells hurricane fencing.'

'We could do with some of that round here if this keeps up.' The barman shakes his head, glances at the windows again.

'Hurricane fencing. Can you believe that? She was a strange one, Marcia.'

'I saw it coming this afternoon,' the barman continues. 'Away down the valley, getting bigger all the time.'

'Like that time she was going to get all those

chickens. Seen something on the TV about them being good for the soil and all of a sudden wanted dozens of them running free.'

'I swear that cloud looked like a goddamn atomic bomb had gone off. Boiling up and angry. And I mean it looked *angry*.'

The old man nods. 'It must be sitting across the whole valley by now. Maybe even further if it's high enough to reach over the mountains.'

'Maybe so.'

The valley has always been unkind. For three hundred years it has never been home to more than a couple of dozen souls at any one time, a handful of unincorporated buildings and a few acres of subsistence farming. Not even an attempt at building a larger, more permanent settlement. The soil is thick, rich wet clay holding fast to the mountains' bedrock. The north end, where the land rises into the near-constant clouds, is carpeted with old-growth forest that has stood since before the lands were first settled. The south, sloping gently away to the plains beyond, is grassland, which turns to marshes at the valley's foot where its twin rivers meet. People driving across this stretch of land on the highway might wonder why no one has ever made more use of it. Herds of cattle. Majestic old farm buildings overlooking rich pasture. But then they'd cross one of the rivers that mark its edges, climb up into the mountain passes, and they'd forget all about it. Save perhaps for a lingering feeling that they are somehow better to be gone, away from the long shadows of the peaks and the strangely bleak emptiness between them. The valley is green the way a cemetery is green and it does not do to disturb the surface of such places for fear of exposing what lies beneath. No one stops for long in country like this.

Townsfolk over in Fairlight or Hornchester don't talk about the valley. They might stop at the gas station there or drop into the roadhouse for a beer on the way home if the need or the chance presents itself, but none of them would ever consider, even for a moment, living there. Some unconscious impulse, an evolutionary remnant lurking in the human hindbrain, tells them: this place is wrong.

The soil is thick, but crops grow poorly, as if the land were suffocating the seeds while they were in the earth. Almost everything built here fails, one way or another. The woods are old and thick but unpleasant walking country, dark and gnarled and uninviting. The twin rivers do not burble, they slither, churning thick and angry against the banks. An unspoken, unformed, centuries-old local superstition has it that no one comes to live in the valley unless no place left on earth will take them, and that those few who are born here had best leave if they're to escape the same damnation as their parents. No one stays in this place, where old sin and years of regret have soaked into the bones of the land itself, not unless they have something to atone for and nowhere else left to do it.

The old man sighs as he repeats, 'Ayuh. It's a bad one. Where the hell's Chris got to? How long does it take to check on one damn dog?'

'Women.' The barman shrugs. 'You know how it goes.'

'How it *always* goes. Maybe we're both gettin' senile,' the old man says.

'You and me? Sure, I'm not as young as I was, but that's uncalled for.'

'Naw, you jackass, me and Chris.'

'You've been married to her since dinosaurs roamed the earth, Will. You should be used to it by now.'

'Bah. I always was a slow learner.'

The barman's still laughing at the old man's joke when the front door bangs open and a bearded guy strides inside, pinching the rain from his eyes with one meaty hand. Keys jangle from the other, half a dozen of them dangling from a fob marked with the Mack logo. He runs his gaze over the place before he reaches the counter. As though he's looking for someone, or making sure there's no one here he doesn't want to meet. Whatever he's searching for, he doesn't seem to find it. Just shrugs as his shoulders relax and his concern passes. The locals repay his gaze in kind, wondering who he is and why he's here on a night like this, where he could be heading. What he's done to deserve a stop here in the valley. He walks up to the bar, drops on to a stool and asks for a coffee.

'Sure, it'll just be a couple of minutes,' the barman says. He turns as a bright, mousy brunette comes through the door behind the counter and drops her keys next to the register. 'Hey, Ashley. You find that sweater OK?'

She gestures at her chest and the blue woollen number that covers it. Moisture is beaded in a V from her neck downwards and she sweeps damp hair back out of her face. 'Yeah. Shit, it's really bad out there. The wind's built up something fierce.'

'That's what Will was just saying. We can hear it in here.'

'We sure can.' The old man raises his mug and smiles, comfortable and easy. Like he's settling into a well-worn chair. 'Nothing like '75 though.'

'Nothing ever is, Will. You know that.'

'Damn straight. That storm was so bad . . .'

Ashley smiles wryly at the barman and whispers a fraction ahead of the old man, 'Harry Dillon's house blew down.'

'. . . the wind blew Harry Dillon's house clean apart . . .'

'Only thing left was the tub.' She winks as the truck driver stifles a smile.

'. . . The only thing left of it was his bathtub, just sticking out of the rubble, full of rainwater like he was planning on taking a soak in it . . .'

'Of course, I'm too young to remember it.'

'. . . Of course, you're too young to remember it. Poor old Maud, too . . .'

'Drowned in the river,' Ashley whispers.

'. . . got swept away when the Easy broke its banks. Drowned, poor woman.' Will's face breaks into a sly grin as he rounds on her. 'And don't think I can't hear you, girl. I'm old, but I ain't so soft in the head yet that I don't know I've told that story plenty of times before.' The barman chuckles to himself and the young guy smiles.

'So why tell it again?'

'For the benefit and entertainment of newcomers like our friends here,' Will gestures theatrically at the truck driver and the guy in the leather jacket, then pauses, his wrinkled face expectant.

'Gene,' the trucker says. 'The name's Gene.'

The young guy follows suit after a moment. 'Vince,' he says. Thirty minutes since he shuffled in from the night. His short blond hair's still plastered to his skull, and only his jacket's no longer running with rain. He dresses smartly, the 'young professional going casual' image the cities seem to love, looking very out of place in here. But try as he might to cover it with an easy smile and a friendly manner, his body language gives him an edge, says that he's not just some white-collar guy out for a drive on his day off. When he came in, he regarded the bar and the warm glow of the gas fire in the corner like a drowning sailor seeing an approaching lifeboat. The bar and its occupants regarded him like a sinking ship seeing one of its rats returning.

'Some audience,' Ashley says, shaking her head.

'Two whole new pairs of ears for you to bore stupid. You going to take your one-man show on the road with crowds like that?'

'Two, ten, a hundred. It's all the same.'

'Depends how much they pay for tickets.'

'Where the *hell* is Christine?'

'She's not back yet?' Ashley asks.

Will waves at the near-empty bar and simply shakes his head.

'She's probably taking time to pretty herself up for you.'

'We could be here all night then.'

'If you're not careful,' Ashley warns him, 'I'll tell her you said that.'

He shrugs. 'You wouldn't be so cruel.'

'I could try. How much you want to bet?'

'I'll take my chances,' Will says. 'I'll give Chris a couple more minutes, finish my coffee, then I'll go look for her.'

Ashley nods. 'Might be an idea to check on the brothers, too.'

'Why's that?'

'To make sure there's nothing they need at their place.'

'They'll be fine. They're always stocked up, those two.'

'They are?'

'Sure.'

'I've lived here nine months and I haven't so much as seen through their windows. They're your cousins and you've lived here since time began. But how long's it been since you were last inside their house?'

The old man's expression hardens. 'A while.'

'So how do you know they're OK?'

'That's the impression they've always given me, being family.' He shrugs. 'They're just that sort of people. You'll understand when you've been here longer, seen a few more storms like this one.'

'Still, in a storm like this, it's best we know for sure.'

Vince waves his empty glass and Ashley goes to serve him as the barman hands the trucker his coffee. Good strong stuff, a hot drink to match the weather.

'I'm Isaac,' he says. 'Is that your rig out there?'

'Yeah. I'm glad I don't have a trailer, not with this wind.'

'You're on the way to a pick-up?'

'Yeah, that's right.'

'Where're you headed?'

Gene pauses for a moment and concentrates on the coffee. 'South, down towards Philly. But not until this storm dies out. Catch that wind from the side and bang, over you go.'

'Is that a real danger? I mean, those things've gotta be pretty heavy. I've seen panel trucks flip in the wind, and rigs with trailers, but never a rig on its own.'

'It can happen.'

'I never knew that.'

'If the wind's strong enough it can. The high sides catch it at the right angle, with enough force, and the wheels leave the road. Then that's it. Nothing you can do but hang on. I don't want to risk it.'

The young guy shivers. 'Quiet tonight,' he says to Ashley. 'Guess the weather must be keeping everyone away.'

'It's never that busy at the best of times,' she says. 'The weather don't make any difference.'

'With quality decor like this?' He waves at the room, but his eyes never leave her. He smiles. 'You gotta be kidding me.'

''Fraid not. What can I get you?'

'It's a tragedy.' He eyeballs the room again and checks his watch, then orders another shot of Scotch and a coffee. Something to take the chill off.

'Meeting someone?'

'I'm supposed to be, yeah.'

'Friend of yours from round here?'

'Yeah. But I guess with the weather being what it is, there's no guarantee he'll show up. If that's the case I'll just have to entertain myself.'

'I'm sure you're good at that.' Ashley turns towards Will, who's struggling into a warm coat, muttering complaints about his creaking joints under his breath. 'I can go check on Christine if you like,' she says. 'I'll drop in on the brothers as well, see how they're doing.'

The old man looks relieved. 'You sure, Ash?'

'We can't have you catching cold and moping around the place for the next week saying that you're dying of pneumonia.'

'Now that only happened once. It's my age. A cold can be lethal at my age, you'll see.'

She doesn't rise to it. 'Give me a few minutes and I'll go.'

'Well, if you insist. Be careful, though, the way that storm is.'

'Don't you worry about a thing,' she says. 'There's nothing out there to be afraid of.'

Lightning shrieks across the sky over the darkened parking lot, flash-freezing the world in place for a second, as a man in a trenchcoat walks calmly towards the roadhouse. In the sudden brilliance his eyes pick out the unlit sign – ISAAC'S BAR AND GRILL – under which some local wit has scrawled, 'Pop.: 6.' He grins to himself and resumes his stride as the strobe-stopped raindrops go back to smashing against the gravel. The wind howls around him, ripped into strange eddies by the storm's thrashing above. His smile has an edge to it, and only a trace of humour. A nervousness, a wariness he's trying to hide. He glances briefly around the parking lot and to the valley beyond, scanning the darkness, then shoulders his way into the bar.

The music on the radio cuts out in a final, triumphant burst of static and never comes back. Everyone takes a moment to glance at the latest newcomer, checking him out. He doesn't bother to return the gesture, just walks up to the counter and takes a seat. 'A beer,' he says when Ashley asks what she can get him. He doesn't look at her, at any of them.

'You're not planning on driving?' Isaac says while she pulls him a pint.

'No.'

'No? Not that it really matters. I can't remember the last time anyone here got pulled over for a DUI.'

'You'd have to be drunk to be out on the roads in this, and even then you'd probably wish you'd stayed home.'

Isaac nods. 'It's pretty bad out there.'

'You don't say.' The man takes a sip of his drink and closes his eyes like he's planning on falling asleep where he sits.

2

Two men watch the figure on the road. He stands on the far side of a short bridge over a narrow cleft cutting into the hillside next to them. An indistinct shape hidden in a plastic poncho beaten by the wind and rain, rooted in place among the dirt and blowing leaves. A man's voice, howling and bellowing like a dying animal, screaming between gusts and the cracks of thunder above. They can't make out any of his words, only the pain, the hurt and anger, contained within them. In one hand, the figure has a naked flame, torn to shreds by the wind but still burning bright and yellow. In the other, something long and metallic that glistens red in the glow.

'What do you think we should do?' one man asks the other, the older of the two. Neither of them make a move towards the interloper.

His companion is silent for a while, then shrugs, looks uncertainly at the first. 'Christ knows. He could be drunk, could be . . . Christ knows. Whoever he is, he's been like this all this time?'

'As far as I know, yeah. I heard it over the wind when I went to check on the hens. Saw him and figured we'd best have a couple of us deal with it if we can. I don't think he's moved at all since I first saw him.'

The figure shrieks a single, drawn-out word and half-sinks to his knees as though all the fight's gone out of him. It could be a name. It could be nothing, a non-verbal expression of some unfathomable emotional torment.

'You want to try talking to him?'

'No.' The second man shakes his head. 'No, I don't want to do that at all. Look at him.'

'Yeah. What if he tries coming to the house?'

'I guess we'll have to deal with him.'

'How?'

'Christ knows.'

The figure whips back the hand that holds the flame and throws something towards them. A bottle, arcing out across the ravine. Both men watch it land well short of where they stand, if it was ever intended for them in the first place. When it smashes against the ground, fire boils across the wet leaves, the flames painting everything a monstrous orange and white. The two men instinctively flinch, even though they're too far back to feel the heat. On the other side of the ravine, they see the figure rise to its feet again and lift the object held in its other hand, slowly, deliberately. The fire dances grimly from the blade of the axe as the man steps forwards.

3

Isaac has given up on the bar's newest arrival and gone back to the young man. Will engages Gene in small talk and everything returns to normal. The barman asks Vince where he's from. He sniffs his scotch, knocks it back and says, 'Baltimore, usually.'

'You're out of your way round here, aren't you? Hell of a drive.'

'Damn straight. I'm staying at a place near Smithford for a few days.'

'And this is the best bar in these parts, which is why you drove thirty miles on a pilgrimage out here? I'm flattered. If I'd have known, I'd have cleaned the place better.'

He laughs a couple of times, shakes his head. 'Shit, if this was the best I'd be gone from these parts as soon as I could.'

'Ouch. Thanks.'

'No, I'm supposed to be meeting someone out here.' Vince smiles, slow and easy, like his teeth have been oiled. 'I've been looking at farms for thirty, forty miles in either direction. Thinking of buying land, getting away from the city, you know?'

'Out of the rat race?'

'Something like that, yeah. There's a man who's

looking to sell his father's old land in the next valley over, and he suggested we meet up here so we can go over the particulars. Look at some photos, talk prices, all that. If I'm interested, I'll take a look at it tomorrow.' Again, the smile. 'And besides, I spent the afternoon surrounded by cow shit and being yammered at by real estate agents, so I figured I owed myself a drink.'

'Looking to buy around here, huh?'

'Yeah. Thinking about it.' He doesn't explain further, just asks, 'How about you ... did you grow up around here? Got any pointers you could give me? Guy like you in a job like yours must know a few things.'

'No, I'm not from around here,' he says. 'I'm from Cincinatti, originally. We moved around a lot when I was younger, though. Why'd you want to move away from Baltimore?'

'I'm just thinking about it. The big city can get you down after a while. Too crowded, too many people.'

'You're downsizing and this is the best you could find?'

'Something like that. It's not so bad out here.'

The barman raises his eyebrows. 'I never thought I'd hear anyone say that. So what do you do? What're you downsizing from?'

'Nothing very exciting.'

Isaac smiles. 'Really? You get dental with that?'

He shrugs. 'I work in insurance. Checking claims,

adjusting premiums and payouts. That sort of thing. Like I said, not very exciting.'

'You've done it long?'

Vince sips at his coffee, about to say something in reply, when the sound of someone yelling comes from outside. The voice is distorted by the storm, wordless. The barman and Gene both turn to peer in the direction of the windows, hoping to see something in the darkness of the lot outside. The shouting gets louder and a figure runs past the glass. A thin guy in a suit slams open the front door, stares wildly around the bar and yells, 'There's an old woman outside, lying in the parking lot. She needs help!'

4

The man looks like a startled deer, eyes white and jumpy. Panicking, not knowing what to do. Isaac stares at him for a moment. 'An old woman?' he says. 'Christ. Christine.'

'She's just lying there.' The man gestures at the door behind him. 'I don't know what happened to her. She's not moving.'

Will jumps off his stool with surprising speed for his age. Isaac hurries around the counter to join him. 'Gene, can you give us a hand? We might need to bring her inside.'

'Should I call nine-one-one?' Ashley asks.

'Let's see what's wrong first.'

The three men sweep out of the door. The guy in the suit watches them go past with his mouth still hanging open. Ashley hands him a glass of brandy, but he barely seems to notice.

Outside, the storm howls across the parking lot, the wind and rain ripping at the skin of the trio like wild animals. Isaac tugs a couple of grass stalks blown from the fields to the south from his hair and swears at the heavens. The words are torn from his throat even as he utters them.

'What'd you expect, Isaac?' Will yells, cupping his

hands around his mouth to be heard over the gale. 'You knew it wasn't sunshine and flowers out here. I didn't realize it was this bad, but still. I *told* you this was a bad one. It weren't no secret.'

If the barman retorts, it's lost to the elements. Then they reach Christine. She's lying splayed out on the gravel, eyes closed, coat and skirt both soaked dark by the rain. There's nothing obvious wrong with her, but when Isaac bends down next to her to check her pulse he sees a ragged cut and a nasty-looking bruise on the back of her neck. Nothing that looks broken, no major damage. Will crouches beside her and smoothes her hair out of her face. Worry pinches his features and for a second he looks his age, worn out and surprisingly fragile. His wife is cold to the touch but he hopes that's just from lying out in the rain like this.

'How is she, Isaac?' he says hoarsely.

The barman stays there for a moment, then scoops his hands beneath her head and shoulders. 'I have no idea. I can't tell in all this. We've got to get her inside.'

Gene helps him carry the old woman into the bar. In the light, her condition looks better, but not by much. Her face is pale, but she's breathing steadily and doesn't seem to be worsening noticeably.

'Christ,' Vince mutters.

They lay Christine on one of the bench seats. Isaac takes a closer look at her injury. 'It doesn't look so bad to me, Will,' he says. 'But then I'm no doctor, so what do I know? I mean, she's alive, right?'

'The worst a blow like that could've done is broken her neck,' Gene says after a moment. 'And if that'd happened, we'd probably have known when we moved her.'

'Jesus. Maybe we shouldn't have touched her.'

'It's just a guess at the worst it could've been. That and maybe a fractured skull, but that's not definitely life-threatening. I think we did right.'

'You guess?'

'I was training to be a vet, years ago. People are different to animals but the principle's the same.'

'A vet?'

'Yeah, not a doctor. And I never finished the course.'

Will cradles his wife's head in his hands. 'I don't think she'll care about the difference,' he says. 'Can you fix her up?'

'Uh . . . I'll try. You should probably get her some dry clothes. She'll get cold like that. That won't do her any good.'

Then the old woman's eyes flick open. Will practically collapses with relief as her gaze meets his. 'Chris, sweetheart. Are you OK?'

'Lord,' she says. 'What happened?'

'We found you unconscious outside. What happened to you?'

She slowly picks herself up into a seated position, unconsciously smoothing out her skirt. 'I . . . I don't know. I'd checked on Brandon. He was hiding in his basket. I was coming back, and then . . . nothing.'

'You don't remember a thing?' Isaac says.

'A noise?' She doesn't look at all certain and her tone makes it sound like guesswork, another question, not an answer. 'Footsteps?'

'There was someone out there with you?'

'There was ... oh God, my keys! Where are my keys?' Christine pats her pockets. Her hands are shaking and her teeth chatter together. 'My keys are gone. Will, my keys are gone.'

Will looks at her, at Issac. 'Someone *attacked* her? To get into the gas station?'

'It looks that way, doesn't it?'

'They could've killed her, hitting her like that. How could anyone do that to an old woman? *Who'd* do it?'

'Jesus.' Isaac shakes his head. 'You'd have to be some kind of psycho ...'

Isaac's voice trails away as he looks around the bar. At Ashley and Vince at the counter. Then the newest arrivals. The guy in the suit, shaking a little but looking relieved as he clutches his brandy. Gene, doing much the same as Isaac, gaze narrowed. The guy in the trenchcoat, still sitting with his eyes closed at the far end of the counter as he nurses his half-drunk pint.

Gene and Will follow his line of sight. The three of them edge towards the stranger, Isaac in the lead. The man doesn't move as they approach, either oblivious or uncaring. Finally, when he's just beyond arm's reach, Isaac says, 'Hey.'

He's close enough to smell the damp rising from

the guy's coat as it dries. Close enough to see the individual bubbles on the surface of his beer. Close enough to see the stubble on the guy's chin, a good couple of days' worth. Close enough to see that the guy has his free hand hidden inside his coat, down below the level of the bar.

'Hey. Hey, buddy.' Isaac edges forward and reaches out a hand towards the guy's shoulder.

The eyes snap open in sharp focus.

5

In my head, the bar crumbles and fades. Metal turns to blood-coloured rust, glass smears and smudges with grime, the air turns foul and rotten. I sit in a room with nothing but corpses for company, nursing an empty bottle with a jagged neck. My mouth's full of the taste of iron. The door swings open, clattering in a wind I can neither feel nor hear, and in the entryway stands a child. A dead girl perhaps ten or eleven years old. Instead of eyes she has empty black holes reaching back into nothingness I can feel like the pull of twin black holes.

She walks towards me, her feet echoing dully on the rusted floor, and there is nothing I can do but sit there and wait for her. She holds out hands dripping with blood as she draws closer. Finally, she reaches up and clasps me by the shoulders.

'Yeah?' I say and look up at the barman, trying to remember for a second where I am, what I'm doing here. The boredom I'd seen previously in Isaac's eyes has been replaced by fear. There's a faded tattoo on the back of one of his hands, but I can't make out the design.

'I, uh, don't suppose you know anything about what happened to the woman outside? To Christine?'

'What? No.'

'Really?'

I shake my head. 'Why would I? What did happen to her?'

'Someone beat her over the head and stole her keys. She must've been out there when you came in. Did you happen to see anything out in the lot? Anyone else?'

Christine's sitting up, looking pale and dazed, but alive. Is this what I came here for? Is this just the start of things to come? If that is the case, she should be dead. I look back at Isaac and realize he's still waiting for a response. Say, 'Look, I'm not likely to attack an old woman then leave her out there in the rain while I stop for a drink, am I?'

'Yeah, I guess,' he says.

'I think you should call nine-one-one. Even if she's not hurt badly, the person who did that to her is still around here somewhere. If they're capable of that sort of thing and they've taken her keys then they're probably planning on going through her house.'

'I know that,' the barman says, but off to one side I see Ashley pick up the phone. 'I just wanted to be sure what anyone might know first. You said you didn't see anything when you came in?'

'No. I didn't see a thing,' I tell him. 'If I had, I'd have came in yelling just like that guy. Anyone would.' I point at the man in the suit. As I do it, I wonder whether he's the one I'm looking for. If he's 'Sam'.

The veterinary student turned trucker leans past

Isaac and wedges his face squarely in front of mine. His wiry red hair is thinning and his beard is the sort that would do a porn star proud.

'You're taking this awfully calmly for someone who didn't do nothing,' he spits at me. Everything about him radiates aggression.

'Hey, hey,' I say, holding up my hands. I don't want this whole situation getting out of hand because some guy has a short fuse and needs to lash out at anyone he doesn't trust. 'Yeah, I am taking it pretty calmly. It's just that I've seen this sort of thing happen before, and I know jack about medicine. So I'm not going to panic and I can't dive in to help. Anything else I can do, I will.'

The girl behind the bar calls out, 'The phones are dead, Isaac. I can't get through to anyone.'

'The storm must've taken out the lines,' Will says from the back of the trio. I don't speak at all, but there's a cold, sick feeling in the pit of my stomach. At the convenience of its timing and the cold air of menace which is now rapidly gathering in the bar.

'Cell phone?' Isaac asks the barmaid.

She shakes her head. 'No signal. Hasn't been for a while.'

'Radio?'

'Nothing works, Isaac.'

The barman rubs his face. 'Nothing?'

'No.'

'Fuck. The transmitter on the hills must be out.'

The threesome gathered around me breaks up.

Isaac picks up the phone behind the bar as though hoping it might have sprung back into life in the last few seconds. From the look on his face, it hasn't, and he slams it back in the cradle. 'Fuck,' he says again.

I should've considered this possibility ahead of time. A place like this can be very easy to close off from the outside world if someone wants to. I wonder who knows I'm here. I've talked to several people about the valley during the past couple of weeks, but I doubt any of them would remember anything about it or be able to say exactly where it was I'd gone. Cut off from those who know me, I could vanish here and it would be like I fell off the face of the planet. By the time anyone came anywhere close to finding me, I'd be bones and dust.

No one says anything for a moment, then Gene asks, 'So now what?'

'Someone'll have to drive to Fairlight and get help,' the old man says. 'While they're gone, we can check the gas station ourselves to see if the feller who attacked Chris took anything.'

'Or if they're still there.'

'Yeah.'

That pause that always follows a request for volunteers, everyone waiting in the hope that someone else will step up to the plate. The urge to get out, to let someone know what I'm doing here, to leave some record of my passing, grips me and I say, 'I'll go.'

'You?' the guy in the suit says from the back of

the room. 'You were probably the one that did this in the first place.'

'Don't let's start that again, fellers,' the old man says. To me he adds, 'But he has a point. For all we know, you were the one hit my wife and robbed my store, and you're just going to drive off and leave us. No offence, but how do we know you can be trusted?'

'You don't. But if I wanted to drive off and leave you, I'd have done it by now without needing an excuse. Why would I even stop for a drink? I'm not that stupid.'

He inclines his head. 'Fair point.'

'Anyway, I've got a full tank of gas and I drive real fast. You need the cops and maybe a paramedic, we can't call them from here and I'm happy to get them. How far's Fairlight?'

The old man looks at me for a moment, then says, 'Twenty miles or so. The next valley along. Once you're over the hills, try calling the cops again on your cell phone. You might be able to get a signal there, without the ridge in the way. I'm Will, by the way.'

'Alex. I'll be back before long.'

No one says anything more to me as I swing out into the screaming night. As the cold air hits me, I realize how greatly relieved I feel to be out of the building and heading away from any trap prepared for me there.

The wind slaps into me like a freight train, throwing

me forwards into empty blackness. I lean in and fight it, walking bowed and stiff to my car, trying to keep my feet on the ground. The rain no longer falls as drops but comes now as solid lines of steel, metal rods lancing down out of the gloom with deadly force. Then there's an ear-splitting roar above and lightning slashes across the roof of the world. The boiling, swirling cloud is painted a vivid emerald-green and I'm looking straight up into the deep vaulted core of the storm. I see explosive billows thrusting out of its walls, pushing and growing against each other like some kind of volcanic bloom at the bottom of the ocean. Thick shreds of dark cloud whip and whirl beneath its base, circling the heart of the maelstrom.

Then the flashes are gone again and I'm inside my car, a piece of shit Chevy I picked up second hand for a couple of hundred bucks a few days ago. Five years and fifty thousand miles past the time it should have been turned into scrap. So far it's managed to hold together OK, but sitting there with the wind crashing against its frame, shaking it from side to side, I offer up a silent prayer that it sticks to the road. That it doesn't just blow away into nothing and take me with it.

The engine whines as I floor the gas and fly east up the highway. The wipers are going as hard as they can and the headlights are on full, but neither makes much of an impression on the rain. Periodically, a green-white flash will light up the whole valley and the accompanying crack of thunder kills all other sound, silencing even the engine, but otherwise I'm running almost blind. In truth, I've been running blind since before I reached the roadhouse. Since I took the plunge and headed out here on a fool's errand.

I curse myself for not planning properly ahead. For becoming so distracted by the whole business that dragged me to this place that I made mistakes. Stupid mistakes that anyone with half a brain would've avoided. No backup, no cavalry waiting to come find me if things turn sour, no one expecting a call to tell them I'm OK. For buying this lousy car without realizing I'd have to try and coax the thing up to speed while the world tore itself to pieces around me.

I shouldn't have come.

One of the periodic flashes shows me running water up ahead, a ribbon of white glowing briefly in the black, and I kill my speed. Ahead, the highway crosses a river that runs down from the highlands at the northern head of the valley. The waters are dark and massively swollen, topped here and there by rips of silver foam. I roll slowly forwards until the car's headlights are able to illuminate the scene properly, wanting a clear look at things before I continue. The bridge is short and low, a simple arc of concrete maybe twenty yards from end to end. The river has yet to break over its top, but it sucks and churns against the base of the structure with a deep, menacing bass rumbling. The concrete looks as though it's shaking with the continual impact of the water and I wonder how long before the seemingly inevitable occurs. Hard to tell with the rain hammering from its surface. I don't fancy having the thing collapse beneath the Chevy as I drive across, so I take a flashlight out of the glove compartment and step out into the storm for a closer look before I risk the crossing.

The wind slams into me, bringing with it the full force of the deluge like it's been waiting to have me back in its grasp ever since I escaped into the shelter of the car. I trudge forwards, hauling my coat close around me, face and ears stinging with the pounding of the cold rain. I hunker down where the road launches out over the water. The noise is deafening here, like Niagara Falls in the middle of a hurricane, and the only slices of what passes for the real world I can see around me are the circles picked out by the beam of the flash and the dull gleam of the car's headlights. I press my hand flat against the road surface and try to sense it moving.

Lightning streaks across the deep green sky above in a fresh and vicious series of bolts, leaping from one side of the aquatic inferno to another. One jagged fork cracks into the ground on the opposite bank of the river, throwing up dirt and smoke like a bomb going off. The boom of the thunder drowns out the noise of the flood for the briefest of moments, and I feel the bridge trembling, shaking and juddering.

Then there's a sudden horrifying lurch and the ground beneath me shifts with a deafening tearing sound like a huge tree being uprooted. I have just enough time to see the bridge drunkenly pinwheel away in slow motion, to see the banks, road and everything for twenty yards on every side of me tear apart and fold in on themselves, to see my car's head-lights wink out. To see everything around me thrown asunder. Then the river roars in angry triumph as I go tumbling down into the foaming blackness.

I shouldn't have come.

6

Cold. Cold so sudden and intense it threatens to lock my every muscle tight and leave me helpless and sinking. There's no light, none at all, and my head whirls dizzily. The immense force of the water has me bucking and spinning, and I can't tell which way is up or down. I'm lost in another world where nothing makes sense and I wonder if this is what death feels like. Already I can feel my lungs pushing against my ribcage, burning for air, and my limbs turning to lead. Something brushes past my face; it might be part of my coat trying to bob clear to the surface. Equally, it might not be, but I kick out anyway. My legs are like rubber matchsticks, my arms trying to claw for purchase against the water as if I'm rock-climbing. Red and white spots dance in front of my eyes and the need to open my mouth, to breathe, to suck air, is close to overwhelming.

And then something hard and rough slams into one outstretched hand, solid and unyielding against the current, and I grab it fast. My arms burn as I use every ounce of strength to haul myself up, towards the surface. My mouth's full of cold, earthy fluid and I don't know if I'm breathing or not, when suddenly there's air on my face and I'm choking out water as

I gulp sweet oxygen down into my aching chest. I'm gripping a thick tree root exposed by the flood as the bank washed away, retching as my gut tries to purge itself of river water. I drag myself up it and along this lifeline, away from the torrent, for as far as I can before it's lost in the mud.

I lie there for a while, face pressed against the sodden dirt, every muscle screaming with exhaustion. My chest is cold and heavy and breathing's a massive effort. My ribs don't want to move. My lungs are poured concrete. But I remember the ground vanishing beneath me and I know I have to get properly clear of the river. Too tired to stand and fight against the wind, I crawl, arm over arm in utter blackness, up the shattered muddy incline the flood waters have made of the banks. Every inch makes my muscles burn with the effort, but every inch is another inch closer to complete safety.

My right elbow pushes against something soft, which holds for a second before giving way with a dull slopping sound. My heart jumps into my mouth as I imagine the ground collapsing again, falling back into the river, and knowing that this time it'd kill me for sure. Everything I am, snuffed out in a moment in the whirling liquid thunder of the Easy.

Then the smell hits me.

Damp, rotten, fungal. Spores I can almost feel lodging in the back of my throat, infesting my body in a way I'll never be able to eliminate. And behind it, a thick, cloying odour, acid like sour milk and vomit. Bile and old meat. An oily sulphurous miasma so wet with vapour that I'll be tasting it for hours.

The scent of death, of a once-living being in the rampant grip of decay, is something you never forget.

I stop where I am and clamp my jaw down against the desperate impulse to throw up.

Then my hair jumps on end and the world turns blinding white as a bolt of lightning slams into the ground maybe six feet away. It strikes with a noise like a flashbang grenade detonating and my eardrums turn to spikes drilling into my brain. I flinch as the thunder's shockwave hits me and, as my senses return, I can hear the ground sizzling as the water boils around the impact site. The afterglow stays burned into my retinas in pure and dazzling white, an instant and perfect portrait of a world without shadows, a world where every detail is brought into sharp focus.

I'm almost at the top of the muddy crater that makes up the collapsed remains of this chunk of riverbank. The tip of my right elbow is wedged into the mottled, bloated chest cavity of a man's corpse, slime and fluids oozing thickly from the point of impact.

The lower half of his body is still wedged in solid earth, so far spared by the swollen river that exposed the rest of him and by the pounding rain drumming from his decayed flesh. And just before the after-image fades, I see the top of another head protruding from the mud a few yards further along.

One side of the dead man's face is a shattered hole, a blackened mess of bone fragments and rotting meat. It's a gunshot wound.

A vice clamps around my stomach, acid fills my throat. I wrench my head away from the corpse and vomit on to the slope, heaving over and over again until there's nothing coming up but burning fumes.

When I finally stop retching and I'm feeling nothing worse than the sick, post-purge wrenching in my gut like pulled muscles, I look back at the two corpses, examining them by the flickering light of the storm.

The ground-beef hole blown in the side of his head may have killed the guy, but it wasn't his only injury. His right forearm is warped and twisted where the bone beneath is broken. His ribcage is strangely distorted and I'm guessing he has at least three fractured ribs. Without proper tissue to support them, the fragments must have broken free and sunk into the stew. Quite apart from the damage I did with my elbow when I crawled over him.

The second body is barely exposed at all, but I can see straight off it's a woman. A ragged, sodden mat of blonde hair clotted with dirt covers most of a face that might have been reasonably pretty alive but which is now just a blotchy and distorted mess. Even in its current state, though, the ugly crevice in her skull left by the blow that killed her is still clear, a deep dark-green fissure in the waxy flesh. Something blunt or heavy, swung with a lot of force. I can't see any sign of clothing, so she's been stripped, at least partially. It's possible that there are a few minor injuries – lines that could be defence wounds from a knife, dark patches that could be bruising – but nothing like the damage the guy next to her suffered before he was killed.

Someone brutally murdered these two people. And if it hadn't been for the storm, they'd never have been found.

7

Six months earlier, I walked away from a police cell and out into the night air a free man. They'd thought I was a murderer.

I wasn't, not in the way they knew, but it took a long, difficult interrogation to convince them of the fact. It was a frame-up, and a clumsy one at that. There were records — phone calls, credit-card receipts, CCTV footage — that gave me an alibi and my attorney a field day with the two cops working the case. Detective Perigo; if he'd used his first name around me, I hadn't heard it. His partner, Morton, let him do most of the talking. Perigo didn't sound happy, but then I wondered if he ever did. Everything I saw about him suggested he was tense, gruff and overbearing as a matter of habit. A jerk. Morton was harder to read. I'd been to the scene after the fact and I hadn't reported it, but that wasn't a crime, and that was that. They'd wasted days looking for me because they were short on leads and lazy as all hell. I'd turned myself in. Faced the music. Danced.

When they were done with their questions, a uniformed cop took me back down the sterile concrete corridors to my holding cell. The place echoed with the unintelligible voices of other inmates, overwhelmed now and again by the shouting of a drunk guy somewhere further within. Sound bouncing and warped like insane whalesong. The place smelled of sweat and old, dead air, the scent of crushed dreams.

It took a long time, but the lock on my door eventually ratcheted back and another uniform took me upstairs again. Perigo and Morton must have finished checking my story because they were waiting for me by the front desk, and they did not look happy to see me.

'OK, Mr Rourke,' Morton said. 'You're free to go – for now. We're not charging you with anything yet. *Yet.*'

Perigo just smiled wolfishly. 'Be seeing you.'

The charges were never raised again, not by the cops and not by anyone else; of course they weren't. There was nothing more to pin on me, and they had only been after me for want of a better suspect. Because they had jack all else to go on, and the real killers would never surface. They'd needed to show some sign of progress, and I'd been it. That was all. Maybe they knew that, maybe not, but it didn't matter.

Mud sticks. Not too badly, and probably not for too long. But it's a stain and a jolt to the character, and you feel it when it affects you. It makes you re-evaluate everything you used to believe about yourself. About the way you live. For me it wasn't just the charges, but everything that came before and around them. Events that had made me look again at what I was, what I'd been. What I'd done.

I had some savings, I had insurance money from the fire that hit my old apartment. I rented a new place, and I just drifted for a while. Let everything slide in the search for that elusive *something* I had lost. The missing sense of having a core, a centre to my being I could depend on. Something I'd given away by choice. Lines that I'd chosen to cross, never to go back. For a while, it felt like being back in the asylum after my breakdown, years ago. The same indefinable feeling of having already passed a fundamental point of change, trying to trace it and understand it through the ripples left behind on the surface, never knowing where it could eventually lead me. Of stepping into a world outside the one I'd known, with no way of knowing what I'd find there.

All horseshit, of course. Last time that happened, the brave new world was one in which my parents were dead and my Bureau career was over. Short-lived existential angst you either get over, or die trying. Naturally I had to adjust and adapt as well as deal with my loss and I had to figure out my place in the new nature of things. But life went on. The world was still the same place when I opened my eyes every morning, and I was still a part of it, like it or not.

This was no different, I eventually realized. What was done was done, but there we all still were, trying to get by. And sooner or later I'd have to deal with that, one way or another.

'You should get back to work,' my friend Sophie told me over coffee one morning. 'Get back to what you're good at.'

'To tell the truth, I'm not sure what I'm good at any more. Not sure how much of it all was just the lies I told to make it through the world.'

'Alex,' she said, 'that's bullshit. You sound like a lovesick teenager.'

'No it isn't. You know that better than most.'

'You're just feeling guilty for things you shouldn't,' she said.

I shake my head. 'If I'm feeling guilty, it's for things I damn sure should be guilty for.'

'It'll pass, and it'll do it more easily if you're busy. Look, maybe Rob could . . .'

'No,' I said. 'No. Not yet. Maybe not ever.'

She pouted. Probably mostly for show, her way of trying to get me to see reason, but I could see she was genuinely upset underneath the act. She cared, and that was something at least.

I shrugged, said, 'Right now it feels like that's all past history.'

'It doesn't have to be.'

'Maybe not, but it still seems like an era that's over. And it should stay that way. I can get used to what's coming, not what's been.'

'This is just some mid-life-crisis thing, you know that, right?'

'That's not the first time you've told me that.'

'Maybe one day you'll believe me.'

I smiled. Didn't feel like it much, but I smiled. 'When I grow the ponytail and start dating the stripper, then I'll start listening to you.'

'Maybe.' She smiled back, but her eyes were full of worry. 'You've got to sort something out at some point, though. You can't live on nothing but air, y'know.'

She was right. I knew it then, and I actually started to think about it properly a couple of nights later. I stood down by the river, watching a couple of storehouses on the opposite bank burn, great twisting streaks of orange and red lashing at the sky like dancers. I remembered feeling that way myself not so long before, everything within turning to ash and flame, remembered how I'd been willing to let the whole damn lot go up around me. How little else had mattered.

And it damn near had all turned to smoke. Nearly, but not quite. There's no mileage in that kind of thinking. You can't stick with it for too long. Either it destroys you, or, more likely, just makes you insufferable to all those who might otherwise have helped you.

The next day I phoned around, called some people I knew in the investigation-stroke-security business. Work contacts, acquaintances. Names I knew from business cards or websites. Friends of friends of friends. My first steps back into the normal working world.

So I found myself travelling to Detroit to trace a

nineteen-year-old girl involved in a relationship with a much older man. He had links to the sex trade, and we were going to extract her from it. It was a simple, honest job. Something I could feel good about, free of guilt or unpleasant moral judgement calls.

For all that, Detroit felt strange. A city not quite at ease with itself. Half-way between a troubled recent past and an uncertain future. A war being fought for its soul. The divisions in the city's social fabric had made it the most dangerous major metropolitan area in America, and I could feel it. The undercurrent of division, tides tugging this way and that. On my first night there, a man was injured in a stabbing at the Holiday Inn where I was staying. The victim was a black guy around college age. The perpetrator was a white man in a suit and tie. He didn't seem to know why he'd done it. He just sat, slumped in the lobby with the staff watching over him, until the cops showed up to take him away. He looked as though he was trying not to cry.

Deke and Ulrich were the other two guys employed by the girl's father for this job. I met them in a diner on Young Street that smelled of old burgers and fresh coffee. Night was coming on and the sky was like burning copper. Deke was a local investigator of sorts; he'd handled the initial task of finding our target. A rough, wiry guy with a voracious appetite for chilli dogs,

'They've got everything,' he would explain to me

later on stakeout duty. 'Lots of protein, enough carbs to keep you running, not too fatty. Practically a health food, pal. And you can't beat the taste.'

I wanted to say something about vitamins and fibre, green vegetables and cholesterol. But I was smoking and I would've felt like a hypocrite. Besides, they weren't *my* arteries.

Ulrich was a big guy, tall and broad. A little obtrusive for surveillance or detective work, but that wasn't why he was here. He was muscle, an intimidating presence designed to put anyone off the idea of causing us trouble when the curtain went up. He spoke with an accent that sounded German or Scandinavian, but he never said anything about where he was from. Never said anything much at all, except when he'd been drinking, and then I could only make out about one word in three.

We took staggered shifts watching the old man and the girl at their hotel, learning his routine, the size of his entourage and the frequency of his visitors. The girl had two minders with her at all times, and never left the hotel, not even their room, unless he was present.

'A guy like this is always paranoid,' Deke said. 'They don't want their property trying to run off before they've been broken and don't have no place to run to.'

'Yeah, I know the sort.'

He gave me a strange look, but changed the subject.

Eventually, the time came to make a move. We decided to do it in full public view in the lobby, where neither of us could cause much trouble. If it didn't work, we'd take them on the road, far less politely. I spoke with the hotel's manager. Said something about quietly clearing the matter up before the place acquired a reputation for harbouring pimps and thugs. Before the corporate office got wind of things. Keep it out of official channels. I made it sound like the situation was the hotel's mess, that the manager's job was on the line, and they seemed to buy it. For now, anyway. There was a little crowd of interested staff, maybe a half-dozen of them, 'working' behind the main desk when the time came to act, all there to see the show.

When the party of four emerged from the elevators, we went to meet them. Cut them off half-way across the lobby. I ignored the three men, addressed the girl directly. 'We're here to take you home, away from all this, Nikki,' I said. 'Your dad's worried about you and he sent us to look after you.'

'Mind your own damn business,' the old guy said and grabbed her by the arm. 'And stay the hell away from ours.'

I kept ignoring him. Made sure their path was still blocked though. 'Do you want to come with us, Nikki? Don't worry about him or his friends. Nothing's going to happen to you.'

She glanced at him, at me. Said nothing, but I

saw her nod, quickly, only a fraction, like she was already bracing for the consequences.

'You sold her to the highest bidder yet, Fuller?' Deke said next to me. 'Were you planning on having her end up like Mary McClellan while you enjoyed the cash?'

I had no idea who he was talking about, but I knew Nikki probably wasn't the first girl Fuller had come to possess like this. The old man ignored Deke. 'I don't have to put up with this,' he said. 'Get out of our way or I'll have Security turn you over to the cops for harassment.'

'Let them,' I said. 'Right now it's not us who's breaking the law. Nikki wants to come with us, so I'd let go of her if I were you.' I held out my hand towards hers.

Fuller glanced past me, probably looking for some sign of support from the hotel staff. Then he nudged the minder next to him, a squat guy like an old-style union enforcer. Slow, though, and I saw the punch coming a mile away. Stepped to the side and crashed my elbow into the guy's stomach to leave him doubled over, coughing. Ulrich stepped up in front of Fuller and the other minder, shaking his head gently, and it was over.

Nikki thanked us when we got out to the car. Then she cried most of the way out to the airport. I didn't ask her what had happened to her, or how things had been with Fuller. Either she needed to talk about it, or she didn't, and I had no need to push.

It was a good job. No blood was spilled and everyone except Fuller went home happy. For me, it was the beginning of a return to the world outside, the long process of absolution, and a small reminder that not everything works out badly, not everything is tainted. A start I thought I could build on.

Then, a couple of weeks later, the note arrived. In the morning post, just like a regular letter. I ripped the envelope open and quickly forgot about the rest of the mail in my hands, unread. Words in hard black ballpoint, short and simple and chilling.

PEOPLE ARE DEAD, it read. YOU HAVE TO KNOW WHAT I DID. YOU HAVE TO FIND THE CROSSES. FIND THEM OR OTHER PEOPLE COULD DIE. I HEAR YOU'RE GOOD AT THIS.

8

The note was signed: SAM. With it, a photocopied map of the middle of nowhere. Just a highway running through an empty valley and a tiny legend saying 'rest stop' circled. The envelope had a remailing agency label on it. No other clue to the sender. No other contents. I felt a shiver come over me, pictured the wildly silly scenario of the sender watching my apartment, waiting across the street, eyeballing my every move.

Was it a joke in bad taste or a psycho's love letter sitting on my doormat? I couldn't figure out why someone would send it to me in either case. It had never happened to me before. If it was the former, it was weird but harmless. If it was the latter, people could die if I didn't do what it suggested. No chance of going to the cops with it; a weird note wasn't something they'd chase up, not without more to go on or bodies already dropping in the streets. And besides, I had no idea if they'd even talk to me. 'Alex Rourke? That ex-Fed I saw on the news, wanted for murder?' they'd say. 'Well, well. And you want me to help you out?'

Why the hell would someone want me out in the middle of nowhere like that? The clever son of a bitch was obviously smart enough not to threaten me but to threaten others. Appeal to my sense of guilt. And for what?

Maybe I should've torn it up, forgotten about it, figured it was just sent by some crackpot as a joke. Stuck to regaining my handle on life and returning to my regular career. Maybe I should've. But I didn't.

I did what I could to research the place on the map. News, crime, reports. In the past five years there were no reported murders or missing persons in the area, no men called Sam in any of the patchy records I had access to, and the nearest crosses were on the outskirts of a town called Fairlight twenty miles away. The valley was a total blank.

The more I thought about it, the more my mind twisted into knots. I tried to figure it for a joke and forget about it. Concentrate on normal, regular, everyday matters and not let it get to me.

And then the dreams started.

By themselves, nothing significant. I'm no flake; dreams are just dreams. But they're a clue to the currents running in the subconscious, and these were classic anxiety dreams heavily laced with implied guilt.

In them, the world around me was riddled with decay. Metal rusted, stone cracked and crumbled, wood rotted and blistered. Always I was surrounded by corpses, never seeing another living being. The only other movement in this strange and alien world was a young girl with dead black holes for eyes. Always coming after me, finding where I was, holding out blood-drenched hands towards me. And always I had the feeling that I had, in some way, been responsible for what happened to her.

No matter how much I might have wanted to pretend the note meant nothing and to go on with life, my own head just wouldn't let it drop. Not while it was possible it was real, that people's lives could be at risk if I did nothing.

9

On the artificial grass of the Kuretich Downs driving range, Lieutenant Aidan Silva stood smashing ball after ball down towards the line of scrub-covered dunes bordering Dorchester Bay like he was hoping to hit a passing ship. The cold salt wind tugged at me as I leaned against the rail next to him with my hands in my pockets, trying to keep them warm. The day was grey and wild, the sky like wet iron and the promise of winter.

'This kind of shit doesn't just happen,' Silva said as his latest volley whipped through the air towards the ocean. The difference between a good drive and a bad drive was lost on me. 'Not like this.'

'Crazies get in touch with cops all the time. You can barely run an ongoing investigation in this country without someone coming out of the woodwork to claim the CIA made them do it.'

'That's different.' He sighted up on another golf ball, then let fly with the club. I lost sight of the ball against the colourless sky; it might have been blasted into orbit for all I knew. 'The goal of nuts like that is always one of two things: either they want the attention, or they have some clever theory and want to show you how smart they are and how complex it all is. This "Sam" of yours wants you out in some place that probably doesn't even have running water.'

I shrugged. 'Something like that.'

'Right, so where's he going to get his attention? There's *no one* around. Unless he lives there, there's nothing for him to gain. And if he was the second type of crazy, where's his clever theory? Where's his fourteen-page explanation in crayon showing you how smart he is and how dumb you are?'

I shrugged with shoulders stiff from the cold. 'Maybe it got lost in the mail.'

'Right.' He smiled grimly. 'And like I said, this kind of shit doesn't just happen. Why send something like that to you, now? Why not to me? Why not to the goddamn White House? People like you and me, we don't get that sort of thing unless some nutcase has just seen us on the evening news.' He glanced at me again, then slapped another ball down-range. 'Although I will say you're a real trouble magnet, Alex. You, you I can believe attract that sort of thing just by waking up in the morning.'

'Tell me about it.' I stared out to sea. I couldn't see a horizon; grey merged into grey. Rain was coming in. 'So what do you think I should do about this? Is there any chance the department could check out the note, get some information on who sent it? Fingerprints, point of origin, anything of use?'

'Sorry, no. It's not worth the time and effort, and

what would we get from it?' He softened his voice, but his next words still hurt. 'Besides, you're persona non grata with the force right now. I don't know if the BPD would look good working with you.'

'I was innocent.'

'They're all innocent.' He looked at me again, brawny face etched with sympathy. 'You know how it goes, Alex. You've got to give it time for people to forget.'

'So what do you think I should do about the note?'

'Forget about it. If it turns out to be something, you can deal with it then. But it won't. They never do, and you should remember that.'

'I can't,' I said, tapping my head. 'It's gotten buried in here. Funny, isn't it, how the smallest things can have such a hold on you? If this thing's real I don't want to take the risk with other people's lives.'

'It's not, at least not in the way you mean. I said you needed to get on the evening news to draw this kind of attention. Have you done any jobs, worked on anything recently that could have put someone after you?' *Whack*, and another golf ball sailed into oblivion to join its friends. 'Revenge, payback. You pissed anyone off enough that they'd want you out, away from any help?'

'I took some time off.'

He played it diplomatically, said nothing and just concentrated on his next drive.

'I had a job in Detroit at the end of last month,' I said. 'The first thing I've done in a while. Apart from that, nothing.'

'You kill anyone?' He looked back and smiled, not entirely convincingly. 'Kidding.'

'No, I didn't. Me and two other guys helped get a girl out of the clutches of a would-be pimp on behalf of her concerned parents. Nothing got out of hand. No violence, nothing. You think someone's after me for *that*?'

'Sure, why not? I'm not a psychic, Alex.' The air got a little colder, the wind tasting of ice. 'Point is, this is the only thing in months you've been involved with. And that note of yours shows up afterwards? Maybe it's nothing, but I'd call that suspicious. You talked to those other guys you worked with?'

'Not yet.'

'You should. And get some sleep, Alex. You look like shit.' He struck the last ball with so much force I thought his driver would snap. The ball seemed to bounce and roll clear past the end of the range and off into the scrub bordering the beach. A cold, lonely rain began to fall, painting the world the same colour as the soulless ocean.

I called Deke when I got back to the car. Asked him if he'd noticed anything happening after the Detroit job. Any payback, anything strange, anything to make him worried.

'Nah,' he said, sounding confused. 'A lowlife like Fuller can't do much even if he wanted to. But a guy like him only gets even with the girls he thinks he owns. They misbehave, try to run out on him . . . Them, he'll hurt. Maybe even worse if he's in a bad mood. Like Mary McClellan. But guys like us, we're not worth anything to him. We're just the messengers. I could imagine him going after that girl's pop, or after her, but that's it. And he's probably too busy moving on to the next one in line. Why?'

'Probably nothing. Some weird tip, I think, but I don't know what it's supposed to be about or who it's from. I was wondering if Fuller was trying to set me up. But if he's left you alone . . .'

Deke thought for a second. I wondered if I sounded nuts. 'I could call Ulrich, see if he's seen anything. But it's all good here with me, man.'

I thanked him and hung up, left with a lot of questions and still only one way to answer them for sure. A way I wasn't sure I wanted to take.

When I got home, there was a dead girl waiting on my doorstep. She had the same empty eyes, held her hands out towards me in exactly the way I'd seen before. There was blood on them, mixing with the rain dripping on to the front step. I stopped and stared at her for a time, then turned the key in the ignition and headed for the airport, Kansas City and the only other person I could think of to turn to for advice.

10

The corridors were bright and cold, harsh and airy at the same time, like the passages of some cathedral to the sick. Voices and footsteps echoed through them, mixed and garbled as though their owners were speaking in tongues. The man in front of me put his papers away when I sat down, then asked me how I was.

I explained the note, the uncertainty I felt about both that and myself in general, the way I'd been for the past few months. I told him that I knew the note was almost certainly bullshit, either a joke or a trap, but that I still couldn't let it go because *what if*. If it were real, I'd be playing with people's lives and ignoring a genuine danger and a genuine crime. Then I added, 'And I've been seeing a dead girl.'

'Cultural transference.'

'What?'

He sighed and adjusted his glasses. 'I mean, it's *always* a dead girl, Alex. In this culture, it always has been. Especially for people who've led the life you have, and who've led it in the profession you've chosen. The white knight. The slain angel figure. The one avenging the other. When your subconscious is trying to push you into becoming involved with something of this nature, it's no wonder it turns to such archetypal imagery to do so. The romantic ideal of something pure and defenceless and innocent to avenge is a powerful one. You're undecided, but your subconscious already knows what it wants to do.'

I didn't need to ask if it could really do that; I'd seen it enough at first hand to know it could. Somewhere in the depths of the building, a voice broke into raucous song for a few bars before erupting into gales of uncontrollable laughter. 'I don't know why it would happen though,' I said. 'I mean, it's just a note and a name. If I had a victim, a photograph, something to fix on . . . I could buy that.'

'It's been a while since you've come to see me, Alex, but I still know you well enough to know that's baloney.' He smiled as a mother bird teaching its child to fly came in to land on his windowsill. The young student began to preen itself while its parent looked on. 'How many cases have you been involved in down the years which have involved dead girls, dead women? How many of them remain unresolved? That business last year, even. You were convinced that the girl — what was her name, Holly?'

'Holly Tynon,' I said.

'You were convinced she was alive. You made that your truth and it ate away at you for weeks. You said so yourself. Because you wanted to chase the notion of the classic romantic lost cause. But in the end you were wrong. It wasn't real and she was just as dead as all the others.'

I didn't say anything, just bowed my head.

'Would you have felt the same way if it had been *Henry* Tynon or *Harry* Tynon, Alex?' he said pointedly. 'Because I very much doubt it. I'm not saying you're a bad person or that there's anything wrong with thinking that way; quite the opposite, in fact. It's entirely natural, practically hardwired into our genes to project these feelings, these needs to protect or to avenge, on to the opposite sex and on to those members thereof who are young enough to fulfil the role of the wronged innocent. To remind us of what we ourselves have lost. Children, to a different extent and deriving from a different root, serve the same purpose in such fantasies of the subconscious. But you've never had children, have you?'

An old ache tugged at my chest for a moment as I answered, 'No.'

'So for you the romantic-knight impulse is the one that remains dominant. You see — or your subconscious tells you that you see — the dead girl for this reason. You feel guilty for all those others you've been unable to lay to rest, and always will, I suspect, unless you find some way of releasing your feelings of responsibility for them. And so your own mind drives you on, to strive once more to succeed where you have failed in the past. Because doing so is the only way to assuage your deep-seated feelings of remorse.'

An orderly wheeled a cart past the room, whistling to himself. The sound bounced off the walls. Cheery, like the sunlight outside. Like the two birds by the window.

'So what do you think I should do?' I said.

'What do I *think*, Alex? I think you should seek serious, in all likelihood residential, counselling for what appears to be a borderline obsession which I can only see worsening, further eroding your mental state, layering guilt upon guilt until you suffer another breakdown or put a bullet in your own head. You have a history of problems with exactly this sort of emotional issue and I think you need to deal with it once and for all before it's the end of you.'

He shook his head and sighed. The two birds steadied themselves and flew away again. 'What do I *know* you'll do? Ah, now that is something entirely different,' he said. 'I know you'll go looking for this imaginary dead girl of yours, or whatever it is she represents in reality. You'll go because you lack the capacity to ignore an unresolved injustice, even one you can't be sure exists. You'll go because the guilt you feel from your past forces you to, like an addict, knowing that each time you do so only makes it worse, but you're still incapable of stopping yourself. You'll go and maybe you'll find the writer of this note of yours, and maybe you'll find the dead they insist are there, and maybe you'll stop them killing any more. But the dead will still be dead and you'll still be unable to bring them back and you'll still feel some responsibility for not having done more sooner or some regret that all the justice in the world can't make up for what they suffered, and you'll add another layer to the pile of guilt in your head and you'll love it and hate it at the same time.'

I wanted to mount some kind of defence, but I knew that he was at least partially right. I couldn't deny the pattern in my own behaviour down the years. And I knew that I would be going to the place on the map, lost cause or not.

'You're a pain junkie, Alex,' he continued. 'Addicted to remorse and plagued by notions that you are in some way capable of preventing every terrible thing in this world from happening, no matter how bizarre or laughable this idea may seem. That is why you seek them out. And make no mistake about it — these things come to you because on one level or another, you want them to. You face them because you choose to, not because cruel fate continues to deal you bad hands.'

A nurse put her head around the door and said, 'Visiting time's almost over, Doctor Kessler.'

The man nodded at her and said, 'Indeed.'

'Thanks,' I said, standing to leave. The two of us shook hands. 'I appreciate your insight, as always.'

'Go, do what we both know you're going to,' he said, waving away my gratitude. 'But please, for your own sake, try to at least take some comfort from it this time. Let go of some of that burden you insist on carrying around with you.'

*

I had plenty of time to waste, no desire to see anyone killed, and I couldn't just let it drop. I hadn't had a good night's sleep in six days and I was feeling it. My thoughts were beginning to jumble, the world reaching me through a grey mist of fatigue. I'd done my share of being riddled with guilt in the past few months and I didn't want to add to it by pretending this was nothing. As for the risk of the note being a trap of some sort, well, the hell with it. I figured if I changed car, dressed and acted differently enough that someone looking for me might miss me on a casual glance, I could get a look at the scene unmolested and maybe smoke any betrayal out into the open. And sometimes you just figure you've got nothing much to lose and no reason not to stick your head over the ramparts, and this was one of those times.

The further away from Massachusetts I drove, the more I felt as though I was passing into another world, leaving behind everything I knew to be real. Heading into the unknown in a blind leap of faith, preparing to face a spiritual test or whatever kind of penance I'd earned for my past misdeeds. The highway narrowed, twisting as it climbed into the highlands. Passing through crumbling towns every ten, fifteen miles, which looked more and more like something out of a Springsteen song the further away from civilization I drove. The colour draining from them to leave nothing but weather-stained russet-brown and cracked concrete. The life of those within them disappearing with it, the people becoming more and more depressed, and more and more depressing. Poverty, collapse, the crushed, dead heart of the American Dream.

I stopped on the outskirts of a small town called Hardwick to fill up my crumbling Chevy and grab an early dinner. It was fast turning to dusk. I couldn't have had more than thirty or forty miles to go until I reached the valley. It seemed like hours since I'd last seen another vehicle heading in the same direction as me; the few I had seen were all travelling the other way. Like driving into a disaster zone while everyone else flees to safety. A lonely highway into nowhere. The diner attached to the gas station was about the size of a toolshed and reeked of old fat and bad coffee. Red and white plastic furniture, the livery of some statewide chain of similar establishments. Most of them, I guessed, better staffed and appointed than this one. It was tended by one man, young and lanky, although I could hear someone else clattering around in the kitchen out back. No chatter, no voices, neither of them talking to the other. Just the ring of metal on metal and the crackle of a radio.

'What can I getcha?' the guy asked.

I didn't fancy my chances with anything much on the menu, but I ordered a baked potato and coffee anyway. Then, since he was the only person I had to share space with for the next hour, I showed him the map and asked if he knew anything at all about the area.

The guy looked at the map for a while, then flashed

me a grin like the grille of a tractor. Said, 'You're heading to the valley?'

'Doesn't it have a name?'

He looked like I'd just asked him if he'd ever met the Premier of China. 'Not round here it doesn't. You say "the valley" and most people'll know where you mean.'

'Yeah?'

'It's the only one that doesn't have a name.'

'Seems kind of odd to me.'

'All the others have names. But there ain't no sense wasting one on a place like that.'

I raised an eyebrow, prepared for the stock local shaggy-dog story I felt sure was coming. 'Is that so? How come?'

'There's nothing there,' he said. 'Nothing there now, nothing ever will be. What'd you want to go to a place like that for? You on your way someplace else?'

I shook my head. 'There's someone I'm hoping to meet there, that's all.'

'Get them to meet you somewhere else is my advice. You don't want to go there.' He leaned over the counter a little. The smile was gone now and his eyes were mocking. I could feel the contempt radiating from him. 'They say the land there don't take kindly to anyone who's not supposed to be there. There's creatures live in the woods up the mountains. They come for you, wreck anything anyone tries to do. Like a proper curse. Best thing you can do with a place like that is to keep on driving and leave it as far behind you as you can.'

'Anyone ever die out there?'

'I don't know. You know how stories go. Could be dozens of people dead in that valley, could be it's all just talk. I never been there myself.'

The potato arrived. It didn't look too appetizing, but it could've been worse. The guy wished me luck and walked away. As he pushed open the door to the kitchen, he looked back at me and said, 'Funny. You ain't the first person to be asking about the valley in here today.'

By the time I registered what he said, the door was swinging closed behind him. I tried calling after him but there was no reply. Even the clattering made by the diner's other employee had stopped. I ate in silence, then waited around for a while to see if either of them were going to return. Nothing. Like being the last man on earth. I dropped a ten on the counter and left without seeing another sign of anyone.

The drive out the rest of the way to the valley was even emptier than before. I felt like Columbus sailing into the unknown, no one for a thousand miles in any direction. Like falling off the edge of the world.

In a strange way, it felt good.

It was full-blown night and howling like all heaven was come to hunt on earth by the time I swung the

Chevy into the parking lot at Isaac's and killed the engine. The valley was dead, dark and empty except for the driving rain and a lingering sense of dread. I'd miscalculated; I could see it straight away. There was no chance in hell that anyone lying in wait for me was going to miss me if they came into the bar. It was too small, too empty, too isolated. Everything was. There was nothing here but a gas station and maybe a half dozen dwellings, and then big stretches of fuck all for miles either side. They could kill me right here and it would be like I'd been plucked from the planet, never to be seen again.

Only two types of people live out in a place like this. Those who were born here and have never known anything better. And those who came here to get away from somewhere or something even worse.

Nothing about it felt right. Nothing at all.

Walking into the bar confirmed my suspicions. A barman built like a Viking warrior, with an attitude to match. A tough guy, big man in a small place. The kind of man I could imagine beating his wife and having a stack of military-grade firearms in his basement, justifying both because 'Out here, man's gotta look after himself.' If I was going to peg anyone out here as a murderer on first impressions, it would've been him. His accent wasn't local; sounded like maybe somewhere out west. He might have owned the place, but he hadn't lived here all his life.

The woman working for him was pretty cute.

Sharp eyes under hair still soaked from the rain. Her voice was backwoods trailer trash but lively and quick. Something that seemed rare enough in these parts. At first I couldn't figure out whether her and the barman might be married, or family, connected in some way beyond the employer-employee relationship. But after a while it became clear the vibe just wasn't there between them. She looked like she belonged here, and equally that she didn't want to.

Everything about the youngest guy in the room, probably in his early twenties, screamed 'stranger'. Leather jacket, decent clothes. Certainly didn't match his surroundings. He was talking to the barman when I came in, but it was pretty damned obvious they didn't know one another. He was hard to read, in part because of the smooth-talker act he was pulling. But when he mentioned working in insurance, looking to buy land and move out here, something inside me told me he was lying. About who he was, about what he was doing here, the person he was supposed to be meeting. Nothing about him sat right with me. I couldn't tell if he really was from Baltimore, but he certainly had an urban air and a dangerous gleam to his eyes, like a big cat when it turns away from the light.

Down the bar, an old guy who looked like Johnny Cash's moustachioed seventy-year-old brother and talked like Perry Mason. Seemed harmless enough, but still — local guy, local sensibilities. Local loyalties.

Guy lives in a place like this for long enough and he starts to become a part of it.

Then the other non-local. A heavy-set guy with a face like a brown bear — nice enough when he smiled but taking on a whole darker aspect, eyes hooded, mouth drawn, when he wasn't. He was twitchy, too. Looked round as I walked in, head turning fast, that threatening mask dropping over his features like a curtain. Something on his mind.

If one of these people was 'Sam', I couldn't put my finger on which it was. I sat there, shut my eyes like I didn't want to be bothered, and tried to catch as much of their conversation as possible. I sat, nursing my beer, and felt weary beyond anything. I could feel my head nodding before the visions started and the bar turned to rusted metal and death. There she was, my dead girl, my siren in the night. She'd just reached me when I was suddenly brought out of it and there were people wanting to know if I knew anything about someone being attacked in the parking lot.

'Sweet horsefucking Jesus,' Isaac says as I walk through the door to the bar. The sucking roar as I shoulder in out of the night has everyone looking at me. They don't stop even when I close it again. I must look like death on legs. 'What happened to you?'

The walk back was an exhausting trudge, sloshing through the rain with every item of clothing sticking to me, the wind still frenzied and the cloud above angry and violent. Every time lightning crackled I expected to be hit. Every time the flash hit my eyes, I saw the corpses' shattered faces again. I'm cold and exhausted and soaked but I manage a wry smile and say, 'The bridge is out.'

For a moment no one says anything and we all just keep staring at one another. I wonder whether it was one of the locals eyeballing me now who killed those people. If one of them could be 'Sam', leading me out here to admire his handiwork. It seems unlikely it could've been anyone from outside the valley; the burial site's simply too remote, too obscure. Even with the reputation the place has in the surrounding area, I can't believe anyone would pick it deliberately, especially since they'd have to hide at least one vehicle while they did it. I imagine Will's old hands gripping the wrench that killed the woman. Isaac's muscled frame jerking as he slams his weight into every blow pounding her husband. Ashley's eyes glinting madly as she pulls the trigger.

But I guess it's possible they're all imagining the same things about me, that I attacked the old woman in the parking lot. Maybe worse. It's also possible that none of them are 'Sam', that he's still waiting out there in the dark. Or that he doesn't exist except on a piece of paper and I'm out here chasing a phantom. That everything else is just coincidence.

'The river's that high?' Isaac says. 'Jesus.'

'Yeah, it is. Anyone got a blanket or something? Some dry clothes?'

'Ashley,' he says to the girl behind the bar. She nods and vanishes into a back room. Pretty much everyone is gathered near the counter, except for Vince and the guy in the suit. I go and find a seat near the gas fire, try to warm myself up. Christine's sitting by her husband at the bar with a rough dressing on her injuries. She's got some colour back.

'So the east bridge is flooded –' Will says.

'It's gone completely,' I cut him off. 'Swept away underneath me when I tried crossing it.'

'OK, it's gone. What about the west one?'

'No idea, but I don't rate the chances. There's a lot of rain out there.'

'It might be OK.'

Isaac shakes his head. 'The Clay Stream's bigger than the Easy, Will, even when the sky's not dropping a million gallons of water into it. If the east bridge has washed away, there's no way the one over the Clay is going to have survived.'

'Not necessarily.'

'How do you figure that?'

'It was built higher up, it's got better supports,' the old man says, clenching a fist by way of demonstration.

'I'm telling you, it won't have made any difference.'

'Someone should check it, find out for sure. Anyone fancy running out there in their car?'

There's not exactly a chorus of volunteers. I'm sitting there, dripping on the floor, hardly a great advertisement for going to look at flooded bridges. And, personally, I've got no intention of trying the second one myself unless there's no other choice. I've had my dunking for today.

Then the guy in the suit stands up, the one who found Christine in the lot. He's fairly young, I guess mid-twenties, with an immaculately shaved head and glasses. He looks like one of those college students who goes straight into teaching after graduation. 'I'll go,' he says.

'Sure?'

'Yeah. What happens if the other bridge's gone? Would we be stuck here or what?'

'Unless you can fly, that's right,' Isaac replies. 'You've got sheer mountains at one end of the valley. At the other the Clay and the Easy join up and head on down to the plains. The place where they meet'll be totally under water now.'

Ashley emerges from the back with an old blanket and a bundle of clothes and weaves her way towards me.

'Right,' the guy says. 'Yeah, I'll go. We should get the cops. And I don't much want to be stuck out here.' He glances at Christine.

'When whoever attacked her is still around someplace,' I finish for him. I don't say anything about the chances of it being Sam, or the chances of someone being killed.

'Yeah.'

'We might not have a choice in the matter.' I turn to the others. 'Was anything taken from the gas station?'

Will nods. 'Cash. Not much. A bunch of things tossed off the shelves. Maybe they took some of it, but I don't know for sure. I think we might've been missing a few things from the pharmacy shelf – first aid, some painkillers.'

'You don't carry any heavier drugs?'

'No, no. Bathroom cabinet pills, nothing more.'

The young guy checks his keys. Says, 'I'll come back to let you know how it looks,' and vanishes out into the night without a backward glance.

Ashley drapes the blanket around me, then catches hold of my right arm and peers at the mess on my coat sleeve, or what remains of it after my walk in the rain. 'What's that?'

'That's the other thing we've got to deal with. There's at least two bodies buried near the river. I . . . stumbled across them when I was trying not to drown.'

Everyone goes quiet for a moment. People look at each other, at me. Ashley gasps and drops my arm like it was red-hot. I look at her expression of horror and I remember the faces of the dead couple. The smell hits my nostrils again and I feel the urge to retch.

I'm cold and wet in a strange place and someone here probably killed those people and buried them in the dirt. A couple of the others see my expression fall. I have no idea what they make of it. Isaac frowns and looks away.

Then Ashley says, 'Really? Dead people?'

'Really.'

'Was it . . . bad?'

'A man and a woman, and they sure as shit didn't die in an accident, as far as I can tell,' I reply. 'They weren't in good shape when they went into the ground and they're certainly not in good shape now they're out of it. I'm certainly not going to be sleeping tonight. So yeah, I'd say that was bad.'

I can't read what I see on people's faces. Shock and worry, sure, but no telling whether it's genuine. Will and Isaac seem to have mastered themselves better than most, but that could be bravado. Don't want to look freaked in front of strangers; a couple of good old tough mountain guys. Stand firm; fear's for wimps.

'What's to say they weren't just washed up with the flood?' Will says. 'They might have been hikers or some other folk caught up in the mountains and dropped there by the river.'

'They're buried. The river just uncovered them. And they've been dead a while.'

'They're probably just people who died in an accident of some sort,' Christine says. 'In another flood in the past, or a landslide. It happens.'

'You don't get a lot of landslides in flat fields.'

'Well, maybe not that.' She looks hurt. 'But some other sort of accident.'

'I'm sorry, but the dead man out by the river was shot in the face. Unless he was cleaning his gun and it went off, that was no accident. Neither was the damage the two of them had suffered, nor the fact that they were naked,' I tell her. 'And like I said, someone must've buried them there. That certainly wasn't a matter of chance. Does anyone own that land south of the road?'

Will places a hand on his wife's shoulder and pulls her gently towards him. Her face relaxes slightly at his touch, and she lays one of her hands on his. 'No one,' he says. 'Not for a long while. It's empty.'

Amongst the murmuring going on around me, I make out Ashley saying, 'Jesus. Who'd shoot a couple like that?'

'How long has it been unused, Will?' I ask.

'The last person to own it was Charlie Banks, but he died a couple of years ago.'

'He died? How?'

'He had a weak heart,' Will says. 'But Banks wouldn't have had anything to do with . . . what you're talking about. He had a wife.'

Which doesn't have anything to do with anything, but I don't say so. 'You're probably right,' I tell him. 'Especially if that land's been unoccupied for a couple of years.'

'His wife's down in Florida now with a guy that owns his own hurricane-fencing company.'

I'm about to ask more about Mr Banks when the front door bangs open again and three guys shoulder in out of the night. Young, in their mid-twenties at most. Jeans and cargo pants, T-shirts and jackets. And all absolutely soaked to the skin. They've been out in the rain for a long, long time and they look half-drowned. Almost as bad as I must've done when I came in.

Isaac turns his attention to them and the spell breaks. He says, 'Jesus, guys. You've gotta be frozen. What happened?'

'Car died. We had to walk.'

'How far down the road?'

'Far enough.' While his two friends collapse into a booth, the spokesman for the trio, a tall, wiry guy with a black goatee and a face like a bad-tempered eagle's walks over to the counter, opens his wallet. His hands are stiff, struggling with cold-tensed muscles. 'Can we get a bottle of Jack or something? Enough to warm up.'

'Sure, sure. Ash, go see if you can find some more blankets for these guys.'

She nods and vanishes out the back again. I notice that she keeps one eye fixed on the three newcomers as she goes, instantly wary of them. Barmaid's intuition, perhaps, spotting likely trouble before it happens. From the looks of them, I can understand why she'd be feeling it.

I head for the restrooms and do what I can to wash my coat sleeve. The stain is oily, the colour of jaundice, and no matter what I try I can't seem to do more than just smear it around, making it worse. Then I strip off and change into the clothes Ashley brought for me. They're not a bad fit; a little loose around the shoulders but a damn sight better and warmer than my own sodden rags. They smell musty and I wonder where they came from.

12

When I return, Isaac is still talking as he hands the newcomer a bottle and three tumblers. 'We'll wait for this to blow over,' he says. 'Then we can take a truck out and tow your car back here, let Will have a look at it, see if he can find out what's wrong. With a bit of luck you won't be stuck here. Nearest repair service is in Fairlight and they might be busy after this storm.'

'That'd be real kind of you,' the guy says. His accent's not local. Southern, I think, maybe the Carolinas. 'Guess there's no sense doing it until the storm's done.'

'Yeah. It's not as if there's anywhere much to go for now, anyway. The east bridge is out and my guess is the west will have followed it by now. So get comfortable.'

'So I suppose anyone coming through is stopping here now?'

'I guess so, yeah. Why?'

'We were planning on meeting a friend over in Fairlight, but he'd be coming in this direction, so maybe he'll show up here too. Guy called Walker.' The man keeps his gaze on Isaac's face as though he's searching for a reaction. He doesn't seem to get one.

'Maybe, yeah. We've had a couple of people come in tonight like you guys. There could always be more. I'm Isaac, by the way.'

'JC. Thanks for the Jack.'

I watch him walk back over to the booth and sit down with his friends. They talk in voices too low to catch while he doles out the whiskey, looking alternately back at the counter and then at the door. Ashley eventually returns and hands them their blankets without a word.

'The Bankses,' I say to Will. 'Did they have a house round here? Something that's still here?'

'Of course. Ain't no one living in it, but it's still here. Why?'

'I'm just trying to get my head round all this. I mean, I don't know the area at all or what might've gone on here. Who everyone is, that kind of thing. I'm sure it's nothing, that I'm just a little dazed after that tumble into the river.' I try a smile. 'I can't keep giving you the third degree; I think I'll go for a walk, try to get my bearings.'

I'm heading for the door when Ashley calls after me, 'If you're looking for a guide, I'll come with you.'

'Are you sure? It's nasty weather out there. Real nasty.' I don't really want anyone following me, but as I say it, I realize it might be useful to have someone with a car. Someone who can hold a flashlight. Mine are now at the bottom of the river.

'Why not?' she says. 'Can't spend all evening cooped up in here anyway.'

'Be careful though,' Will says. 'It wasn't Charlie Banks had anything to do with those dead folk, but I know people who might, and who might have jumped Christine just to rob us. The MacBrides.'

'What?' I say.

Ashley shakes her head. 'Not again, Will.'

'All I'm saying is it could've been the MacBrides. There's no one else round here capable of that sort of thing.'

'If you believe they are.'

'Believe? You can't argue with the damn facts, girl, and you'd know it too, be saying the same as me, if you'd lived here longer. You'll learn.'

She shrugs. 'I know they're weird, Will, but there's weird and then there's killing.'

'And I say they're capable of both.'

She just shrugs, says nothing more.

'What are you talking about?' I say.

Isaac shakes his head. 'There's a family live way up the valley, in the woods past the Foundations. The MacBrides. They don't come down here, just stay on their land. Don't like visitors, either.'

'I don't know,' Ashley says. 'I'm pretty sure there have been times when someone's tried to get into my trailer when I've been there and I guess it's been one of them. Or when someone's tried to look through the windows at night. I hear scraping against the glass and I know someone's tried jiggling the catch before now when I've been getting ready for bed.'

'That might just be one of the brothers,' Isaac

says. He grins, but no one else follows suit.

'I'm convinced they come down here at night sometimes,' Christine says. 'I let Brandon stay out one night . . .'

'Brandon?' I ask.

'Our dog. I let him stay out one night a few years ago – do you remember, Will? He was barely more than a puppy back then – tied up at the back of the station. It was a lovely summer night and I thought he might prefer it out there and not cooped up in the house with us.'

'He doesn't like the heat much,' Will cuts in. 'Even back then. Now he's a big old hairy thing, but he's always hated hot weather. It gets him all worn out.'

'So I left him outside. He seemed happy enough. But then in the middle of the night Will and I heard him yelping and howling. A terrible sound, it was. We went out to see what was wrong. I wondered if he might have found something and hurt himself – a sharp piece of metal or something – and he couldn't get free of it again. But it wasn't. He was lying on the ground with one of his paws over his face and . . . oh, what had happened to him . . .' She shakes her head, one hand pressed to her lips.

'He had scratches and cuts all down his back, Alex,' Will says. 'Like some son of a bitch had whipped him good and hard. And he wasn't breathing right; the vet said he had a couple of broken ribs. Took quite a beating. But that wasn't the worst of it. One of his ears was ripped off. He had blood all down his face, poor thing, and all this torn flesh where his ear used to be. It was horrible.'

'We thought it might have been another animal, like a bear or a coyote. But Will said, no, that couldn't have been it. He hadn't fought with anything, not that we were able to see, and if it had been an animal then it would have finished him off or tried to eat him.'

'There was a stick,' Will says. 'I found it out the back of the station, near where the grass gets longer. It had Brandon's blood on it. One of those MacBrides used that stick to beat our dog half to death for no reason at all, just for fun. They're nothing but bad.'

'You're right about that,' Isaac says, nodding. 'And it's not just animals either. When I bought this place, Peter was clearing his things out and showing me where everything was after the agent gave me the keys. He warned me about them. I was asking him about the Foundations, and he told me to steer clear of them. In daylight, a grown man scared of empty fields. And at night, he said, I shouldn't dare set foot in there.'

'Damn straight,' Will says. 'You wouldn't get me in there for anything. Not after dark. Those sons of bitches can see in the dark something unnatural. Like they've been bred for it.'

'Yeah. He said there were a couple of kids from Fairlight decided to do it for a bet. To hide out in there one night to prove whatever the hell it is kids need to prove to one another. I guess you all know the sort of thing. They went out there in the evening and found themselves somewhere to hunker down.'

'I think I remember this,' Will mutters.

'So Peter's asleep upstairs when he hears this almighty banging on the doors. This is two, three in the morning. Down there he finds one of the kids. He's crying. He's actually crying. White as a sheet, and he's got cuts on his face like he's run into a rose bush. And he tells Peter that they've been attacked. They were hiding in a trench out of sight of just about everything, trying not to make any noise, just hunkered down, when they started hearing these sounds around them. At first they thought it was just animals – snuffling, grunting, moving in the under-growth. But then they heard laughing. Close, all around them. And then, the kid said, a hand touched his head. Someone reached over the edge of the trench, out of the dark and the bushes, and touched him on the head.

'So they ran. The two of them just upped and ran away along this trench. And the laughter kept coming from all around them. The kid said things kept hitting him from behind, like they were being beaten with sticks by whoever was chasing them and whoever was doing it was enjoying it. They were both panicking and screaming and everything, the kid said; and for a kid to admit that, you know they must've been shit scared.

'And then they get separated. The kid talking with Peter scrambled up and away, out through the bushes, but the other one didn't follow him. The kid ran, and he could see shapes like people all over the place, and all sorts of other strange things. And whatever they were they were still laughing like a pack of goddamn hyenas. Then suddenly it changed, and there was all this whooping and hollering like they'd got something to celebrate. They must've caught his friend, the kid said. They must've caught him and set on him like animals at a kill. He reached the road, dog-tired, and managed to run here to the bar.'

'Fucking hell,' Vince says, his voice low, shocked. 'Is that true?'

'Yeah. You should've seen the look on Peter's face when he was telling me this. He said he didn't know what to do. He didn't want to go out there himself, but what could he do?'

'He could've come got me,' Will says. 'Christine could've looked after the kid.'

Isaac shrugs. 'Well, he didn't. He got his gun and a couple of lights for the pair of them, and Peter told the kid to take him back to where they'd been hiding and maybe they'd be able to find his friend.

'He said it was the most goddamn creepy thing he'd ever done. The place was dead quiet, like there were no animals out there at all, and *nothing* – owls, bugs, nothing – was making a noise. There was just the breeze in the bushes. And then, every once in a while, he'd hear laughing or whispering, so close he felt it was right next to him. And here and there he'd see movement, changes in the shadows. Like they were all around him but they were happy just to toy with him, to make him afraid. Nothing touched him or the kid, but he said they knew that they could have if they'd wanted to.

'They found the other one eventually. He was lying at the bottom of one of the old pits like he fell down. Out cold, either from the fall or from someone hitting him. Whatever it had been, Pete couldn't say, and neither could the kid when he woke up. He had the same kind of scratches on him as well. But that wasn't all. First, his cap was gone, something his brother had brought back from Canada. That – well, that he might just have lost, dropped while he was running, and maybe Peter just couldn't find it. But even without that, there was the cross.'

'The cross?' My ears prick up.

'When they found the second kid, someone had laid these two pieces of wood on his back in the shape of a cross. And that *can't* have happened when he fell. They left that on there as a warning, Peter reckoned. You're alive this time, but you could easily have wound up dead.'

Counting coup. A little ritual marking someone as dead, symbolically, without actually killing them. Passing on a message to people trespassing on land that's not theirs.

Or maybe the whole thing's nothing but a half-assed story concocted by the old wino who used to run this place and the cross is just a coincidence. It's not like it's an unusual symbol.

'Have they used that kind of marking any other time?'

'I dunno.' Isaac shrugs. 'Not that I've seen since I've been here, and Peter just told me that one story. He seemed to think that was enough for him.'

'What are their names?'

'The MacBrides?' Will says.

'Yeah.'

'Why?'

'I'm just curious.'

'The old man's called Stuart. I don't know about the rest of his brood.'

'Anyone called Sam?'

'No.' Will's eyes drop for a second. 'I don't know of any Sams out here. Not up the other end of the valley or down here with us.'

'I can't remember the last time they left the woods for certain except to drive into Fairlight in that horrible truck of theirs,' Christine says. 'They simply don't come down past the Foundations these days.'

'Except for the times you talked about,' I point out. 'Creeping around in the dark and attacking your dog.'

'Well, yes. I suppose I mean not that any of us can be sure of. They don't come down to talk to us.'

'What are the Foundations?'

'An old building site, massive thing, in the fields to the north,' Isaac says. 'They were going to put in a country club here, what, nearly fifteen years ago.'

'This place seems kinda remote for something like that.'

'I thought that was the point of them.' He shrugs. 'Some "retreat" for rich types to holiday in luxury at for a couple of weeks at a time. I guess you have to be far enough away from the city for them to think it's worth it.'

I nod. 'True.'

'Anyway, good idea or not, I know they bought up a bunch of land and started putting in some of the foundations, laid electric and gas mains, but the whole deal fell apart. The foundations are still there. Weird maze of trenches and concrete that used to be a construction site. The MacBrides don't own them, but . . . well, we don't go there. Some of them do, like I said.'

'Stop trying to scare him,' Ashley says as she goes to fetch her coat. 'There's nothing out there. Not really.'

As Ashley hauls on her jacket I see her eyes flick towards the three newcomers again. Her expression is nervous, gaze wary and cautious. When I follow her towards the door, I catch snatches of their conversation. *Why here? . . . damn water . . . money . . . turn tail and run . . .*

I stop by their booth. Try a friendly smile. 'Pardon me for asking, but none of you guys would be called Sam by any chance, would you?'

'What's it matter to you?' JC says. His eyes are hard and everything about him screams 'go away'. None of them react to the name.

'I'm just here answering a personal ad. Guy called Sam. Bit of a blind date, y'know?'

'Any of us *look* like fags to you?'

I just smile again, knowingly. Let that answer his question for him. One of them seems to pick up on the suggestion and finds it funny. He grins and digs his elbow into the ribs of the guy next to him, who hisses, 'Shut the fuck up, Spin. You want me to break your fucking nose?'

'Just kidding, Craig, man. Say, you sure your middle name ain't Sam? Fine figure of a guy like you . . .'

JC silences them with a look, then watches me all the way to the door. I can see the bar's lights catch on something underneath his jacket as I turn to leave.

13

We duck out into the night. Ashley swears and hunkers down into her coat as the rain hits her again like a wall of water. I've been soaked once already and I'm getting used to it. The wind is almost constant, racing past us and up, away into the heart of the storm. As we struggle across the parking lot there's a squealing noise like a thousand nails dragging down a thousand chalkboards and a buckled, twisted sheet of corrugated iron arcs past us from one of the old outbuildings near the bar and vanishes into the black. Even though it's not that close, Ashley ducks. She looks at me and shouts something that gets lost on the wind.

We're scurrying across the highway, the elements tearing at the blacktop with a whirling shriek, when the first lightning sets the storm alight. Ashley stares, hypnotized, at the rotating mass of deep green and black and its tattered daughters above us. Between gusts I hear her murmur, 'Jesus. Would you look at that.'

'Yeah,' I shout back.

'It's like something out of the Apocalypse.'

I grab her by the shoulder and steer her in the direction of the roadside and the scant shelter offered by the bushes. 'Let's just hope it doesn't get any worse, huh?'

She glances at me. 'How could it get any worse?'

'The bar could blow away. We could all be killed by flying debris.'

'Nice.'

She pulls a flashlight out of her pocket and scans the undergrowth as we push into the night. I see nothing but rippling black shapes, leaves whipping to and fro like moths disturbed by the light. I guess they're enough for her to navigate by. Around us, the valley is almost entirely dark. The bar and gas station glow steadily in the gloom, but aside from these two hollow shelters in the middle of the void there's barely a glimmer. A single nightlight at the door of a trailer, half hidden in the scrub, perhaps. The cat's eye glint of a lamp left shining in the windows of one of the handful of buildings out here. Tiny scraps of civilization dotted around pure blackened chaos. Ashley seems alert, eyes darting from side to side, watching for something, anything.

We walk maybe four hundred yards along the road before Ashley steers me off to the left, on to a badly overgrown dirt track surrounded by tall grass. 'The Bankses' old house is down here,' she says in a brief break in the storm.

The track runs for no more than fifty yards, rising slowly, until a final bend climbing a thick earth bank. At the top, the house itself comes into view. Two low storeys of battered wood and thin aluminium sagging at one end, its front door locked with a rusting padlock. Beyond, empty pasture split here and there in the flickering storm light by dark shapes; trees, farming structures, junk, figures so indistinct it's as though a race of giants are marching through the fields towards us. I can believe it.

The padlock's strong, but the nails holding the chain in place are less so, and then we're inside. For a moment, the comparative silence is absolute and the storm is shut out completely. Then my hearing adjusts and the bass rumbling and rattling comes back with a muted vengeance, tugging fitfully at the deserted structure.

'That's better,' I say, try a friendly smile at Ashley. She's not looking at me but running the light around the room we're standing in, still scattered with the last few remnants of someone else's life. A couple of boxes, a faded list discarded on the floor, a small bookshelf too broken or bulky to consider taking. Chilled air smelling of fresh damp. Windblown dirt and shreds of grass plaster the window next to me, stuck, twitching, to the panes.

'You want to look around?' Ashley says. She doesn't sound keen.

'Might as well.'

She sticks close behind me, working the flashlight, as we wander around the desolate building. The wind booms against the walls and dust drops from the ceiling. The former front room at the entrance doesn't seem to have been touched since Mrs Banks moved away with her hurricane-fencing salesman. The fire's dead and cold and the room feels abandoned. The kitchen at the back of the house looks much the same, but there's something out of place. A smell like milk gone bad, faint but there, hovering on the edge of the olfactory horizon. Nothing in the room to produce it, though.

The light pans quickly around the room. Ashley says, 'Nothing here.'

'No.'

Another gust of wind tugs at the building, juddering the windows and setting the back door rattling in its frame. I try the handle, expecting another padlock, no luck, but it swings inwards with only a groan of protest.

'Unlocked,' I say, feeling my palms twitch as I shut it again. No one locks only one door. Someone's been here since the house was abandoned. Sam? It'd make a great hideaway if it was. 'Was it left like this?'

'I don't know.'

I walk over to the only other door in the kitchen, listen at the wood. Nothing apart from the sound of the structure as it creaks and shifts with the battering it's taking. The smell's stronger here though, wafting out from under the door. I look back at Ashley. She's holding the flash high, like she's ready to hit someone with it if they come bursting out of hiding. Almost cop style.

No one jumps out when I open the door and look at what used to be the dining room beyond, but the air turns worse, sticks in the back of my throat like tar. In the beam of the flashlight, I can see a small drift of trash against the far wall. A bundle of clothing near by.

Dark stains on the floor. Dried blood.

14

The trash is a mixture of paper, food wrappers, empty bottles and a couple of porno magazines. I poke through them with the end of a ballpoint. It's this month's date on the magazines. In the corner, there are tufts of what look like hair or fur, clumps matted with blood. I can't tell what it is exactly, but it doesn't look human. A dog, maybe, or a rabbit. There's more of it by the dark stains on the woodwork, which are definitely blood, but dry. Quite a lot of it, too. The clothing pile looks to be a complete set of men's clothing – jeans, shirt, sweater – speckled here and there with more blood.

It looks as though someone was staying here until recently. They killed an animal – tore it to shreds, almost, to judge by the remains – then changed and left rather than clean up their hideout, either eating the animal or taking it with them. I think about Sam and his promises of more people to die. I wonder if he was staying here when he wrote that note. If this was like what happened to Will's dog, Brandon, taken to the extreme.

Ashley looks at me like she's trying to read my mind. 'Interesting,' I say.

'*Interesting?* Disgusting, more like. Why're you here, mister?'

'Alex. I'm looking for a guy called Sam. You know anyone by that name in the valley?'

She shakes her head.

'It looks like someone's been staying here or, at least, visiting regularly. Maybe it was him.' I shrug. 'I don't know. Are there any crosses in the valley? That's the only other thing I know to look for.'

'I don't think so.'

We leave the room and go to check the upper storey. It's a little cramped, rooms wedged up against the pitch of the ceilings and thoroughly riddled with damp in places where the roof is beginning to collapse.

'You can't get many nights like tonight out here,' I say to Ashley. In the glimmer of the flashlight she looks even mousier than she did in the bar. Small button nose, soft, delicate features under a tousled bob of light brown hair. She can't be older than her early twenties and she smells like rain.

'Do you mean the storm, or everything else?'

'Take your pick.'

She laughs once. 'Yeah, it's a lot different to anything I've seen since I started working here.'

'You weren't always local?'

'No, not really.'

'I had you pegged as some relative of Isaac's.'

'Not quite. I grew up in the next valley across. But a relative of mine used to live near here. My uncle David.'

'Yeah?'

'It was him set me up with the job at the bar and

somewhere to stay last winter after my divorce. I needed it.' She shakes her head, stares off into nothing much.

'He's not around now? Is he a friend of Isaac's?'

'He didn't live out here all the time, but he knew Isaac, sure. Hard not to, somewhere this small.'

'You're talking about him in the past – "didn't", "knew". What happened?'

'My uncle David had a stroke about a month after I moved,' she says. 'He's in a nursing home down in Virginia where his ex-wife lives. She keeps an eye on him, I think. I don't get much chance to go down to visit him.'

Lightning arcs in the scrap of pasture I can see through the bedroom window. The land around is blanched and laid bare for a moment, chaos-tossed abstract shapes bleached of colour. The upper storey doesn't seem to have been touched by anyone in months. The dust and grime have been undisturbed for ages.

'So you came back out here after your divorce?'

'Uh-huh. Great place to wind up, huh?'

'Shit, you must've gotten killed in the settlement. He got the house, the yacht and the Ferrari, huh?' I wink at her, let her know I'm kidding.

She laughs. 'I wish we'd had all that to start with. At least I could have had some fun for a while. Got something out of it.'

'No such luck?'

'Yeah, you might say that. The whole thing was a

dumb idea from start to finish. He was a nice enough guy, at least when we first met. But I never really wanted him or liked him enough to marry him.'

'Seriously?' I raise my eyebrows. 'You married a guy you didn't like enough to marry.'

'Yeah.' Ashley laughs again. 'Sounds kinda stupid, doesn't it?'

'I didn't want to have to say it that way, but yeah, it does.'

'Well, I had my reasons.'

'You'd have to.'

'One thing I was sure about when I left high school and started doing the adult thing was that I didn't want to be stuck here if I could help it. So many people get that way, y'know? So many people just end up staying. They talk about leaving, but they never manage it.'

'Yeah, I know the sort of thing.' I nod. We move into the last room on this floor. There's still been nothing up here to compare with what we found in the dining room. No more sign of the anonymous visitor. 'I've seen it happen often enough. Places like this have a strange gravity well of their own.'

'Yeah?' she says.

'Grew up in a tiny place at the unfashionable end of Maine. I got out of there as soon as I could, but that didn't involve marriage. I just got a job down south. You went with the aisle-and-a-cake idea, I guess.'

'Yeah. A few years after high school, I met this

guy, Kevin. He seemed nice enough, but more importantly he had plans. He was going to get a job working at a friend's store in Oklahoma City. So we could move down there, save up to buy a little place of our own, have a family and stay away from the place we'd both grown up. Sweet deal.'

'I can understand that. Except for the whole not liking him enough to marry him side of things.'

She shrugs. 'Yeah, well, I didn't say I'd thought through the plan all that well.'

'How come it fell through?'

'We got married and we moved, and that was all fine. Kevin started work, I found a job at a lingerie store . . .'

'Really? Lingerie?'

'Uh-huh.' She grins. 'Shocked that us mountain girls know about that sort of thing? Think it's all thermal underwear?'

'I'm stunned.'

'We're more adventurous than you might think.'

'I guess. Was it a good job?'

'Yeah, not so bad. Pay wasn't bad, staff discount on the stock . . .'

'That must've made Kevin happy.'

'You'd think.' She shrugs. 'But that wasn't the case, far as I could tell. Almost as soon as we got to the city, he changed. Started drinking – and I mean *serious* drinking – with his buddies from work, pissing away all our money, and chasing anything with a skirt and a pretty smile. When he did come home it was just so he could have his dinner or get his laundry cleaned. Son of a bitch hardly talked to me except to tell me what he wanted.'

'Sounds nasty,' I say. 'Must've been a lonely life.'

'It was. But I guess it could've been worse. He never hit me or anything. But I was miserable as hell. Didn't know anyone much, so I didn't go out even though things were lousy at home. And we weren't saving for a house – the way Kevin got through money, we were having a hard time just paying the rent.'

'So you left him.'

'That I did. Up and walked out one day. He never fought the divorce – I guess he was as glad to be rid of me as I was of him, and it wasn't like either of us had the cash for lawyers.'

'How come you didn't stay in Oklahoma?'

'I would've done, but I lost my job at the store. Lay-offs. Last in, first out. And I was running real low on money with nowhere much to go when my uncle offered to help me out.' She shrugs. 'So here I am, twenty-five and stuck back in the place I hoped I'd never be stuck in, with even less chance of finding a way out than last time. I guess it just ain't supposed to happen.'

'You're not tempted to try the husband route again? Might get more lucky second time around.'

'Round here? You really *are* a stranger to these parts, Alex.'

I nod. 'No kidding.'

'So how come it worked for you, Alex?' Ashley says.

'How come what worked?'

'Escaping. Leaving this kind of place. How come you managed it and I didn't?'

I decide not to say anything about joining the Bureau. Not before I'm more sure of what's going on and what anyone here might have to do with it. 'I went to college,' I say. 'That got me away, for starters. Did this and that for a while, ended up working with an old friend of mine for a few years, although that's all over with now. But I didn't have any family to fall back on if everything went wrong, so it was much harder to wind up back where I started. And I never had anyone else screwing things up for me.'

'Sounds nice.'

'Coming from here ... Well, on the way up here I heard some things about this place. It's got a reputation.'

'You heard the stories?'

I nod. 'Everyone seems to think the valley's not a good place. That there's nothing good ever comes of anything out here.'

' "There's evil in them thar mountains!" '

'That's the stuff.'

Another bolt of lightning shrieks into the pasture. Ashley's eyes fix on the window and she says, 'What was that?' as the sound of splintering glass comes from downstairs.

15

'What did you see?'

'I . . . I don't know. It looked like someone moving out there, out in the fields. What happened to the window?'

More noises from downstairs. Shuffling. Scraping. Dull and heavy against the bare wood. Like there's a large, ponderous animal prowling around below us. I can see the fear etched in Ashley's face and she's biting her lower lip hard enough I expect her to draw blood. The knuckles on the hand holding her flashlight are pinched white. A thick odour begins to ooze its way through the floorboards beneath us, wet and putrid like stale pond water. My head is full of images of a huge, hunched-over monster from the river, dripping with mud and weeds, shambling around the house below, trying to find us. I picture it being led around like a pet by the hand by a dead girl with darkened eyes and I have to suppress a shudder.

The heavy noises reach the bottom of the stairs. I daren't move, I daren't breathe for fear of alerting the *thing* making them. Ashley slips her hand into mine and holds it tight. Neither of us says a word, but we exchange a look, eyes seeking each other for reassurance. Then the sounds fade away, growing quieter, eventually seeming to leave the house altogether. The sense of menace recedes with them. Thunder rolls and the building breathes again.

'What the hell was that?' Ashley says, letting go of my hand.

'No idea. No idea at all.'

'Did you smell that?'

I nod. 'Yeah. Christ. Let's get out of here.'

'No,' she says, pulling me back. 'Don't. Not yet. Let's wait a couple of minutes and be sure they're gone. Please?'

We do just that. I wait by the window, hoping to catch sight of whatever – whoever – the mysterious visitor was by the rippling lights of the storm. Peering through the glass as though I'll spot it making its way back out through the fields. But I see nothing at all.

When we make our way downstairs, the front room and kitchen floor are covered in great sloppy swooshes of mud like long, dragging footprints. The mud reeks of rancid water and slime. The glass in the kitchen door is broken, pieces lying all over the floor. There's no sign of what smashed it. But that's not all.

Tucked by the front door, leaning against the wall like an umbrella left there by a returning homeowner, is a large heavy-bladed axe gleaming in the light of the flash. Its head and haft both look to have been wiped down with a damp cloth; there are dark, wet smears of what could be mud, could be something worse, all over it, as though the cloth itself was too sodden to do a good job of cleaning it.

Ashley asks me if there's blood on it when she sees it.

'I don't think so,' I tell her. 'I can't tell; it's just smears. But I can't see any red.'

'So what's it doing here, Alex? It's not like axes just appear, not on a night like this.'

'Yeah, you can say that again.'

'So?' she repeats.

'I don't know. Let's go. I think we've spent long enough inside.'

'Yeah, I think you're right.'

We open the front door. My heart jumps into my mouth when I see that there's a figure standing no more than ten yards away. Its back is to us, but it looks big; a tall, heavy-set man, broad and hard. The sort of person who could wield that axe in just one hand. The figure spins round when the flashlight hits it, and then a man's voice says, 'Jesus Christ, Ashley, you scared me half to death.'

'Tony?'

'Yeah.' In the light, his shape seems to shrink and resolve itself into a guy somewhere in his early forties, a little shorter than me, dressed for the weather in a heavy coat and mud-splattered trousers, work boots to match. He looks pale and has an uncertain smile hovering on his lips.

'What the hell are you doing out here?'

'I could ask you the same thing. What were you doing in there?' He points at the house. 'And who's this with you?'

'Alex,' I say. 'Ashley was showing me the lay of the land. We were looking around for anything strange.'

'Someone knocked Christine out cold and robbed the gas station,' Ashley adds. 'And Alex found some . . . people buried out by the Easy.'

'Jesus.' Tony shakes his head. 'For real?'

'That's right. Have you seen anything tonight?' I ask him. 'You've been out and about, right?'

'I'm looking for Ben.' He looks at Ashley when he says it.

'His,' she tells me. 'Tony's the younger of the two.'

'He went out to check on the fields a while ago and he hasn't come back. With the storm and all . . . I thought I saw a light from here, which I guess was you guys. Anyway, I was thinking of heading back. My flashlight's batteries have died.' He pulls it out of his pocket and waves it at us to demonstrate. 'Maybe he's home by now. It was probably stupid of me to be worrying.'

'Did you come inside the building here?' I ask.

'What? No. When?'

'Someone broke in while we were in there,' Ashley says.

'Serious?'

She shows Tony into the derelict front room and the mess left there. I follow behind him. He stops just inside the doorway and stares at the mud slopped over the floor, shaking his head, then double-takes when he sees the axe.

'Hey, that's mine,' he says. 'That's my firewood axe. What's that doing here?'

'It's yours?'

'Sure.' He looks at me. 'I haven't seen it for a week or two. I thought I'd lost it somewhere.'

'Could your brother have had it?'

'He helped me look for it, so I don't think so. How'd it get here?'

'Whoever came in left it behind. It wasn't there when we arrived.'

'What do you think they wanted with it?' he says. Neither of us answers. After a while, he just shrugs and looks at us. 'Well, I'm going to go home, see if Ben's come back. Should I take that,' he says, gesturing at the axe, 'or leave it where it is? This whole thing's pretty weird.'

'Might as well leave it,' I tell him. 'Tonight's not a night for cutting wood anyway.'

'Yeah, that's for sure. Maybe I'll see you back at Isaac's, Ashley. So long.'

He waves goodbye and walks back out into the storm as if the whole episode had never occurred. It seems forced to me, the Hundred Yard Nonchalant Walk. I wonder about him and the other brother, Ben. And Sam.

For a moment, I think I hear a strange whooping cry in the distance, carried by the wind. It comes from the opposite direction to that taken by Tony as he trudges away. Ashley doesn't seem to notice it at all.

'Is he always like that?' I ask her.

She shrugs. 'He's kinda strange, but he's harmless.' She puffs out her cheeks and hugs her chest. 'Still, it's good knowing he's out here too.'

'Yeah.'

'After what happened when we were upstairs, it's nice to know there's someone else around. Let's go back to Isaac's.'

'Have you got a car, Ashley?'

'Sure. Why?'

'Because there's one other thing I'd like to do before we go back, if you don't mind helping me again,' I say, running my hand through my hair. 'I didn't want to mention it when we were back at the bar – it'd lead to too many awkward questions – but I want to have a proper look at the bodies by the river.'

'Jesus.' She looks shocked. 'Why the hell'd you want to do that?'

'I didn't have a light with me when I found them, so I couldn't see much then, but I want to see if I can tell how long they've been out there. And, maybe, what exactly it was that happened to them.'

'Can't the cops do that?'

'Sure, yeah, but if they take a while getting here with the bridge being out, it might be better to know now,' I say. She's wavering and I can see it won't take much to push her into helping me. 'It won't take long.'

'I don't know . . .'

'It could be important. With people like the axe guy around, I think it's best we know as much as we can. Please? All you have to do is hold the light for me.'

She thinks for a moment more, then nods reluctantly. 'OK. I guess it can't be any creepier than being in this place. But I don't touch squat, right?'

'Right.'

We pick up her Neon from outside her trailer and drive east towards the river. Ashley talks less and less as we get closer to the end of the road. She seems to be concentrating on her driving, but I can see her knuckles tightening on the wheel as the Easy draws nearer. Lightning shudders against the hills as she pulls up maybe thirty or forty yards from the scar left by the bridge's destruction. She says, 'Where're we going from here?'

'I'd guess it's a couple of hundred yards, maybe more, downstream. If we follow the bank south we'll find the spot without too much trouble. I'll recognize the tree that helped me get out of the river easily enough.'

'Walking?' she says.

'With the ground in the state it's in, I wouldn't trust driving anything short of a bulldozer off the road. It shouldn't be too bad to walk, though. So long as you don't mind the mud.'

'I can take mud. I'm not so keen on dead people.'

'You won't have to touch a thing,' I remind her. 'And this won't take long. Promise.'

Then we hike out on to the sodden earth, faces more or less square into the wind. My clothes feel like ice, already soaked just as my last set were. I can't feel my hands. Ashley has her teeth gritted and every once in a while her flashlight beam whips away from the path ahead and off to the sides, seeking out some half-glimpsed movement in the dark.

'Whoever was at the house won't have come out here,' I tell her.

'You don't know that for sure.'

'No,' I concede, 'but it's not likely. It's a long way on foot from there to here, and why bother, even if they did know we'd found the bodies? He won't come.'

'Says you. There are two dead people here and someone killed them, and someone was wandering around in the dark with an axe not so long ago. I don't want to take chances.'

'They've been dead a long time.'

'There's no harm in being careful.' She trails off.

The gale snaps at our legs as we walk, and at one point the ground crumbles beneath me. For a second my heart jolts as I imagine sliding down into the churning river again, but the collapse stops and I manage to recover my footing. Then we reach the muddy hollow where the bodies are buried. I see the same hollow gouges carved in the land and the tree that saved me from drowning just beyond them.

'This is the spot,' I say. 'Watch the slope. You don't want to end up in the river.'

Ashley takes my hand and I help steady her against the slippery ground as we shuffle wetly along the incline towards the burial site. I'm thankful the storm is wiping away any lingering smell. Ashley, on the other hand, could probably use some forewarning of what's coming. Without the odour, she's got nothing to prepare her for what she's about to see.

The light dances on the exposed upper torso of the first corpse, swollen, black and distended, and glistening slickly in the rain. She says, 'Oh, Christ,' and is instantly and violently sick.

I wait for her to finish, then say, 'Sorry. I tried to make it clear this wasn't going to be pretty. I did the same when I found them.'

'This is horrible, Alex.'

She stands up again, face pale, the light shaking in her hand. Tries to focus on the scene in front of us. And then we see it. The empty hole in the earth where the woman's corpse had been.

It's gone.

16

'There was a second body here,' I say.

'What?'

'The woman's body.' I point at the hole in the ground, barely able to believe what I'm seeing. 'It's gone. Jesus Christ.'

'What do you mean, it's gone? Who'd take a body?' She waves at the darkness around us. 'Who the fuck takes a body, Alex? Why would they?'

'I don't know,' I say. 'But the bank hasn't collapsed any further, so it must have been someone who did this. It hasn't just slid into the river.'

Ashley clasps her hand over her mouth. I think of whoever came into the house, the muddy trail they left across the floor, the axe. They didn't leave anything else behind, but still . . .

Ashley's beam is fixed on the empty scar in the mud. I can hardly hear her voice over the wind. She glances at me, eyes wide and dark, then scans around her as if she's expecting to see the woman's corpse walking through the fields.

'Yeah, someone took her,' I say. 'Maybe they watched me find the corpses and waited until I'd gone before they took her. Or maybe they just came across it after I'd left. It could be anything.'

'Could it have been ... whoever came to the house?'

I don't answer for a moment. 'I guess, yes.'

'Holy shit,' she says. 'Holy shit. You mean he could've been ...'

I try to remember if there was anything strange or unusual about the woman's corpse. If there was some detail about it that would make someone want to remove hers but leave the man's. Some distinguishing feature of her death that her killer wouldn't want to risk anyone seeing. I can't do it.

The hole gouged in the earth is ragged and uneven, not cut with a shovel or a similar tool. It looks as if someone has clawed the mud free by hand. There are definite fingermarks gouged in the dirt, fistfuls of soil thrown aside. I can't tell if the churned earth around the burial site is due merely to the tracks I left earlier, or if it's the fault of whoever took her.

Not a trace of the woman remains.

Why the hell would someone want her body? And if they'd gone to so much trouble to bury these two in the first place, why risk exposure by coming back for one of them now?

I look at the hole, at the fields, and back again. There doesn't seem to be anything to be done. 'Christ. We'd best do what we came here for.'

'What about the woman?'

'I don't know. I really don't. One thing at a time.'

'Oh, Jesus. Oh, Jesus.' She's white and her eyes are

huge and staring. 'I don't think I can do this, Alex. I can't handle this kind of . . . Oh, Jesus.'

'Look, you don't have to do much.' I place a hand on her shoulder and soften my voice as much as I can over the wind and the river. 'You just hold the flashlight and let me do the rest. You feel ill, you look away. Just keep the light on, OK? This won't take long.'

She nods, and I bend down beside the corpse, my stomach already beginning to churn again. Up close, it looks like it's had a few months' decomposition at most. But the soil is sticky, thick clay. Real heavy tannin-rich stuff. The sort that slows down the whole process by weeks at a time. Maybe even months. And at this altitude, chances are the whole thing freezes over at the start of the fall and doesn't thaw out until spring, meaning they could've been here for a year or so, well before Sam wrote his note to me.

Lightning crashes somewhere near by as I scrape some of the worst of the mud away from the man's limbs with a stick. Up close, the stench coming off him is horrific. Ammonia and milk gone all kinds of bad. His skin is swollen and waxy, in parts mottled brown and in others oily piss-like yellow where everything inside has broken down. Digging further, he's completely naked.

His injuries, quite apart from the gunshot wound that killed him, are massive and numerous. His right arm is broken, like I saw when I found him, and I can't find out anything more from his warped ribcage.

Down beneath the dirt, his genitals are mangled like they've been crushed by a lump hammer. There are a couple of what could be gashes on his legs and ugly blotching elsewhere, but I can't tell if they're injuries or just the result of decay. The cracked bones certainly don't seem to be – it's not like the person who buried him in this field would've had to fold him up to save space.

No, someone took great pleasure in beating the shit out of this guy and then blew his brains out.

Lightning snaps overhead, the flashlight beam jumps crazily to one side, and in the booming silence that follows the thundercrack I hear Ashley murmur, 'Oh shit, no . . .'

Behind the flickering curtain of white-lit streaks of rain, picked out in the shaking circle of light, a child's arm and leg protrude from the dirt.

17

From his size, I'm guessing the boy was between four and six years old when he was killed. He's naked, exactly the same as the guy I guess was his father, but unlike him or the mother there's no obvious cause of death. His flesh is puckered and grey-green, but it's unmarked. Given the unsophisticated nature of his parents' murders, I'd guess he was probably smothered. All that time still to come, all that life stretched out in front of him, snatched away. Everything he'd ever be, gone before he had the chance to be it. A whole innocent future wiped out. I saw plenty of child murders in my days with the FBI, but they're something it's impossible to forget – from the initial crime scene to that tragically tiny coffin at the funeral, the slaying of someone so young is a different kind of horror.

Looking at what happened to the three of them in this case, the guy was obviously the focus of the assault; the damage suffered by the woman, as I remember it, was nowhere near as bad. The prolonged nature of the beating suggests that either the person responsible was a random sadist who enjoyed inflicting that level of pain, or the killer was taking revenge for something personal.

Beating someone to death is usually a personal thing. Sometimes a crime of passion, sometimes not. But if you're just setting out to kill a stranger, and you've got a gun, you shoot them straight out and be done with it. That's the accepted logic, anyway, even if it is a gross generalization. Enough crimes follow the pattern to make it a reasonable rule of thumb.

The wife may have been cracked in the skull to shut her up, or just to despatch her once the husband was dealt with; a single killing blow suggests there wasn't a lot of anger in the attack, but that it was controlled. But then why batter her like that when you already have the gun you used on the husband? Maybe the killer needed her to go quietly. And if the kid was smothered, that must just have been to cover his tracks, cold and methodical. Almost an after-thought, to eliminate the last possible witness.

Since you couldn't leave a car – which either the killer or the family must have had – on the road in a place as empty as this without someone spotting it, the killer must have had somewhere near by they could leave it. A house, a barn, someplace to stash the vehicle so he could bury the three corpses without attracting suspicion.

Which means he's almost certainly one of the locals. Or someone local enough to know the area well. Sam. Were these the dead people he talked about in his note? And if so, what the hell did he mean by 'finding the crosses'?

Ashley has one hand pressed to her face and no

longer seems to be reacting to the wind and rain battering against her. She's retreated inside, cutting off as much of the world outside her head as she can. I've seen people do it before. Shock at being confronted with the grim reality of death. You're promised a white light, happy relatives, and maybe you see the dead all nicely dressed in a funeral parlour somewhere. The reality is usually an ugly stinking mess in a hole in the ground.

'Hey,' I say. 'Ashley.'

It takes a moment or two, but she eventually realizes I'm talking to her, answers in a daze, 'What? What is it?'

'It's done. Let's go back.'

'Really?' She sounds relieved, and also slightly unconvinced.

'Yeah.'

I take the flashlight from her unresisting hands and scan it quickly over the top of the dirt bank, the original ground level of the field by the river.

'What're you doing?'

'Checking there aren't any markers here. Crosses, anything like that to show where these people were buried.'

She shakes her head and says, 'There's no crosses around here.'

As she says it, I think I see something moving at the edge of the light. When I whip the beam back again, though, the light just vanishes into empty darkness. Nothing there to catch it.

'What?' Ashley says.

I sweep the light across again. Still nothing. I tell myself it was probably leaves or something picked up by the wind; there's all kinds of stuff being blown around out here, ripped from the ground by the force of the storm. 'Nothing,' I say. 'Let's go back.'

'Sure.'

We slosh through the darkness to Ashley's car in complete silence. Ashley gnaws on her nails like they're cough candy. Once we're back inside and the Neon's shuddered into gear she finally breaks the quiet and asks, 'Who . . . who'd do that, Alex?'

'People have the capacity to do all kinds of things,' I say. 'Sometimes they've got a reason for it, one that we might be able to understand, sometimes they don't. Sometimes something happens that makes it come out of them. They snap and all the bad wiring they've kept covered suddenly has control.'

Ashley rests her free arm against the window, oblivious to or simply ignoring the wind thrumming at the glass. 'But to kill a family like that . . . how can there be a reason for that? I don't get it. It's . . . well, it's just not right.'

'Imagine you tried to rob them. The father fights back, so you kill him. And now the wife and the kid are witnesses to a murder and you can't allow the cops to find out, so you do the only thing you can. You make sure no one can identify you. It does happen. It's tragic, but it's not uncommon. There was a family on vacation somewhere near Atlanta a few years ago,' I say. 'Almost that exact thing happened to them. Nasty case.'

'Robbery?'

'Robbery gone wrong, yeah. A guy tried to carjack them. The husband went for a gun he had in the glove compartment so the guy shot him in the face. Then he panicked.'

'Panicked? I didn't think people like that did panic.'

'He wasn't expecting to kill anyone, I guess.' I shrug. 'It shocked him, losing control like that. Anyway, he just started firing wildly at the rest of the family. The wife took three bullets, their eight-year-old another two, but most just hit metal. One of them blew a hole clean through the ignition and he couldn't get the car started when he tried to drive off, so he had to leave it there.'

'Jesus.' She shakes her head.

'Thing was, the little girl survived. She was in the ICU for a while, but she gave the cops a real good description of the 'jacker and they managed to find him three months later. Now he's doing life for the killings.'

'What happened to the little girl?' Ashley asks.

'I don't remember. Point is, though, that kind of thing does happen. Not for any good reason, but it does. More often than you might think, too. It's a strange world and it's unpleasant at times.'

'I wonder who they were,' Ashley says. 'The dead people, I mean.'

'I don't know,' I say. 'Maybe they lived round here.'

'Someone in the bar would've said something. They must've known if anyone here had gone missing. They'd have said. Even if it was a year ago or more.' She shakes her head.

'So they must have been passing through, I guess. Or they were hikers, like Will said.' I can't imagine anyone coming to these parts on vacation, not given everything I've heard about the valley, but I suppose it's possible. Outside, the fields are painted a dim green for a second as lightning courses through the high-up reaches of the storm. The valley's a jumble of barren pasture and belts of scraggy woodland to either side, all tossed by the wind.

'Are you going to be OK?' I ask.

'Yeah.' She sniffs. 'I just need someone to talk to. This is helping, Alex. Thanks.'

'Hey, don't mention it.'

'How about you?' she asks. 'You ever need to talk to someone, a shoulder to cry on?'

I shrug. 'I guess, sometimes.'

'Girlfriend? Family?'

It's my turn to shake my head. 'Not any more. Even friends are in short supply these days.'

'That's pretty rough,' she murmurs. 'You got religion?'

'Never seen the point.'

'Therapist?'

'Not these days.'

'So who do you talk to when you need someone?'

'I have a very understanding sock monkey.'

Ashley laughs despite the shock she's feeling. 'You serious?'

'Not really, no. But I've been thinking about getting one. Maybe when I get home. The world needs more sock monkeys.'

The lights of Isaac's Bar and Grill at last begin to shine clear and bright through the curtain of rain and Ashley swings the Neon into the parking lot. It's dead, home to nothing more than abandoned vehicles and the howling storm. A couple of figures, those nearest the windows, are dimly visible through the glass. Nothing seems to have changed since we left. Still no cops, still no sign of help. I wonder if we'll see any such thing until morning.

'There's no place like home,' I say and look over at Ashley. She's staring up through the windshield with calm, dark eyes. The flickering tongues of lightning crackling within and between the walls of the storm's heart are almost constant now, thin and weak-looking, but ceaseless. The shreds of cloud circling the base have grown and swollen into thick curtains beneath one side of the core, spinning with greater purpose and intensity, so low they could almost be clipping the tops of the buildings. I can nearly believe that the world's flipped, that we're about to fall down into the maelstrom.

'It's like we're there,' Ashley says, voice almost a

whisper. 'Like we're inside the storm. Flying in the clouds.'

I gently tug on her arm. The display's hypnotic, but dangerous. 'Ashley, let's go.'

Without the car to muffle it, the wind screeches like a bandsaw and feels almost as strong. Part of the plastic 'GAS' sign from Will's place rips clear of its mountings with a crack and vanishes up into the night as we trudge into the bar. Leaning forward, the wind ripping at my coat as it tries to haul me up and away, I find myself worrying that the roadhouse itself really could be torn to pieces, scattered by the gale, just as I'd suggested earlier.

'Did you two enjoy your little stroll?' Isaac says as I shut the door behind us. He eyes up our muddy shoes and rain-soaked clothes with a wry expression on his face. 'You look frozen.'

'Yeah,' Ashley says. She heads straight for the door behind the counter, stripping off her coat. Doesn't spare a glance for anyone much, and I wonder how badly she's still feeling the shock. I can see JC and his friends watching her as she goes. He glances at me, leering slightly, but says nothing. Goes back to his drink and signals to his friends to do likewise.

'Did you go up to the Banks house?' Will asks as I join the others by the bar. 'See everything you wanted to?'

I wonder how much to tell them. How much to give away. 'Yeah,' I say. 'It's looking pretty battered.'

'It sure is. Be a small miracle if anyone buys it

before it falls down completely, especially after tonight. Is the weather still as bad out there as it was?'

'Worse. No sign of the cops yet?'

He shakes his head. 'No, no cops. That young feller hasn't been back yet. I'm starting to wonder if we haven't seen the last of him.'

'You think he might have driven off and left us?'

'It's been long enough that he should've been back by now.'

'The Clay bridge could've gone after he crossed it,' Isaac chips in. 'He might just not be able to get back to this side.'

The old man weighs up the chances, then shrugs. 'I suppose. Someone ought to go and see how it's holding up. Chris needs a doctor and I guess we all need the police now.'

'We saw Tony,' Ashley says, coming back into the bar. She's looking calmer and steadier now, properly in control of herself again after our trip to the river. My worry subsides. 'I think the brothers are OK.'

'No Ben?'

'He said he was out checking on their fields. Tony was looking for him, since he'd been gone so long.'

'I'll go look at the bridge,' Isaac says. 'Are you OK to watch the bar for a few minutes, Ash?'

She nods.

'I'll go too,' I say. 'If that's OK with you.'

Isaac shrugs. 'Anyone else?'

'Why not?' Vince says. 'I sure could do with

stretching my legs a little.' When he says it, his eyes jerk briefly towards JC's table then back suddenly, as if he realized what he'd done and didn't want it to show.

18

We head out to the bridge over the Clay Stream in Isaac's jeep. As we're shouldering our way to the vehicle, Isaac looks up at the flickering sky and says, 'Jesus. Last time I was in a storm half as bad as this was Oklahoma. I've never seen one like it here. Summer lightning, sure, but this is just insane.'

'Guess there's a first time for everything,' I say.

'Half as bad?' Vince yells over the wind. 'Jesus Christ. What happened that time?'

'It dropped a twister that killed a bunch of folks in a trailer park, flattened half the town, and lightning set the school on fire. Took them over a year to rebuild.'

'Christ. That won't happen here, though. Will it?'

Isaac shrugs. 'We don't have a school, so I guess not.'

'Ha, ha.'

Isaac smiles grimly. 'No one needs to worry. If worse comes to worst, everyone can hole up at the bar until this blows over.'

'Is it stormproof?' I ask.

'No idea. It's never really been tested until now.'

'I guess we'll have to hope.'

'Think of the fun we can have finding out.'

Isaac's expression is anything but fun.

'I'm just praying the bridge stays up so I can get out of here. I mean, maybe I can still make that meeting tomorrow or something,' Vince says. A hangdog expression settles on his features as he remembers what he's doing out here. I don't find it very convincing. 'I only have a few days before I have to go home.'

'There's not much you can do if it's gone. They won't even be able to get a helicopter out here until the storm's over. Your friend might have to wait a while to talk property with you.'

'I suppose.' His face gains a couple of notches of hang, loses a touch of dog.

We drive in silence for a couple of minutes. Then Isaac says, 'The sheriff's department should be able to fix up a temporary bridge. A couple of years ago the one across the Dawkins Stream the next valley over was hit by a barge and they had to close it. Everyone was crossing on pontoons for a month.'

'So long as they get some uniforms, forensics, the works as well.'

Isaac shrugs. 'Once we find out what's going on with the bridge, we'll know what the cops can –'

He slams on the brakes, sends us skidding to a halt, as the rear end of another car suddenly appears in the headlights. It's a white Honda compact, just like one I saw in the parking lot when I arrived. I guess it's the guy who went to check on the bridge. There's something in front of it, maybe another vehicle, but it's hard to tell through the rain sheeting against our windshield.

'Is that him?' Isaac says.

'Only one way to find out,' I say.

'I never saw his car, but I guess it's him. Unless it's them other guys' car. The one that broke down.'

I shrug. 'It's facing the wrong way if it is. They didn't pass me on my way out to the Easy so they must have been coming from this direction. How close to the river are we?'

Isaac doesn't say. It turns out not to matter; as soon as I open the door I can hear the water. A dull bass rumble, constant through the howling of the elements. Through the dazzling sheets of rain picked out by our headlights, I can see that it is indeed a second car beyond the Honda, skewed sideways across the road. Beyond it, at the very edge of the beams' reach, two forlorn and twisted shreds of steel girder jut like jagged teeth against the sky. The bridge is gone.

And so is the guy who came to check on it.

19

It's clear as soon as I shine Isaac's flashlight through its rear windshield, clearer still as I move around the Honda to get a proper look. There's no one inside. I think about the mystery axe-carrying visitor at the Banks house, about the missing corpse. Every sense is on high alert, my instincts screaming that something is very wrong here. That this place, this whole valley, is genuinely damned. I scan the darkness around the road as well as I can manage with the flashlight. All I see is a lot of standing water, flat grass, empty air, all picked out in harsh monochrome like old movie film. No monsters, but I can easily believe they could exist in such a place, rationality be damned. The dark is all around.

I try the driver's door on the Honda. Unlocked. The keys are still in the ignition, but the engine's dead and cold. The parking brake is on and the gearshift's in neutral. There's no sign of anything wrong, any blood, marks, damage – aside from the front where it T-boned the second car – but there's equally no sign of the driver. Like he got out and simply flew away into the night.

The other vehicle, an Escort which had seen better days even before tonight, is even more puzzling. Its front end is badly crumpled, even though the Honda caught it square on in the passenger door. The driver's door is ajar, the airbag's blown, and the mess inside makes it look as though it was abandoned in a hurry.

From the look of the car, there probably wasn't more than one occupant. Too much junk on too many seats. I move round to check on the trunk. It's unlocked and empty apart from some black plastic sacks scrunched up in a corner.

'What the hell happened here?' Isaac asks behind me. 'Is there any sign of him?'

I sweep the flashlight under both cars, just in case. 'Nothing,' I say. 'From what we've got here, there's no way of knowing where he might have got to.'

'Do you think ... Do you think *they* were here? Maybe they got him.' He looks around at the fields bordering the road as if expecting something to burst out at him. I don't share his immediate apprehension, but I still feel a shudder go through me. As though there's something waiting for us all out there in the dark.

'The MacBrides?'

'Yeah,' he says. His tone makes them sound like avenging spirits.

I walk over to the remains of the bridge supports. At the bottom of one of them I find a harsh, ragged dent, an impact mark lined with paint. It's the same colour as the Escort. The night's too dark and the road's too wet to make out any tyre marks.

I rock back on my heels and try to piece it all together. The Escort was crossing the river, and it must've been going pretty fast. Did the driver lose control? Did he make a mistake in the rain? Or was it something else, something that made him race across regardless of the danger?

At the bridge over the Easy, I played it cautious, or tried to, and checked it first before I tried to drive across. Maybe the driver saw this one was weakening, saw it about to collapse, and went for it. Hammered his foot on the gas and just tried to make it to the other side in time. Because he had some vital reason to make it into the valley. He floored it, hung on for dear life, prayed. Then he lost control as everything fell to pieces behind him and smashed into one of the final supports, bouncing out into the road in a spin that left him broadside across the highway.

But alive; thank the Lord for modern safety equipment. So he hauled his shit out of his busted vehicle and disappeared into the night.

Was it the driver of the Escort who attacked Christine in the parking lot and helped himself to some first-aid gear? And if so, why do that rather than come into the roadhouse and simply ask for help? And where is he now?

Either way, it seems that when the guy came out to check on the bridge and fetch the cops, he wasn't expecting another car to be blocking the road like that – the same as we weren't expecting to see the Honda when we arrived. He hit it, not too bad, and got out of his car to look at the scene, engine off, but keys still in the ignition. Maybe he checked the Escort, maybe not, but he must've seen the tattered metal that used to form part of the bridge.

Did he go to see up close how severe the damage was? How badly did he want there to be a way across, a way to fetch the cops?

And then . . . something. Something happened to him. He can't just have vanished into thin air. Was the other driver waiting out here for him? The visitor at the Banks house? The people from up the valley? Sam? Or did he just lose his footing and end up in the river?

'What've you found, Alex?' Isaac calls out behind me. 'You got something there?'

'Not really, no. I think that the other car hit the bridge coming across and finished up beached in the middle of the road.'

'You think? What about the guy who came out here to check on the bridge, where'd he go?'

'I have no idea. He's sure as shit not here now though.'

'And neither's the bridge. Let's go back.'

The words hit home, stark and true. It's gone and none of us are getting out of here until morning at least. And no help's going to be getting in. 'Sure,' I say. 'I'm just wondering, if the bridge has been down since our guy went to look at it, how JC and his friends made the crossing. They got here somehow.'

'Maybe that Escort was their car,' Vince says.

'Maybe it was, but don't you think it's strange they didn't mention the bridge collapsing or the fact that they drove into one of the supports in their hurry to get across? However they did it, they've been oddly quiet about what happened.'

Isaac nods. Thunder booms across the valley. 'I'd say they've got some questions to answer when we get in.'

'You've got that right.'

As we drive back to the roadhouse, Isaac glances at me and says, 'What do you think's going on out here? Where'd that guy go?'

'I don't know.'

'Maybe he ended up in the Clay. Got too close and fell in.'

'It's possible.' I shrug. 'It'd be a strange coincidence if that was the case though. Tonight of all nights? I don't buy it. I don't buy it at all.'

Lightning arcs overhead in shimmering emerald. The whole valley lights up with the strange and terrible glow. In the flash, I see the land to the north engraved in stark lines, weirdly jumbled and twisted. A chaotic mix of rolling curves, geometric shapes and sudden rips and crumples in the ground, some almost as tall as a house and all overgrown with twisted clumps of weeds and thorns. Like barbed wire scattered across an old battlefield from some nightmarish past war. For the briefest fraction of a second in which the image remains frozen on my retina, I think I can see figures picked out in silhouette, dotted around the madness. The shadowy sentries standing guard on this shattered landscape.

'What the hell's that to the north?' I say.

Isaac glances out of the window, but the lightning's gone and there's nothing left to see there. He says, 'What?'

'The ground up there. It's like ... I don't know. Ruins. All broken and jumbled up.'

'That's the Foundations.'

'That place you were telling me stories about? The construction site for ... what was it going to be, a health retreat?'

'Something like that. A country club, I think. Big place for rich types out in the middle of nowhere, anyway.'

'Jesus. I had no idea it was so large. That's a huge area it covers.'

'Pretty massive, huh? And that was only going to be the beginning of it.'

'Why did they stop work on it?'

Isaac shrugs. 'Before my time. But the way I hear it from Will, the guy who owned the project upped and vanished one day, taking a shitload of cash that was supposed to be going to the workforce or to buy more property or something. Whatever it was, it was enough to put the company even worse in debt than it was before, and left it with no one in charge. The whole deal folded and everything went bust. They didn't even have the cash to fill in the holes they left.'

'They never caught him?'

'I don't think so. Not that I ever heard, anyway.'

I look out the window again, waiting for another bolt to momentarily cut away the shadows. 'Who was the developer?'

'I don't know the company. The guy?'

'Yeah, him. You remember?'

He shrugs again. 'Like I said, it was before my time. I wasn't out here back then. No one famous, as far as I know. Not exactly movie-of-the-week material, and not the kind of thing that makes it on to *Cops*. Will might remember, but it was a long time ago. Fifteen years, more or less.'

'That's a long time for a development like that to stay forgotten.'

'That's the way it is here,' he says. 'That's just the way it is.'

20

Will stands up as we return, asks, 'How's the bridge?'

'Gone,' Isaac says.

I see Ashley glance at me, eyes searching for some sign of hope, but I just shake my head. There's no way to repair the damage without a team of engineers, a lot of time and tons of machinery.

'Jesus. Why didn't the feller who went to look at it come back? He get across?'

Isaac looks at me. I say, 'No, he didn't. His car's out by the river. The last car to come across that bridge swiped one of the supports when it reached this side, leaving it beached in the middle of the road. The guy who drove out there collided with it. Not badly, but he left the car there.'

'So where is he?'

'Gone,' I say, echoing Isaac's earlier comment. 'I've got no idea where, but he's disappeared.'

'Maybe he swam across,' Christine says.

Isaac shakes his head. 'The Clay's running so strong there's no one could make it, I reckon. Which also means we're all stuck here until someone comes to fix the road again. Still, I suppose it's not as though we don't all live out here already.'

'All right for you to say,' Will replies. 'But if we've got some lunatic MacBride running around in the storm doing all sorts of harm then we really need the cops.'

'There's something else we need,' I say. Isaac looks at me, then over at the table where JC and his two friends are taking a great deal of interest in our conversation. I call over to them, 'You guys were the last ones to arrive here. Where's your car? Broke down out on the road?'

JC says nothing, just shrugs.

'Which is strange, because we didn't see it. The only two cars out there were the one that struck the bridge and the one belonging to the guy who went to check on it. You showed up after he left.'

'Your point?'

Isaac follows me over to their table, a looming presence to my left. I keep my eyes fixed on the three young men. 'Was it you who hit the bridge as it collapsed?'

'Shut your mouth, man,' JC says.

'And if it was, why didn't you think to mention it to us before now? You all seem mighty calm for a bunch of guys who nearly died crossing a river,' I say. 'If it wasn't you, and you – what? – swam across the river? I mean, there's no other cars out there – so then why in God's name didn't you mention either the bridge being out or the two crashed vehicles? Slip your mind? You figured you'd get a couple of drinks in, relax and maybe it'd all come out in conversation?'

'Get fucked.'

'And come to that, if the bridge was already out, what the hell's so important you risked drowning just to get here? Talk to me, JC. Because right now I think you're full of shit, and maybe you and your friends here would be best locked up while we wait for the cops.'

JC shakes his head and slowly, very slowly stands up with his hands resting on the table. Spin and Craig stay where they are, but their eyes are tight and glittering dangerously. The air seems to crack with a sudden frost.

'You don't know shit, man,' JC says to me, looking me straight in the eyes. Without blinking he whips his hand round behind him and comes up with a high-calibre pistol, levelling it at my face and cocking back the hammer. I have time to think about going for my own gun, wedged in the waistband of my jeans, but by then it's too late.

21

Everyone freezes for a moment. Time locks up. Every blink takes hours, every breath I take roars in my ears.

I sense Isaac tense beside me. I can't tell what he's thinking without turning to look, but I pray he's not about to get me shot. If JC opens fire, it'll be me who gets it first. I can see all the way down the barrel of his Smith and Wesson. My blood feels like mercury.

'Don't try it,' he says. 'None of you.' The hand holding his gun is rock steady but his voice is taut like something's playing at his nerves.

Spin and Craig climb out of their seats, bringing up pistols of their own to cover the rest of the room, one revolver and another semi-automatic. Behind me I can hear the muffled gasps and epithets, murmurs and moans, of people suddenly afraid of dying at the hands of another.

'Craig,' JC says, 'get them all in a booth together. 'Cept this guy here, and the girl.' His eyes narrow and his mouth pinches into what might be a smile. It doesn't look friendly. 'We've got to have ourselves a little talk.'

The other two men get to work, directing everyone to a table in the corner of the bar. Isaac looks ready to kill but frustrated and powerless, unable to do anything against the three of them. I wonder if he has a gun or some other kind of weapon behind the bar. Whether, if I make a move, he'll join in, help even out the odds. How far we'd make it before we got shot. I can hear Will comforting Christine, mumbling to her with one hand on her arm. Vince has his hands up and is offering no resistance at all. Gene's looking at the three men like he's searching for some kind of opening, fists balled at his side.

Ashley walks up next to me with small, uncertain baby steps. Her eyes are wide and dancing and she's radiating fear. JC waves us both into a seat, then settles in opposite us, keeping the gun out in front of him. He makes no attempt to search me or any of the rest of us, says nothing to the other two about doing the same; I guess he must not consider us a likely threat in that respect. With three guns covering us at all times, perhaps he has a point.

'What's going on, JC?' I say. 'What's all this about?'

He shakes his head. 'You've been doing enough talking this evening, I reckon. I've got some questions for the pair of you, and you're gonna answer them. Right?'

'What do you want to know?'

'The two of you went off real quick after we got here. Real quick and real private.' The barrel of the gun moves from me to Ashley to me again. 'Why was that exactly?'

'I was getting the lay of the land. Having a look around.'

'Nice night for it,' he says.

'I thought so.'

'Try again.' He flexes his hand on the gun and his voice drops a couple of degrees in temperature. I have no doubt at all that he's killed before. There doesn't seem to be any hesitation, any sense of a bluff in what he's doing. The first time, the old saw goes, is the hardest. If I were to guess, I'd say he was well over that hump. 'And don't fuck me around. I don't care about you enough not to shoot you.'

'Just tell him, Alex,' Vince yells from the other side of the room. 'I don't want to die here, right? None of us do.'

'We went to see the place where the last people to own the land along the river lived,' I say. 'I wanted to see it. Ashley came along to show me where it was.'

'And why was that?'

'There's three people who were killed and buried on their land. The storm washed away the banks and revealed them earlier tonight. I wanted to see if there was anything at their home to give us a clue who those people were or why they died.'

'Is that so?'

I nod. 'Yes, it is. Someone beat the living shit out of those folks, broke every bone they could, then shot them in the head and buried them in the dirt.'

'Tonight?' JC raises his eyebrows, looks genuinely intrigued.

'No. A year ago, something like that. But no one much seems to have known about it until tonight. Except whoever did it.'

'That's interesting. That's very interesting. Why were you looking at them – you a cop?'

I shake my head. 'No, I'm not.'

'You talk like a cop.' He raises the gun again, presses it against my forehead. The metal is hard and cold.

I swallow hard. 'I'm not a cop, JC.'

'So why were you looking at dead people in the dark? That's cop work.'

'Someone told me there might be dead people out here before I came. I wanted to see if the ones by the river were the ones they were talking about,' I say. 'I wanted to know what had happened here, and I knew the cops were probably hours away with at least one of the bridges out. So there was no point waiting for them to figure it all out.'

His hand flexes on the butt of the gun, once, twice. Then he takes it away from my head and looks at Ashley. 'And why'd *you* go along to do that sort of thing? You got a thing for rotting meat?'

'He didn't tell me that's what he wanted to do.' She lowers her eyes, can't meet JC's gaze. 'Not at first.'

'You just wanted a walk in the rain, right?' he says. 'Don't bullshit me.'

'I didn't want to stay in here, not all night. That was all.'

'You're damn right to be thinkin' that way. This place is a shithole.'

'Seems fine to me. A bad smell came in earlier though.'

I cut off their exchange before Ashley gets him worked up enough to start shooting. I admire her guts, but there's a time and a place, and this is neither. 'There's more to what we found, JC,' I say. 'Someone's taken one of the bodies.'

I hear someone over in the booth gasp. JC says, 'What?'

'Someone dragged the rotting corpse of a woman out of the mud with their bare hands and carried it away. And they did it within the last couple of hours. Whoever it was is still out there. You might be best off robbing this place or whatever it is you have in mind and then bugging out. You're not the only people up to something tonight.'

'You know shit, mister. We're not here to turn over this place. We got better things to do with our time and I doubt any of you guys have shit worth taking. But we're not leaving until we've got what we *did* come here for.' The storm batters the windows in their frames and I swear I feel the whole building shake.

'So what is it you want, JC?'

'A guy called Evan Walker.' He watches both of us sharply when he says the name. 'Either of you know him?'

'Friend of yours?' I say.

'Not exactly. You know him?'

'No,' I say.

'You?'

Ashley shakes her head.

The biggest of the three, Craig, who looks like a member of the Aryan Brotherhood, glances across at his leader. 'JC, man, what if it was Walker did that?'

'Did what?'

'Took that body. It could've been him.'

'It wasn't. This guy's probably full of shit anyway.'

'But what if it *was*? Maybe he's taken it to where he's hiding.'

'Why the fuck would Walker want a corpse, numb-nuts?'

'Maybe that's what he needed to –'

'He's here, sure, but we already know that,' JC says. 'We find him and we're done. Don't need no bullshit about dead people to do it.'

Craig and the other guy, the one they called Spin, don't look too convinced. Maybe they caught some of the conversation in here earlier. They shut up anyway, though, and go back to keeping watch over the booth with their guns. I can see that the others are pretty tight-packed. In that kind of position, it would be difficult for them to do anything about the three men without getting shot. Too cramped, too little room for manoeuvre.

'So where is he?' JC says.

22

'The only people who've come in tonight,' Isaac replies, 'are us right here. This guy you're after hasn't stopped by.'

'And none of you know him? None of you know the name? Bullshit. We know Walker has a friend round here, maybe more than one. If these two here don't know him, maybe one of the rest of you does. Well?'

No one says a thing. JC points his pistol in their direction. Vince shakes his head, looking terrified, and says, 'Woah, woah. There's no need for that. I don't even live here. I don't have a clue who this guy of yours is.'

'You'd best hope someone sitting near you does, or you're a dead man.'

'Just tell them,' Vince says, turning back to the rest of the table. 'Whatever it is one of you knows, just tell them. It's not worth all of us getting killed over.'

'You mean *you* don't want to get killed over it,' Will says.

'You're damn right I don't.' Vince rounds on the old man. 'And neither should you. Whoever this Walker guy is, if he's connected to people like them then he's not worth taking a bullet for just to protect. I just want to get home alive. The best way to do that is to give them what they want.'

'Well, I've never heard of him and neither has Christine.'

'Me neither,' Gene says. 'I ain't from here either. I just stopped here because of the weather. I don't know no one here.'

'And I already said I've got no idea who you're talking about,' Isaac says.

'You said he hadn't been in tonight,' JC says. The gun swings towards Isaac and JC's finger tightens around the trigger. 'You didn't say nothing about not knowing him.'

'Hey, hey, hey. That's what I meant, though. I haven't seen him, I don't know him, I've got no idea who he is. OK? There's no need to get nasty here. We're all just a little jumpy.'

'We'll just forget about all this like it was some great misunderstanding, huh?' JC shakes his head. 'I don't think so, Mr Barman. You think *this* is getting nasty, you got no idea what nasty is.'

Vince looks at him, at Isaac. Says, 'Look, there's a couple of other people . . .'

'Shut the hell up,' Will cuts in. 'You've done more than enough talking for tonight.'

'No I will not shut the hell up! There're at least two other people living in this place who aren't right here in the bar with us. They live in one of the houses near by. Maybe they're the ones helping him hide.'

Craig looks at his leader. 'Maybe he's got a point. Even if they're not the ones he's here for, I'm thinking we could do with rounding them all up, get everyone under one roof. We don't want any surprises, 'specially if one of them did take that body.'

'Yeah, maybe.'

Spin nods. 'Everyone's here, only guy hiding outside is gonna be Walker. We can find him and the cash and no one's gonna stop us then.'

JC thinks for a moment, eyes flicker as he runs the options over in his head. Then he lowers the gun. I can feel my heart pounding in my chest, sense it slowing as some of the fear leaks out of the room. He says, 'Sure, OK. Spin, you and me'll go fetch the neighbours. Craig, you stay here. Shoot any of these motherfuckers who try to make a move. Clear?'

'Sure, JC.'

The two men stride out of the door and into the howling night without looking back. Craig waits for the door to bang shut behind them, then his mouth breaks into a shark's grin. 'You all better do what you're told like good little kids. JC says for you not to move, you so much as twitch in your seats and I'll kill you all. Don't think I wouldn't.'

He backs away towards the counter. Swings behind it and helps himself to a bottle of vodka and a glass. 'None of you'd make it three steps before I shot you anyway,' he says as he pours himself a drink. 'No point trying anything. Just sit tight. Could be a long evening and you might as well stay comfortable.'

I decide to risk speaking up. Engage with him while the others are gone. Test the waters. 'Could be,' I say, 'but maybe not in the way you think. Someone out there is up to some seriously bad stuff, and chances are they're as much of a danger to you as they are to the rest of us.'

'Sure, right.' He snorts. 'You know shit if that's what you think. Ain't nothing here to worry us. The shit I've seen ... None of you'd last ten minutes in the place I grew up.'

'I know you've got no way out of this valley until someone repairs one of the bridges. Which means the cops. There's no one else going to fix up a river crossing. Cops come here and all this is still going on, you're screwed.'

'You *do* know shit. We swam that river once, we can do it again.'

'You think. It's still raining out there. The water's getting higher all the time.'

'It ain't so hard with a cable to follow to make sure you don't get swept away.'

'There wasn't any cable there when we checked the bridge, Craig. So if you guys left yourselves a way back, I'd say it's washed away. You're stuck here like the rest of us.' He narrows his eyes slightly, probably trying to figure out if this is a trick or not, but says nothing. 'What I can't get is what this guy of yours did that you're willing to pull all this just to find him? I don't get it.' And what, I wonder to myself, does all this have to do with the corpses by the river, Sam's note, and what we saw at the Banks house? If anything.

'Just some business we need to take care of nice and quickly. Walker has something for us, and we've got to make sure our deal's finished before he goes and vanishes for good. Maybe we need to have words with his friends here as well. Just to make sure everything's permanently fixed.'

'That doesn't sound like much to me,' I say. 'Doesn't sound like anything worth dying over. Not even anything worth stubbing a toe over.'

'You're asking a lot of questions, little man,' Craig says, holding up the gun to make sure that I've seen it, that I've not forgotten the situation we're in.

I haven't. I also haven't forgotten that the three of them totally failed to search any of us and that I've got a pistol of my own he doesn't know about. When the time comes to use it, it'll make a fine ace in the hole.

'I'm just talking. Trying to understand what we're all doing here,' I say.

'You've got a big mouth on you. JC ain't going to worry if I was to put a bullet in it, not if you don't start keeping quiet. You bear that in mind.'

I let it drop, act properly cowed. There seems little point in needlessly pushing the matter. I watch Craig as he sits there, waiting for a sign that his attention's wavering, some moment of weakness I can use to make a move. Putting the gun down for a second, getting distracted by something going on outside the windows. Anything to make him less of a threat to all of us. But he doesn't do it; his gaze stays fixed in our direction and his hand never leaves the butt of his pistol. They might have been sloppy about checking their hostages, but JC's crew aren't complete amateurs.

Time ticks on, half an hour or so, and still Craig doesn't let his guard down. I desperately want an opening to present itself before the other two come back and the odds change in their favour once more.

'It's been a while, Craig,' I say, letting an edge of confidence leak into my voice. 'Your friends have been gone an awfully long time. Maybe the night's not going your way after all.'

'They're just being thorough.'

'You're probably right,' I say. 'That's probably what it is. Unless they've already found that friend of yours and whatever it is you wanted from him, and now they've gone and left you. You'll still be sitting here by the time the cops arrive and they'll be off somewhere miles from here, laughing at you. Poor dumb Craig, sitting there and taking the fall for everything.'

He shakes his head, mouth twists into a snarl. 'Shut up, man. That bullshit's not going to work here, not with me.'

'Or maybe they've run into whoever stole that corpse.'

'Is that so?'

'Yeah.' I smile, and not in a friendly way. 'Something real weird's going on out there, and your friends just walked out smack into the middle of it. There's a chance they're not coming back. I've seen some of what's been happening, and I've heard the stories. Weirdoes up the valley, dead people by the river, and strangers out there in the dark. This is a bad night in a bad place you've walked into, Craig. You'd best hope it doesn't get any worse. Not for you and not for your friends. The kind of person who drags a rotten corpse out of the dirt with their bare hands in a storm isn't the sort of person you can scare off with a gun.'

His eyes flick towards the windows, and for a moment I think: *This is it. Here comes your chance.* I gently close my hand around the grip of my pistol behind me. But the chance doesn't come for me, not quite. Instead, the front door slams open and JC stalks into the room with Spin in tow. He looks edgy; his eyes are jumping and narrow. There's no sign of Tony or anyone else behind him, and I wonder if that's what's causing his twitchiness.

'They all stayed where you put them?' he asks Craig.

'Sure, JC. Apart from Mr Mouth here talking shit to me, none of this bunch were gonna give me any trouble.'

'So watch Mr Mouth.' JC glares at me, then back at the big man. 'People like him'll try to make you forget what it is you're supposed to be doing or what you know you can believe. You don't want to be letting them shoot their mouths off. I've told you this before, right? Allowing shit like that to happen's why people don't like working with you guys.'

Craig's face darkens and he glares at JC. 'Well, what about you two? I don't see you with all them people you were going to bring back. Don't see Walker's fucking head in your pocket either. Good fucking work, JC. Real good. Maybe I should give you a medal.'

'Shut your mouth.'

'So where is he?'

'There's no one out there.' Spin looks as though he's got something to say, but JC keeps going. 'Couldn't find no one in any of the trailers and there's no sign of Walker.'

'You couldn't find anyone? But there's supposed to be two more of them at least. Out in one of the houses.'

'There probably is,' JC says, slowly and deliberately, 'but they weren't there. Not when we checked, anyway. Maybe they saw us coming. Maybe Walker's still on their side and they already ran. Maybe they were never there in the first place. It don't matter; we didn't find 'em.'

'There was someone out there,' Spin says. 'We heard them.'

JC shakes his head and snarls, 'It was no one, jackass.'

'No, no, fuck that, JC. There was someone out

there. That weird fucking noise. That was someone.'

'You're that sure over all that goddamn wind? Shut the hell up.'

Spin doesn't seem to agree. 'It was someone making sounds like bird calls to each other. Like they were watching us. Like they was happy to see us out there, wandering around in the dark.'

'I said to shut the hell up.'

'There's something fucked up going on, JC. He,' he says, pointing at me, 'was saying about some dead body going missing, and then we can't find no one, and there was that noise. There's some fucked-up psycho out there, man.'

'Quit saying that or I'll shoot you in the fucking face,' JC yells, snapping his gun up at Spin's head. 'If it was someone, it was Walker. He knows we're after him, and he just wants us to freak so he can get away with fucking us and taking the cash. That's all. He's just trying to mess with your head.'

Spin doesn't move, but his eyes narrow. 'Put that fucking gun down, JC. I ain't Walker and I ain't your enemy. But you keep waving that thing at me and I guess I'm gonna assume that you're mine.'

'You threatening me, Spin?'

'Just sayin'. And it's *you* that's pointing a gun at *me*, JC. You think about that.'

'What'd you hear out there, Spin?' Craig asks.

JC shakes his head. 'Don't you fucking start as well. He heard shit.'

'There were supposed to be other people out there

and they've disappeared. You couldn't find them. And Walker's supposed to be around, and he's gone. And you want to ignore something that could be people? The people we're here to find? Fuck that.'

'It was like a *whoop whoop* sound,' Spin says. 'Like bird calls or something, except there ain't no birds out there in the storm so we know it weren't that.'

'It was shit.'

'You're wrong, JC.'

'It was the wind.'

'It was *people*. It was. Something fucked up is going on.'

'Stop talking like that. This is the last time I'm gonna tell you, Spin. We've got one job to do, we get the money and we're gone.' He doesn't lower the gun, keeps it pointed at Spin. I can feel Ashley holding her breath next to me. Everyone at the other table seems frozen in place. No one wants to break the spell. To draw the ire of the three of them down on us.

'Put the gun down, JC. You're fucking losing it,' Craig says.

'The fuck you say?' JC whips round to face him. 'You want to see what's going on out there?' he says with a voice like mustard gas. 'We deal with every one of these hillbilly sacks of shit right now and we can all go out looking for whoever we want.'

I know he means it, too. Whatever control he possessed earlier is gone, whether through frustration or through simple short temper, and it's plain he'd have no hesitation in killing any or all of us. He'd put us down without a second thought. The hand holding his gun is white with rage and his eyes are black pinpricks.

My pistol slides free of my waistband. I snap my hand round and up in front of me. No time to nestle the gun firmly and securely, like being back on the range, but that doesn't matter. I squeeze the trigger quickly, before any of the three can react, not caring too much whether I hit or miss. So long as it's enough to shock them, make them flinch, while I move into better cover. My shot goes high and wide, crashing into a light fitting above the bar and sending sparks cascading towards the floor. I'm barely aware of yelling something to everyone about getting down, hitting the floor, but otherwise I act on pure instinct, diving sideways and back into another booth where I can move more freely and enjoy better concealment. Get out of the line of sight without putting anyone else in worse danger.

JC's shouting something beginning with 'Don't you fucking . . .' but the rest is lost in the general cacophony as the three of them return fire. Bullets slap through the wood above my head and kick into the floor around me, showering me with splinters. They're firing wild, though, and nothing connects. Not with me, anyway. I can hear Christine murmuring prayers in a high-pitched voice but no one else seems to be making a sound. The only person I can see from my position is Ashley, who's rolled under the table, on to the floor. She's lying with her hands over her head, eyes clamped shut.

I snap my head out of the side of the booth for a fraction of a second, aiming to see what I can of JC's crew and let off another couple of rounds in their direction. The barrel of Spin's revolver is peeping over the top of the partition nearest the front door, and Craig drops behind the counter as I fire. JC I can't see, but I can still hear him yelling to Craig. His voice is an incoherent roar like it's coming from deep underground. I guess they're reasonably close together. Neither Spin nor Craig looks to have much experience of actual fighting to me. Probably nothing but posturing; wave the gun, make a lot of noise. That gives me an edge.

As I pull back into cover, I see JC pop up from behind the bar to fire a couple of chasing shots in my direction, but a bullet of mine shatters the bottles above his head and he drops out of sight again.

'Fuck you,' he yells out. 'You're a dead man. Three of us and one of you.'

'That just means I've got three times as much chance of hitting someone as you do. Give it up while you still can, JC. It doesn't have to be like this. We can all still walk away.'

'You're the one should be giving up. If you don't throw out that gun of yours I'm going to start wasting your friends. They're sitting fucking ducks, man. You willing to let them die on your account?'

'Some deal, JC. You'll shoot me if I do that, and

then we're all dead anyway,' I yell back, as much for the others' benefit as his. To remind them of what's at stake. 'You don't seem like the sort to leave witnesses to me, which means whatever I do, you'd be killing us all before you left regardless. You were ready to do it a moment ago. But so far no one's been hurt and we can still stop all this. Drop the guns and this doesn't have to end badly.'

'Fuck you.' Another bullet sheers through the panelling by my head.

'Craig, Spin, your friend there's going to get you both killed. You don't have to go down with him. You can still get out of this. You've got that option.'

'Shut the hell up,' JC shouts.

I peer around the side of the booth again, eyes on the counter. 'You're screwed, JC. Your whole plan's shot to pieces now. Craig and Spin would be doing themselves a favour by making the smart choice and ending this before they get killed. You're not going to get Walker or his money, not now.'

Then up he pops again. Gun in his hand, blind fury in his eyes. He opens his mouth to scream something at me in triumph, and I put a bullet through it. He drops like a sack of bricks leaving a gout of bloody matter spattered against the wall behind the counter. When he smacks into the ground I hear Spin and Craig freak out completely, yelling in panic. Incoherent staccato bursts of sound like they're speaking in tongues.

Three shots flash well wide of where I'm crouched and I hear the heavy thud as Craig vaults over the counter-top. I punch a couple of rounds in their direction, barely able to identify anything clearly in the soft sparks tumbling from the ceiling except in strobe-like flashes. I see Spin's head as he turns and runs for the door, Craig tugging on his arm. Both of them vanish out into the night, faces full of panic.

It's over.

23

I look over the partition to see Will huddled with his wife, Vince staring at the carnage in horror and Isaac climbing to his feet with a stunned expression etched heavily on his features. Ashley's still prone beneath the table, staring at me with a hand over her mouth as though she's trying not to breathe. No one seems to have been hurt. The bullets mostly flew well wide and were mainly directed at me.

The adrenaline which for those few moments had run like molten steel through my blood begins to boil away, leaving my system, and suddenly my hands are shaking and my heart is racing. My skull feels three sizes too small for my brain and I want to throw up.

'Jesus, Alex,' Isaac says. 'Jesus.'

I look at him, at all of them. Say, 'Can anyone explain to me what the hell that was all about?'

'Jesus. You killed that guy. You shot him in the face.'

'Why were those guys here armed for bear like that? Who were they looking for?'

Suddenly, the muffled noise of the storm outside is broken by distant screaming. One voice, maybe two. Terrible, lingering, ululating cries of agony and terror so piercing they set my bones trembling. Sounds that no human voice should ever make. The shrieks tear through the room like shrapnel. My body washes with ice and we all gaze out through the windows hoping, and at the same time dreading, to see something of what's happening to Spin and Craig in the dark.

There are no gunshots, no other cries apart from those awful shrieks of horror. Then, just like that, they cut out. The bar holds it breath, waiting for something else, some animalistic roar of victory or triumph, but nothing more comes out of the night and the darkness keeps its secrets. Again, I picture the monster from the Banks house. The axe and the smell of death. I picture the two men torn to pieces in howling agony and I picture the rest of us being next, should we dare to venture outside the building and on to the beast's territory.

'Holy . . .' Isaac murmurs. 'What was *that*?'

Ashley picks herself to her feet, eyes wholly locked on mine. Her face is blanched white and I wonder if she's thinking the same thing as me. That the two of us came so close to meeting whatever it is that's out there, lurking in the dark. That those screams could just as easily have been ours, and that we might never have made it back. Christine's praying again, the sound hollow and empty, no weight or conviction behind it at all. The bar is full of the thick, oily smells of gunsmoke and blood, hanging there like dawn mist in the flickering light.

I hear Will mutter, 'MacBrides.' He looks as shocked as the rest of us.

Sam's note said more people would die; either it's coincidence, or it's Sam himself that's lurking out in the storm. I wonder if 'Evan Walker' is, or was, connected to Sam, if JC's aims here in the valley were something to do with the events alluded to in the note and to the dead by the river. He had friends here, he knew the area, just like the killer. Maybe Sam and Walker are the same person. Maybe it was him that Craig and Spin met just now. I wish we'd been able to find out more about him before everything went to hell.

'Is everyone OK?' I say. 'Is anyone hurt?'

The spell that's held over the bar seems to break suddenly, and people start moving again, climbing to their feet. Christine stops praying and people start talking, checking on one another, making sure everyone's unhurt and that the fear of being shot has lifted, hoping the shock's gone. Isaac crosses round behind the counter to check on JC.

I can hear low voices all around me.

'I thought we were going to ...'

'Jesus Christ, he's dead ...'

'What was all that screaming?'

'... need the cops. Someone should ...'

Will eyeballs me carefully. 'What've you got that gun for?' he says. 'If you don't mind me asking, that is.'

'It's licensed.'

'But you're not a cop. You said that.'

'No, I'm not. I used to be, though. A long time ago. But I still carry a gun.'

Isaac shakes his head, looks at the destruction wrought on his establishment. 'What the hell's going on? I mean, what the *hell*?'

'You ever see those guys before tonight?' I say.

'No. I don't think so, anyway. I've got no clue what they came here for.'

'And you don't know this Walker they were looking for?'

He shakes his head again. 'I just don't get it. Not at all.'

'Anyone else?'

No answer.

'We should find the brothers,' Ashley says slowly, voice thick with the effort she's making to keep it under control. 'We should make sure they're OK too. Those guys couldn't find them, so perhaps they saw them coming. Maybe they know something.'

I nod. 'Yeah. If JC and the other guy didn't find them, I guess they must have hidden somewhere. Or maybe they're still out in the fields. There's a chance they saw what happened to ... to those two. Out there.' And a chance they were the ones who did it, I add to myself. Tony's strange demeanour, Ben's apparent absence ...

'Right,' Will says.

Christine rests a hand on his arm. She's not looking at the spray of red on the wall behind the counter. No one seems to want to let their gazes dwell on the bullet holes or the remains of JC, and she's no different. 'Let's all go, if we're going. Let's not ... I don't want us to separate if those men are still here somewhere.'

No one voices any objection to the idea. Isaac reaches down behind the counter and comes back with a polished pump-action shotgun. He checks the slide and then nods. We all trudge out of the bar together. Ashley stays close to me. Everyone still feeling the shock of what happened. And the fear of what the night holds for us all, trapped here with some unknowable, vicious terror now unleashed upon this valley.

24

As soon as we're out of the door, Will leads us sharply to the right, along the side of the building. The storm still seems to be strengthening. The rain's hard and constant, and every one of us is surrounded by a flash-lit silvery halo of shattered drops as they bounce against our clothes. The wind howls around the road-house like a prowling wolf, broken by the occasional rumble as a twisted branch of lightning lashes green against the cloud.

I see Vince looking around him, jumping at shadows. I guess he's searching for any sign of Spin or Craig, or whatever it was they met out here. I don't blame him – I'm doing the same myself. Any dark shape or mark on the highway or the land around it, anything out of place. I want to know what happened to them and what Sam, or whoever it was they met in the night, is capable of. What it was he did to them. But there's no sign of anything much and the dark's too deep.

Vince catches me watching him and laughs nerv-ously. 'Fucked up out here, isn't it?'

'Yeah.'

'Whole evening feels weird now. I've never walked into something like what just happened.'

I nod. 'I've never been involved in anything like that either. And you certainly don't expect it in a place like this.'

'Sure don't. Christ.' He shakes his head. 'I just want to get out of here now. Get home, y'know?'

'Yeah.'

'Look,' he says, 'I hope you know that the way I was acting back there . . . I just wanted everyone to be OK. I didn't want to get shot, and those guys seemed ready to do it. I figured we'd be better off . . .'

'Sure.'

I don't say anything more and Vince clams up again. He's right, there is a surreal feel to the evening. When I showed up here the valley was an empty slice of run-down America, a blank on the map containing nothing but a roadhouse and a handful of homes. Now I'm here, everything about it seems wrong. As though the mountains have allowed a rotten, terrible evil to pool and fester here. Years of bad feng shui, all concentrated in the one place and this half-dozen people. And now, for some reason, it's reached critical mass. Breaking point.

Will leads us off the gravel of the parking lot and down a narrow dirt path. It's lined with shoulder-high grass that I can hear ripping against the earth in the wind. It sounds like dozens of angry rattlesnakes. In the periodic flashes of lightning I can see a dark stand of trees up ahead, an uneven line cut into the near horizon.

The old man and Isaac are talking in low voices, or at least as low as they can in the conditions. In between gusts of wind, though, I can hear snatches of what they're saying. Enough for me to fill in the rest.

'Jesus, Will, what the hell'd we do to get a night like tonight? Someone must've broken a dozen mirrors, y'know?'

'Ayuh. Those guys were crazy. Crazy. But at least it's over now.' He shakes his head.

'Yeah. I guess it is, except for . . . well, you know. But it wasn't just that I meant.'

'The bodies from the river?'

'Yeah. That's something I was never expecting.'

The old man shrugs. 'I doubt anyone was.'

'It came as a shock to me, I can tell you.'

'The cops are going to have a whole bunch of questions after tonight,' Will says.

'Yeah.' Isaac nods. 'I wonder what the brothers'll make of it.'

'I don't. Not for a second.'

I wonder what he means by that as we cut into the trees. The rain lessens a little but we're still being peppered by leaves and small twigs torn free by the wind. Our flashlight beams are scattered by dozens of whirling black shapes and specks of debris. A gravel track runs through the centre of this belt of woodland and Will turns to follow it. There are no lights up ahead, no sign that there's anything up there to be walking to. We pass a derelict shed, half-ruined and creaking in the storm, and then a sharp turn to the left leaves us looking at the brothers' home. A trailer and a couple of wooden buildings just visible through the screen of trees.

'Tony?' Isaac shouts into the dark. 'Ben? It's Isaac.'

No answer from up ahead. Will says, 'They might not have heard you. Hell, they might not be in. Out in the fields somewhere, maybe.'

'You two ran into Tony earlier?' Isaac says, turning to me and Ashley. 'He said he was going home, right?'

'That's what he said. His flashlight batteries were dead and he hadn't had any luck finding his brother.'

'So maybe they are in, but they just saw those guys looking for them and they hid. Anyone know where they might've holed up?'

He gets nothing but shrugs and a shake of the head from Will in reply.

The trailer's the closest of the three structures, cream-coloured fibreglass facing speckled heavily with moss and streaks of damp. We walk up to the door and Isaac knocks. Of the other two, one looks like an ancient cabin, a pioneer-style farmhouse of sorts that's the best part of a hundred years old if it's a day, and the second seems to be a storage shack or maybe even a stables. Both of them are crumbling and mottled with years of weather damage. I can see a white pickup parked under a makeshift awning beside the shack. It's been a good ten years since the vehicle was anything like new and it looks as though it gets a fair amount of use.

'Guys?' Isaac yells again. 'It's us. Them others are gone. Guys?'

His hand's on the latch and he's about to open the door when a voice yells from behind us, 'We're here, Isaac.'

Two men emerge from behind the cabin, both dressed in near-identical working jackets and jeans. Tony is out in front. He looks nervous, but the same fixed smile I last saw on his face is still there, just a little more strained. Behind him is Ben, the other brother. Taller and much broader, he's got to be six five, and has shoulders carved from slabs of concrete. Lurching, slow and powerful, a real mountain bear with a close-cut crop of dark hair shining in the rain. He's holding a shotgun in hands like hams and doesn't look keen on lowering it any time soon.

'Who're those people with you, Isaac?' the big guy asks. His voice is deeper than Tony's. 'I don't know them.'

'This here's Alex, Vince and Gene. They came to the bar this evening. They're OK.'

'They're not with those others?'

'Others?'

'Them guys out here looking for trouble.'

Isaac shakes his head. 'No, Ben. They're with us, OK?'

The big man regards us for a moment, then softens

his grip on the shotgun, apparently satisfied. 'Sure,' he says. 'We just got to be careful, right?'

'Yeah.' Tony walks over to join us. Ben watches for a second, then follows suit. Isaac continues, 'You guys OK out here? A bunch of people tried to hold up the bar and a couple of them came out looking for you.'

'Yeah, we saw them,' Ben says. He turns his gaze to his brother.

'We hid in the basement,' Tony says on cue. 'They didn't know there was a way down there. They didn't manage to find us.'

'Uh-huh.'

'We saw them come round, but they didn't know we were there.'

Ben places his hand on Tony's shoulder. 'We saw they had guns on them. A couple of strangers come round here with pistols and it don't take much to know they're bad news. We'd have gone to check on you guys, but we didn't know if they were still out here.'

I look at them, at the house. 'And you just stayed down in the basement all that time?'

'Yeah,' Tony says. He's still got mud on his boots. They both have. Their coats are wet with rain.

'You didn't hear anything from out here?' The mud could've come from the cellar. The rain might just be what they picked up coming out to meet us. It's hard to tell the truth from the paranoia and the suspicion. In a place like this, with everything that's happened here, it's difficult not to jump at shadows.

'Like what?' Ben says. 'What kind of thing?'

'Shouting, screaming, gunshots. A weird whooping noise like someone making bird calls . . .'

'No, mister, we didn't. The cellar's pretty solid and, with the storm and all, neither of us heard a damn thing. We weren't even sure when those fellers had gone, so we stayed down there a good long time. Made sure we were safe.'

Tony nods. 'Anyway. So it's over? They've gone? We can stop worrying about them?'

Will looks sidelong at me for a moment with an expression I can't read. Then he says to the brothers, 'Yeah, those fellers are gone. One of them was shot, though. We're not sure what happened to the other two. The cops'll be coming out here to deal with it.'

'The bridges are washed away,' Isaac says, waving in the vague direction of the Clay Stream.

'Yeah? Both of them?'

'That's right. The storm took them out. We figure the cops'll have them back up in the morning, but until then we're on our own.'

'And that's not all. Mr Rourke here found some bodies out by the river. Dead awhile and buried in the dirt. A real strange business all round.'

'Three,' I cut in. 'There were three of them. A man, a woman and a boy. But the woman's body has gone missing. Someone dug it up.'

'That's right. So they're going to be looking into that as well. They'll probably want to talk to everyone, I guess.'

'You didn't see anything, did you, Tony?' I say. 'We found out the woman's body was gone not long after me and Ashley saw you near the Banks house.'

He shakes his head.

'Nothing at all? Didn't hear anything either?'

Ben looks down at his brother, eyes glittering, and says, 'You've met this guy before? You were out at the Banks house? Why was that?'

'I was looking for you, Ben. With the storm, I was worried about you being out in the pasture for so long.'

'I was gone half an hour,' the older brother says. '*You* worried *me*, not being here when I got back.'

Tony nods. Ben doesn't do anything. They stand there like a pair of statues.

'Anyway, we were thinking we should probably all stick together back at Isaac's until we know what's going on,' Will finishes. 'Two of them fellers with the guns ran off. We heard *something* happen to them not long after, and it didn't sound pleasant. Figure we'd best not be scattered all over the place, not after everything that's happened. Look after each other, right?'

Tony looks at Ben. The bigger brother nods after a moment's thought, then glances at Will. 'Sure,' he says. 'We'll head back with you. There's safety in numbers, isn't there, Will?'

The two of them fall into step in the middle of our little group for the walk back through the trees. They don't say anything to me or the other two non-locals, although Tony meets my eyes and inclines his head in what could be a greeting. I don't know if Ben sees the gesture or not, but for some reason a look of pure bitterness passes across his face. Just a flicker, just for a moment. The branches above us thrash in the wind and lightning paints the sky green and hideous. Diseased. I glance back at the brothers' dwelling and wish for a moment that I'd been able to have a look inside. The little collection of buildings has a strange atmosphere, even more cloying than the rest of the valley. Like walking into the house where a murder's recently occurred after the place has been cleaned and cleared. Everything looks fine on the surface, but the nagging knowledge of what's happened sets everything on edge. The place crackles with suppressed . . . anger? Hatred? The strange vibe between the two brothers is just one facet of it.

'So what are you three doing here in the valley?' Ben's voice hauls me back to full attention. He laughs a couple of times, adds, 'Guess you didn't come for the weather.'

'I was supposed to meet a guy to talk about buying some land,' Vince says. 'He's not here, though. I guess he won't show up at all now.'

Gene shrugs. 'I'm just passing through.'

'Alex, wasn't it?' Ben looks at me.

'I came here looking for someone called Sam,' I

say, watching his face for a reaction to the name. Like the other locals, if there's anything there he does a good job of hiding it. Like with the rest of them, I'm not sure I believe it. Unless the note was just a joke, someone here must know the name. A place like this, it's impossible to hide.

'There's no one called Sam lives here, not now, not since we first came here,' he replies without hesitation. 'You're out of luck if you're looking for her in these parts.'

'Her?' My heart quickens.

'What?'

'You said "her".'

He shrugs, glances at his brother's back up ahead and doesn't look back. 'Sam can be a girl's name as much as a guy's. It didn't mean anything. Hell, I went to school with a girl named Sam.'

'Fair enough,' I say, though it isn't. 'Anyway, it's not just *her* I'm looking for. Are there any crosses around here? An old churchyard, something like that?'

'Crosses?'

'Yeah. I'm supposed to find some crosses somewhere round here.'

'Is that so? Picked a bad night for it. A real bad night. All three of you. Just bad luck, I guess.' He sounds sad, but doesn't expand further and I can't guess at the reason for his tone. He hunkers his head down and increases his stride until he's shadowing Will. The rain lashes his coat against his figure, making him look like a moving lump of basalt bowed down by the weight of the night.

As I watch Ben, I catch some of the conversation Vince is having with Ashley. He's asking her about our trip out to the river and the Banks house and he sounds full of nerves. When she mentions the signs that someone had been in the abandoned building and the strange visitor who passed through when we were upstairs though, he suddenly becomes much more interested in what she's saying.

'You think it could've been that Walker those guys were talking about?'

The wind drowns her reply, but it doesn't sound especially affirmative.

'He sounded kinda dangerous from what they were saying. Supposed to be a real killer. Maybe it was him who did for Spin and Craig as well, if he's got some-place to hide out here. Where is this house you were at, anyway?'

I think back to the story he was telling earlier about being here to buy property, and I think about the way he behaved when the situation with JC went bad. And I wonder. I wonder what his reasons really are for being here and whether he has a connection to the three dead men. I wonder what he knows. I wonder what he hasn't told us.

25

The bar still smells of cordite when we return. The thick scent hasn't cleared at all, clinging to the walls like the memory of violence. Ashley catches sight of JC's blood and shudders. No one looks behind the counter just yet, with the exception of Ben. He peers behind it and just shakes his head at what he sees.

'What are you doing?' Isaac says.

'Looking.'

'It's disgusting. Christ, the guy almost killed us all. And what's left of him . . . Jesus.'

Ben says nothing, just shrugs. He doesn't seem bothered by the carnage.

I tap Vince on the shoulder and steer him over to a table. 'I heard what you were saying to Ashley,' I tell him. 'You should probably know, she didn't see everything at that house.'

'No?' Vince stares out the window, drumming his fingers on the tabletop in front of him, as though he has little interest in this topic of conversation.

'What would you say if I told you I know where that Walker guy might be hiding?'

'You do?'

'Maybe, yeah. Just maybe.' I eye the rest of the bar suspiciously, lowering my voice to the whisper used for all shared secrets. 'I'm just not sure I can really talk about it. I mean, those guys said someone here was hiding him, so who knows who's listening, right? Maybe it was nothing, anyway.'

I go quiet and wait for a response. Vince holds out for a brief moment then says, with forced nonchalance dripping from every syllable, 'So where is he? You can tell me; I don't even live here. Maybe we could go check it out together and then we'd know for sure, right?'

'Yeah, that's true. Hey,' I add, smiling broadly, 'you might be living here soon too, from what you were saying earlier.'

'Yeah, yeah. That's right,' he says. 'Maybe, if it works out that way.'

'I had a bitch of a time paying for my last place. What are the property taxes like in this state?'

'Oh, you know.' He shrugs. 'So where are we going?'

I harden my tone, drop the bonhomie. 'Nowhere, until you tell me what the taxes are. You're here looking for property to buy? You'll know what the rate is. Assuming, of course, you really are looking to quit insurance and buy a farm and you're not just lying through your teeth.'

Vince holds up his hands. 'It's true.'

'*Bullshit*. You're here looking to buy a farm, you'll know what the property tax rates in this state are. Tell me. It's easy enough.'

He glances left and right. Over his shoulder I can

see the others taking an interest in our conversation. 'Alex . . .'

'It's a simple question. What're the property tax rates in this state?'

'I haven't looked at . . .'

'*What're the property tax rates in this state?*'

'Fuck you, Alex. You're nuts.' He jumps to his feet. 'I'm not putting up with this. I'm getting out of here.'

'Isaac! He's one of JC's friends,' I yell. As soon as he hears that, the barman moves to interpose himself between Vince and the front entrance. The younger man looks from him to me and back again. Isaac grins, and Vince smashes his fist into the barman's chest, leaving him stunned and gasping for a moment. Then he runs full tilt for the door.

26

I whip my pistol out and pursue. Isaac recovers fast enough to snatch his shotgun up again and together we barge through the door after Vince. He's already half-way across the parking lot, feet splashing through the rain.

'You stop where you are, Vince,' I shout. Isaac fires a round into the air, the shotgun's roar mirroring the cacophony of the storm above. Vince ignores us both and jumps into his Mazda. He's frantically turning the ignition, the starter motor just coughing into life, when Isaac plants a slug through the hood and into the engine block, killing it. Through the windshield I see Vince swear and dive for something in the glove box. He comes out with a pistol in his hands, so I shoot him clean through the glass. The bullet catches him in the bicep and throws his arm limp and helpless at his side, blood welling from the hole. He screams with pain, and it only gets worse for him when Isaac grabs him by the neck and hauls him bodily out of the car with one hand to leave him in a heap on the gravel. I kick the pistol away from Vince's good arm and cover him with my own.

'Don't even think about getting up,' Isaac says. 'I'll take your fucking head off.' To me, he adds,

'You're sure he was with them other guys?'

'Yeah, I think so.'

'You think?'

'It certainly fits. There's been something strange about him all evening.'

I look down at Vince, bleeding on the parking lot. The fact that he has a gun doesn't prove that he was involved with what went on earlier, but that and his unhealthy interest in the man they were looking for certainly makes him *look* guilty. And the lies about his reasons for being here do nothing to help him.

'What do we do with him, Alex?'

'Find out who he is and what's going on. Search him, search the car. See what we can find. Unless he wants to save us the effort and tell us himself?' I look at Vince.

He winces against the pain in his arm and lies still. Says, 'I didn't do nothing, you son of a bitch. You're fucking nuts, man. Look what you've done to my arm.'

Rainwater sluices through the bullet hole and on to the driver's seat of Vince's Mazda as I hunt around in the interior. The registration's in his name and he's insured. It looks genuine. He eats Jolly Rancher and called at a Burger King on his way up here. There doesn't seem that much more to learn from what's in here. It's not the neatest car in the world, but I've seen worse. Driven worse.

Isaac taps me on the shoulder. 'Come take a look at the trunk,' he says.

I stand there in the rain, wind snapping at my hair, as Isaac shows me the open gym bag. Three more guns, more ammunition, tape, gloves, black plastic sacks. Almost the full armed robber's overnight bag, just missing the ski masks. With a plastic baggy of white pills for an added bonus.

I pick up the bag and show it to Vince. His face sinks as he sees it. 'Was all this firepower going to help you negotiate real estate? Maybe you wouldn't have to pay taxes at all.'

Thunder barks overhead and the wind screeches through the holed shell of the Mazda and I feel strangely exposed out here. Some primitive human instinct that comes to life in the night when your attention begins to slip from your surroundings. The brain realizing it's not fully aware of what's going on, that the body's at risk. I drag Vince to his feet, holding his hands behind him. He groans with pain as I tighten the hold on his injured arm but doesn't try to fight it.

'Got him?' Isaac says.

'Yeah. If he's stupid enough to make a break for it, take out a leg.'

We push Vince back through the front door. Everyone stares at him, his injury, at us, at the gym bag slung from my free hand. Isaac says, 'I guess we'd better bind this son of a bitch's arm before he loses too much blood.'

When I search him, Vince's jacket contains a spare clip, a cell phone and a folded copy of a map frighteningly similar to my own. I look at it twice just to make sure that it really is a different photocopy from a different map. The cell must have a good two hundred names in its memory, but they're mostly meaningless apart from three – JC, Spin, Craig M. In his wallet, I find about two hundred bucks in cash, a couple of credit cards in the name Vincent Moore, a condom and a handful of random business cards for car repair, dry cleaning and the like, mostly out of state and well away from here. Nothing obviously pertinent to our current situation.

'Anything interesting?' Isaac says.

'Unless you're planning a vacation and want to have your suspension checked while you're doing it, no, not in his wallet. His phone has numbers for JC and the other two guys in its memory. I guess that makes it conclusive.'

Vince doesn't say anything, just shakes his head. I wonder why so few people are capable of accepting that the game's up.

I drop the bag on the table in front of him. 'I'm no expert, Vince, but that's a lot of guns. This Walker guy must be real dangerous if you needed all that just to deal with him.'

'I don't know what you're talking about. Why the hell would I want anything to do with guys like those three? They were total psychos.'

'I suppose you just happened to have traded numbers with them.' He lowers his eyes again. 'And you were carrying these guns for a friend, right? Probably didn't even know they were there. Happens all the time. I'm always finding bags of guns in my car. I blame Triple-A.'

'They weren't anything to do with me,' he says again. 'Nothing.'

'Why were the four of you here, Vince? Who's this Walker guy?' I want to hear something from him that's connected to Sam. I want to know why I'm here and what I'm supposed to be doing. My pulse is up and racing with the possibility of an answer. 'And let me make it clear, Vince,' I say. 'I *know* you were here with JC and his crew. I'm quite happy to guess that you came here separately from them, intending to get the lie of the land and maybe find out where Walker was hiding before they arrived. You were the talker, the one who was going to be all friendly with the locals, and the other three were going to be the muscle. You were going to do your job, then the four of you could go deal with Walker.

'And your three friends were planning on executing every one of us in here, so I doubt any of us are very happy with you. Probably not too inclined to have you breathing the same air as them. You come clean and maybe, *maybe*, I can persuade them to leave you fit and well for the cops to deal with. If you don't, well, I guess there's a chance you won't even last long enough to *see* the cops.'

He doesn't say anything. I frown. 'The other thing you should consider is that something happened to Spin and Craig when they ran off, something really bad. You heard the screams just the same as we did. If it was Walker that did it, then we all have an interest in stopping him. It's pretty obvious something strange is going on tonight, and you've walked into the middle of it. Helping us know the score is the same as helping yourself right now.'

Behind me, Isaac says, 'Are you sure you're not a cop? You certainly know the talk.'

I shake my head. 'I don't even like doughnuts. Vince. Talk.'

He takes a moment to weigh his options, then lowers his eyes. 'Walker used to be a part of JC's crew. They pulled all sorts of shit together down south. Heavy stuff, but nothing too big. They weren't anyone important.'

'And you?'

Vince shrugs with his eyes, keeps his gaze lowered. 'I worked a few jobs with them, though not the last one they did together. Sometimes I dealt with them before or after, helped them get stuff, offload stuff. We were friends, I guess.'

'So why'd they come here?'

'A while back they killed a judge's daughter down in Charlotte. The cops arrested someone who identified Walker as being at the scene, so he ran. Thing is, if they catch him, we know – knew – they'd ask him to testify against the rest of the crew in return for a lighter sentence. Walker's connected. Nothing major, but he knows a lot of people. He could cause a lot of trouble.'

'So you, JC and the others didn't want him surviving in case your names came up and you found yourselves in prison.'

'I don't want to go to jail, especially not thanks to something I wasn't involved in. I've got a girl, Tess, and a daughter. She's only three years old.' He sniffs. 'JC asked me to help, so I said yes. If Walker fingered me for anything, I'd be going down too just the same as everyone else. JC knew Walker was coming here.'

'You're a real saint. Your family must adore you.'

'Hey, screw you. I do what I can,' Vince says. 'What I've got with Tess is something different to anything I ever had before. I want to stay alive and free for her and my little girl. I don't want her growing up without a dad. If it means stopping a guy turning me over for working with him ages ago, so be it.'

'You could try going straight.'

'You know how hard that is when you have a record like mine? You ever tried it?'

'You're a real gentleman. Why did Walker come here, of all places?'

Vince shakes his head. 'He'd been talking about this valley for a couple of months. I'd heard him once or twice, and the others more. He came from round here, I think. But he said he'd done some work with someone here, work they wouldn't want anyone else knowing about. He kept saying that any time he wanted to he could threaten to reveal all and they'd have to pay him off. Like a retirement fund. He had someone here, some friend or family, who'd help him do it, watch his back. JC went after him down south to shut him up and he escaped, so the crew figured he'd come here.'

'Uh-huh.' I look at him, wait for him to continue.

'I always kinda figured the story for bullshit, but then you came in saying you'd found those dead people and I wondered . . .'

I try not to let the surge of excitement show in my face at the mention of the buried corpses. 'What do you mean?'

'That's what he'd always said. That this friend of his killed a whole family and he'd needed his help to hide what he'd done.' I hear gasps from the locals by the counter, can see them swapping glances with each other. 'I don't know if it was Walker that buried them, but I know he took their RV. Drove it two states and ditched it in a neighbourhood that'd strip it for parts in thirty seconds flat, is the way he told it. Point is, he knew everything, and this friend of his needed it to stay quiet, so they'd pay up.'

This friend killed those people by the river. Sam. It must be; it's too small a place for the note, the bodies and Walker's story to be coincidence. It all ties together. 'What did he tell you about this friend of his?'

'Nothing much.'

'A name?'

Vince shakes his head. 'No, nothing. Probably didn't want to tempt anyone into trying the same thing. He just said that he was someone living here.'

I hear someone, possibly Will, say, 'MacBrides.'

'Yeah,' Ben intones. 'They're murderous sons of bitches, the lot of them, up there in the woods. This is just like them.'

'And those people were killed . . . when?' I ask.

'About a year ago, I think.'

'Had he done any work for this friend of his before?'

'I don't know. I think so, the way he told it, but I don't know.'

I lean in closer, lift his face so I'm looking directly into his eyes. 'Did he ever mention the name Sam to you or the others?'

'I don't think so,' he says. 'I don't think so. I mean, maybe, it's possible – people say a lot of names, don't they? – but I can't remember for sure.'

I watch him carefully for a moment, examining his face for any sign that he's holding out at all. I can't see anything there to suggest that he is, and lean back again, look around to the others.

'What do we do with him?' Isaac asks.

I ask Isaac if he's got a padlock and chain or something similar he can spare. He nods and scurries out the back. I say to Ben, 'Bring him over to that radiator in the corner.'

'Hey, hey,' Vince struggles against Ben's grip, but as soon as his injured arm pulls taut he winces with pain and goes limp again. 'You said they wouldn't hurt me. You said you wouldn't let them.'

'Yeah, I said that, and I meant it. We just need you

to stay cuffed in the corner so we can be sure *you* won't hurt *us*. You and your pals have caused enough trouble for tonight for me to take the risk.'

'What trouble am I going to cause anyone with a busted arm?'

I shrug. Isaac comes back in with a rusty chain and a brass padlock in his hands. He tosses them to me. 'Just think how much less you'll be able to cause when that busted arm's what chains you to the wall,' I say.

Ben hauls Vince down to the floor. It seems to take him no effort at all. I wrap the chain in tight loops around his bad hand, just to make sure any move he tries to make will hurt as much as possible, then do the same with the other end around the radiator pipes and click the lock into place. I check the plumbing, making sure he can't unscrew it or slip out of it somehow. He's secure for the night. I wish we all were.

'Isaac,' Ashley says as we return to the others, 'can we do something with . . . him?' She gestures behind the counter to where JC's corpse is lying, shattered, on the floor. 'It's too horrible. We can't have him there all night.'

It's probably been going on all the time and I'd just tuned it out, but the windows rattle and boom with the wind outside. The building shudders a little.

'We could put a sheet over him,' Will says. 'Cover him up.'

'But there's so much blood. It'll soak through. It's too horrible.'

The old man shrugs. 'The cops always say you're not supposed to move anything. We can cover him up then all just move to the other side of the bar. Make like he's not there. It won't be so bad.'

'No, no,' Isaac says. 'She's right. We can't keep a goddamn corpse in here through the night.'

'We can't?'

'It's not healthy. What if it starts to stink or something? I don't want that. We've got to get rid of it somehow.'

'Not just him either,' I say. 'There's the two corpses out by the river. With the bridge out, we know the cops won't be here until morning at least and the longer this rain keeps up, the less trace evidence they're going to have to work with when they do. If they're going to have a hope of finding out who Walker's friend is, we need to go cover them up.'

'"Trace evidence"? Are you on *CSI* now?'

'Believe it or not, I know something about this kind of thing,' I say. 'Anything the cops would want to find will be destroyed by the water come morning and they'll get jack. We need to get them out of the elements as much as we can.'

'You've got to be kidding,' Will says. He shakes his head. 'We can't go doing that.'

'I need plastic sheeting or tarpaulin, something like that. And stakes. Enough to hold it down in this wind. Someone can come with me and we can cover them up together. It won't take long.'

'I think there's some in the repair shop,' Will replies. 'But what the hell's the use? That kind of thing won't hold in the storm. The weather's too rough.'

'And there's the chance the whole damn lot could fall into the river at any point. But it's worth trying though. We can't just give it up as a lost cause. You *do* want Walker's friend caught, don't you?'

Everyone falls silent again. Retreats into their thoughts and the pounding embrace of the storm. Rain crashes against the windows like thrown stones.

'Sure,' Will says eventually. 'We can get some tarp from my shop. Maybe, I guess, we can even keep that guy there.' He jerks a finger in the direction of JC.

'Where?'

'My auto-repair shop at the side of the station. We don't use it for much these days, and he'll be out of the way there. But I'm not happy about it, just make sure you know that.' Christine lays a hand on his arm. He squeezes it.

'Fine. Isaac, are you willing to help me cover those bodies?'

'Me?'

'I can't do it on my own; it's going to be too tough in this storm.'

Isaac shakes his head and his frown deepens. 'Fuck. My life used to be simple, y'know? To tell the truth, I don't fancy it, no. But I guess . . .'

'It's all right, Isaac,' Ben cuts in. He rises from his stool with a face like flint. 'I'll go. We can take my truck. If that's OK with you?'

I nod. 'Sure.'

'I'll go get it. Rest of you might as well get that dead guy out of here and make yourselves comfortable. Looks like it's going to be a long night, doesn't it?'

Will glares at his back as he stalks out of the bar and into the night. Christine's hand tightens on his shoulder, but neither of them says anything further.

Isaac looks at the rest of us. 'I guess we'd better do it. Tony, give me a hand here,' he says, looking over the counter at the corpse. 'Gene, you want to open the door for us?'

'Here.' Will tosses the truck driver a set of keys. 'Open up the shop for those two as well. Lock it when you're done.'

When Isaac and Tony lift JC his head drops backwards. His blank, dead eyes swing round to look at me and there's a nasty wet noise as fluids from his skull leak all over the floor. Ashley gasps and almost immediately clamps her jaw shut like she's either trying to stifle a scream or stop herself vomiting. Tears glitter at the corners of her eyes and I can see her blinking them back as she looks away from the bloody mess.

'Sweet Jesus,' Christine says. 'Be careful, Isaac.'

'Sorry. I didn't know that was gonna happen. You OK, Tony?'

'Yeah.' The younger brother gulps hard.

'Sure? I don't want you dropping this guy.'

'Yeah, sure, Isaac.'

I watch through the windows as the two of them struggle out into the night with their burden slung between them like medieval labourers working at a plague site. The wind tugs at the dead weight but the two men manage to keep it from slipping from their grasp. Gene tracks them with a flashlight all the way across the parking lot, then unlocks the repair shop and stands clear. From here, it doesn't look like it's been used in a while. Probably a bay for repairing vehicles, but with no auto mechanic it seems pretty much derelict, an empty concrete shell attached to the side of the gas station. The two men carry their dead cargo inside. Gene has a word with them, then heads on his own in the direction of his rig, waving off offers of company. Presumably going to check on his vehicle again.

As we watch the other two return Ashley asks me, 'Do you believe in souls, Alex?'

'I said earlier I didn't have religion.'

'Yeah, but that doesn't mean you don't believe that we've all got souls. Not necessarily.'

'True,' I say. 'But I don't, no. Same deal.'

'So what happens when we die?'

'That's it. That's all there is. Nothing immortal. Nothing eternal. We're here for a while and that's all we ever get.'

Tony and Isaac clatter through the bar's front door.

Ashley's eyes flick in their direction, then she says, keeping her voice low, 'You're going out there with Ben for real?'

'Yeah.'

'You should be careful, Alex.' She fixes her eyes on mine. 'Seriously. He's in a really strange mood at the moment. It's creeping me out, the way he's looking at people. I mean, he can be kinda weird most times, but right now . . . Watch yourself, OK?'

I think about the big man, try to remember what he's said or done this evening. 'Really?'

'He's acting like how people are before they go away. Like he's saying goodbye to them.'

The door clatters open again and Ben's standing in the gap. He stares at me, says, 'Let's go.'

27

Will says, gruffly, 'Be careful out there. Watch out for the MacBrides. There's no telling how many of them could be around. They got them other two, so don't let them get close to you.'

We duck out into the rain. Ben's face is unreadable, his long hair whipping around it in sodden strands. Like thorny vines or a jellyfish's stingers. A halo of cold, wet spines.

I can feel the storm up above us still, brooding and waiting. The wind and rain might be as strong as ever, but the lightning seems to have stopped for now and the sky is black as tar. Strange noises come from the cloud though, deep bass groaning and straining like an ocean liner sinking into the depths. Almighty forces twisting and wrenching against one another, pressure building, trapped in this dead-end valley. I wonder when it'll finally explode.

Ben's pickup is the aging and worn-out lump of metal I saw parked by the side of his house. Its white paint is spattered with rust and peeling in places. Inside, it smells like old oil and fresh sweat.

'You sure about covering those people over?' Ben asks as he slips the truck into gear. 'You sure we need to?'

'Yeah.'

'They might've already fallen apart or washed away. They could be in the river by now.'

'We'll have to run that risk. A whole night out in the rain is only going to guarantee there's nothing left for the cops, so we might as well do what we can.'

He nods. 'I suppose.'

As we pull away from the gravel of the parking lot and on to the highway blacktop, the truck's headlights pick out something on the road surface up ahead. Flat and dark, lying in the rain. I tell Ben to stop again, then climb out to take a look.

It's a jacket. Craig's, I think. It's drenched in so much blood not even the rain's been able to wash it clean. The fabric has been rent by slash after slash with something wickedly sharp. A knife, I suppose, no matter how much I picture a huge set of claws carving into him, glimmering in the night.

Maybe six feet away is what looks like one of Spin's shoes. Again, it has blood on it, and a ragged puncture in the heel. Nearby is Craig's gun, left discarded on the roadway. I wonder if he had any ammunition left after the shootout in the bar. If he tried to kill their attacker, only to find his gun was empty, or if he never had the chance to pull the trigger in the first place.

I pan a flashlight over the fields around, but see no further sign of the two men. They seem to have disappeared completely, leaving only these strange, chilling mementoes behind them. In my head, I hear them screaming as they meet a horrible and wholly unexpected end in the dark. Frozen in terror, brains completely locked up, unable even to fire in self-defence as something, someone, boils out of the night like death itself. Craig lying on the ground, shrieking at the agony coming from his gut wounds, Spin yelling in horror as the dark shape picks him up by the throat and finally snaps his neck. Both bodies dragged back away into the dark. Trophies. Food.

'What is it?' Ben asks when I rejoin him in the truck.

'What's left of the other two guys who held up the bar. I think.'

'Bodies?'

'No, no. Just a couple of pieces of clothing and a lot of blood.'

The big man puts the truck into gear and pulls away from the scene. 'What happened to them? You see anything?'

'Christ knows. Whatever it was, it wasn't pretty.' I stare out into pitch blackness, doing my best not to imagine them being torn limb from limb by some unholy beast. To keep my mind from wandering down these routes I change tack; there's nothing to be learned by wild conjecture about what happened to the two of them, after all. 'How come you're so calm about this whole idea, coming out here?' I ask Ben.

'What do you mean?'

'Most people would've baulked at the thought of

having anything to do with corpses as old as these ones. Like Isaac did. Even Ashley only went out there to help me examine them earlier because she didn't know that's what I had in mind when we did it.'

'Ashley saw 'em?'

'Yeah. It rattled her pretty bad. They're not good to look at.'

'Yeah, I guess,' he says.

'So why agree to this?'

'It needs doing, according to you. I can see the logic to what you're saying, and I guess the others do too.'

'Will seemed OK about keeping that guy in his shop.'

'Yeah.'

'I'm surprised he was so easy about it. I mean, that place is his home. Him and Christine ... I figured they wouldn't want a corpse under their roof. Maybe they're just trying to be helpful.'

Ben nods. 'Yeah. But with Will, you can't ever tell.'

'What do you mean?'

'Don't buy into his harmless old fool act; underneath it all, he's a tough old bastard. And he's good at hiding it.' There's a note of bitterness there. Something deeper behind his words. The same thing I saw in him when we went out to his house. 'I'm sure everything that's happened tonight's shook him up. But don't believe everything you see on the surface with him.'

'Really?'

'He can be a cold, calculating son of a bitch when he wants to be, and he'll do what needs to be done when he has to. You mark my words.'

'Like going out on corpse-covering detail without batting an eyelid?'

There's another twisted metal boom from the heavens. The sky remains dark. Ben glances at me and smiles. His expression doesn't do much to fill me with joy.

28

I breathe out, try to change the subject. 'If those people up the valley . . .'

'The MacBrides.'

'Yeah, them. If they're so bad and have done so much wrong, how come you guys haven't turned the police on them? Surely you could get them to stop the sort of things you say they do.'

'The cops have been up there a couple of times before now,' he says after a moment. 'It doesn't make any difference. I know they went to speak to them after the construction guy went missing. Hell, they spoke to all of us back then.'

'Isaac told me about that. He vanished with a load of money and the project folded.'

'And now the Foundations are all that's left, yeah,' he finishes for me. 'This was fifteen, sixteen years ago, something like that. He disappeared one night with a pile of cash he was planning on offering . . . someone, I forget who, for their land. Or to pay his workers, or something. Guess the details are starting to go fuzzy. It was a lot of money, I know that much.'

I nod. 'He took the money and ran?'

'That's what we figure. Of course, the cops looked into it seriously. It wasn't as though everyone liked the idea of selling up, or of him starting construction on what land he'd already got like there was nothing we could do to stop it.' He shakes his head and stares out into the darkness. 'There were some real heavy arguments about it in Peter's – this was before Isaac bought the roadhouse, so it was Peter's place then. Some of us wanted to fight it, some of us wanted to take the money and move somewhere better. He was offering way over the odds for the land. Guess it was real tempting for some folk.'

'You were here back then?'

'Yeah. Grew up round here, and I'd just got out of the army. I didn't want to move. Where'd I go? Me and Tony lived here all our lives.'

'And he wanted the MacBrides' property too?'

Ben shrugs. 'Whole valley if he could've. Turn the whole thing into a golf course with his big ol' country club right smack in the middle. Charge people thousands of dollars for a weekend in the mountains. Could've been a big earner for him.'

'What did they think of it?'

'The MacBrides? They didn't like it.' He glances at me and there's a look in his eyes I haven't seen before. His wariness is gone for a moment and he seems wistful, almost sad. 'Things were different back then. They liked their privacy, sure, but we knew them to talk to. They'd come down the valley sometimes and they weren't unfriendly. That all happened after. But they didn't want to sell. MacBride's wife, Tracy, in particular – she was planning on taking the whole thing to court, trying to organize those of us who didn't want to go, all sorts. It got pretty ugly – Will and Chris wanted out. I think they wanted to make sure . . .' His voice trails away for a moment. Then he says, 'Make sure they had something to retire with; that gas station doesn't make much. Peter was willing to sell. It was just me and Tony and David who wanted to stay.'

'David?'

'Ashley's uncle. He moved away a while back. Had a stroke, I think.'

'So it was you guys against it, you and the MacBrides.'

'Yeah.'

'And the Bankses?'

'Didn't live here then. They arrived here maybe ten years ago, well after all that, then Marcia moved away again right after Charlie died a couple of years back.' He eases off the gas and brings the car to a halt. Up ahead, the road vanishes into empty space. I can hear the river pounding away in the chasm at the edge of the headlights. 'We're here. We're walking?'

'Yeah. The ground won't take a car. I don't think so, anyway.'

'Best not to risk it, huh?'

'Best not.'

'It's going to be tough working sheeting in this wind.'

I shrug. 'That's about the shape of it. We'll manage.'

We climb out into the rain. As Ben's passing me

the thick wooden stakes and the bundled plastic sheets from the back of his truck, he glances at the sky and says, 'What the hell's going on up there?'

The crushing metal noises above are being punctuated by higher, sharper pops and crackles, but still we can't see any lightning.

'Sounds angry,' I say.

'Yeah. Yeah, it does. Sooner or later, it'll snap.'

He's no longer looking at the clouds when he says it. I just nod and we set off into the fields.

'Anyway,' he continues, 'we were all set to argue it out and either sell up and leave or fight the thing, and then Tracy died.'

'MacBride's wife?'

Ben nods. Hunched over in the rain with a sledge-hammer slung over one shoulder, he casts a funereal figure in the black. 'She was killed on the road in a hit and run. Been walking down to the roadhouse, as far as we could tell, when a car hit her and she died on the spot. We all got asked questions, and I guess they must've looked hard at the developer guy since he had reason to want her gone, but they never did figure out who did it. It wasn't him, I know that.'

'No?'

'No. And it wasn't no accident,' he says. He doesn't elaborate further. Instead he goes on, 'It was two, three weeks after she died that the construction guy vanished. Something like that. He held off on trying to persuade the rest of us to sell for maybe a week as some kind of bullshit mark of respect. By then, the cops had done asking questions about what happened. Then one day he was there and they were working on the Foundations same as normal. The next day he was gone. Disappeared overnight, like he'd driven off and never come back, and took all the money with him. Whether that's what happened or not's another story.'

There must've been plenty of people with reason to want him gone. I wonder why the police never figured out who was responsible. Or maybe he really did just take the cash and run. He wouldn't be the first. I say, 'The cops looked into it?'

'Yeah. I think they thought one of us might've killed him or something, but none of us knew anything about it. I guess no one did at all, or else they would've found him by now.'

'They talked to MacBride?' In the flashlight beam, I can see the collapsed river bank up ahead. Almost there.

He nods. 'I think so. I mean, if he thought the guy had killed Tracy, he might've wanted some payback, right? But whatever they asked him, nothing ever came of it.'

'But the whole business killed the building project.'

'Yeah, they were running short on cash by the time that guy vanished. Must've been the last of what they had that he stole. And MacBride did take them to court in the end, just like Tracy had wanted. Me and Tony did too or, at least, we added our names to the papers. The others didn't like it; they still wanted to sell if they could. But we did. It went on for a while, and then the people who took over the development gave up the fight and abandoned the whole mess just as it was. Guess it wasn't worth the bother to them. MacBride and his lot stopped having anything to do with anyone from this end of the valley though. Losing Tracy like that ... well, he figured it was someone here took his wife away and so he cut himself off from the rest of us.'

'That's when the trouble started.'

'Yeah. He don't like our family, me and Tony and Will. Guess he blames us for what happened.'

For a while, I'd forgotten that the two brothers were cousins of Will's. I wonder why they saw the chance to sell up and move differently, say, 'Even though you were on different sides in the land thing?'

'Yeah. Blood's thicker than water.'

'But not enough to make you agree about selling?'

He shrugs. 'Will wanted to retire properly. Me and Tony were too young.'

We slosh through the mud to where the two corpses are half-buried in the dirt. The hole between them where the woman had been is yawning and dark, and half-full of rainwater. The whole bank's slippery and run-off is pouring into the seething river. It looks as though it could collapse again if the rain doesn't ease up soon.

Ben looks at the scene and his expression changes

again. Back to his wary, cold, guarded self. He runs his eyes carefully over the burial site before turning to look at me. 'Let's get them covered then,' he says.

It's not an easy job. We fight with the wind to wrestle the plastic sheeting in place over the two corpses, staking it down as securely as possible. The clay is thick and sticky, and it's difficult to wield the hammer properly without risking sliding down towards the river. Ben is none too graceful as he works and several times I have to stop him hammering in a stake at an angle that could've damaged one of the bodies. We're both soaked and sweating by the time it's all in place, breathing hard while doing our best *not* to breathe hard in the reek. Above, the sky remains dark, but the noises are worse. Horrible, screeching scrapes like two battleships rubbing against each other. I wonder what on earth can be going on up there to make such sounds. The wind's stronger than ever but the air still seems thick, charged. Like the valley could explode at any time.

Walking back seems to take for ever, but in the end, worn out, drenched and covered in clay, we have the tools back in the bed of Ben's pickup and we're ready to go. The big man rubs his hands on his coat and looks at me. He's about to say something when the world shatters like a bomb's detonated next to the truck.

My vision turns to pure light and the air burns. My ears are full of white noise and treacle. A massive bolt of lightning has struck the roof of the pickup, thankfully earthing harmlessly out through the chassis without killing either of us. Across the valley, another four, five, six bolts rip out from the base of the storm like a coordinated artillery barrage. Between the reverberating cracks the metallic tearing from the depths of the cloud reaches an almighty crescendo and the cloud base seems to *drop* suddenly between one second and another, a massive drunken lurch towards us. It's as though it will keep going, plummet into the valley floor and crush everything and everyone. The hammer of God, smashing us all into oblivion. As though the sky itself has turned to lead before our eyes.

'Fucking hell,' I shout. 'Fucking hell.'

Ben doesn't reply. As the lightning continues to ripple across the sky, slamming over and over again from the clouds, the energy within them suddenly let off the leash, he just points away down the valley and yells in terror.

Part silhouette, part living black hole eclipsing every green-purple electric flash lighting the curtain of the sky, a massive wedge of solid darkness extends down from the thick daughter clouds orbiting beneath the core of the storm. It utterly swallows a chunk of the empty fields to the south, its base hidden behind a dark fog of whirling earth and debris maybe a half-mile across.

A tornado. Screaming right at us. A mile away, perhaps a little more, and closing fast.

29

Ben guns the engine as I jump into the truck, it coughs once and for a split second my stomach lurches. I imagine us trapped here, unable to do anything but wait for the wind to tear us to pieces. Then the ignition catches and the tyres squeal against the blacktop. Ben floors the accelerator as we scream west towards the roadhouse as fast as we can. Every once in a while he turns to stare out of the side window and yells, 'Fuck!'

I can't blame him. With every rippling fork of lightning, the view to the south is more and more occluded, turned black by a cloud of encroaching death and chaos. A wedge-shaped column torn into the fabric of the world itself. The size, the height, the enormity of the thing is almost beyond my capacity to comprehend. In the darkness between flashes, it's even worse. All we can hear is the roar, a horrible rumbling howl, a wall of noise broken here and there by a sudden high-pitched squeal as the storm finds something particularly juicy to feed upon. All we can see are the raindrops in the headlights ripped to spray and fog by the wind. Torn to pieces, just like we're about to be.

I've been shot at, been in car crashes, seen all

manner of situations in which I might have been killed. And nothing has ever terrified me or filled me with as much awe as the onrushing shaft of storm-spun chaos that's coming for us now. Its sheer size and lethality are staggering, so far beyond human capabilities as to be almost a religious experience. God is angry, and we must pay.

I don't know if it's me shouting or Ben, but I hear a voice screaming, 'It's following us. It's fucking following us!'

The funnel does indeed seem to be twisting, curving from its original north-easterly path, bending more and more towards the north as it approaches. Turning towards us as we attempt to flee. Some part of my mind is laughing at the irony – we might have been safer staying by the river and letting it pass to the west.

But mostly I'm just more terrified than I've ever been at any time in my life. I don't want to be outside at all, anywhere, as this thing passes by. A cellar, a concrete shelter. Somewhere twister-proof. The bar would be torn to shreds. Anyone outside would be killed by the whipped cloud of debris long before the wind snatched them away into the sky. I know all this, and I wonder if we have a chance at all or if we should just stop fighting it.

My teeth are clamped together as adrenaline pinches my brain into a bright point of light behind my eyes. The roar of the tornado mingles with the angry ocean sounds of blood in my ears until the two are indistinguishable. I look up through the top of the windshield as more lightning courses across the night and I can see the terrible cloud wall hanging over us like an immense wave about to break. More and more of the sky to the left is wholly cut off, vanishing into screaming nothing as the twister zeroes in on us. The funnel is wider at the top than at the base, and we're close enough to it to be right beneath its slope. The noise is a solid sensation, an earthquake more than a sound, and we're driving blind and I know we're going to die.

30

And then suddenly the fog lifts as we shoot out of the edges of the debris cloud. The lights of the bar are glimmering faintly maybe a quarter of a mile ahead. I twist in my seat to watch as the almighty column of blackness crosses the road behind us and thunders into the fields to the north. Even then, I still expect it to swing around again and resume its chase. I can't believe it didn't get us. The twister is so close that when it passes, I can see nothing through the rear windshield. Nothing at all. Not even the road. It's as though the world has just winked out and we're right on the edge.

Then I realize I've stopped breathing and take a huge lungful of air. I'm about ready to pass out with relief.

I look across at Ben and see him doing much the same. He eases off the gas, lets the engine calm down, and glances in the mirror like he's also waiting to see the twister turning to chase us along the road. Just like me, he's finding it difficult to believe that we've escaped it for good. I have to remind myself that it really has gone, lost in the darkness. If I look up, I can still see the upper reaches of the funnel hanging down above us, but it's moving away fast.

'I thought we were dead for sure,' Ben says. 'I thought that was it.'

'Yeah, I know exactly what you mean.'

'The *size* of that thing. Jesus, Alex. I thought we were dead. I really thought we were dead.'

'Yeah, me too.'

'I thought we were dead. I can't feel my hands. Gripping the wheel too hard. I thought we were dead.'

Both of us are breathing hard, puffing with relief. Our narrow escape seems to have left Ben a little less withdrawn again, more open. I take advantage of this and while he's still trembling with relief ask, 'Ben, who's Sam?'

'What?'

'There's no point covering up anything here, just the two of us. When I asked you about someone called Sam earlier this evening you immediately assumed it was a woman.'

'I explained that . . .'

'Come on, Ben. You had someone particular in mind. I can't imagine anyone making that leap who didn't. So tell me.'

He stays silent, goes back to looking at the road. I wonder if he's trying to come up with a workable lie. Figure out an angle, a way out of the verbal trap he made for himself.

'The reason I came out here was because I got a note from someone called Sam and I need to know who that is,' I say. 'Believe me, it's real important.

Not just to me, but to all of us, including you and your brother. We're trapped in this valley until the roads are repaired, and I need to know what it is brought me out here. And you know who Sam is. So tell me.'

He swings the truck into the parking lot and kills the engine. Then he fixes his eyes on mine, dark and glittering. Says, 'It's not for me to tell you if Will hasn't already. You ask him. It's up to him. Not me.'

'Does she live out here? Or maybe she used to?'

'Ask Will,' he repeats.

'What about crosses?'

He says nothing, just swings out of the truck, jumpy, on edge. Isaac's doesn't seem any the worse for wear following the tornado. Maybe some more wind-blown detritus washed up against its walls, but the funnel passed a fair way from the building. Will opens the door before we reach it. The old man's face is flushed.

'Did you hear that just now?' he says. 'That sound? Sounded like a goddamn freight train. Was that a twister?'

'Yeah,' I say. 'Yeah, it was.'

'Honest to God?'

I nod. 'It nearly caught us, too. A real live tornado.'

'Sweet Jesus. We all heard the noise, but with it being so dark . . .' He shakes his head. 'I don't think we've ever seen anything like that here. I did hear of a couple over in Moore County in some really bad storms a few years back, but this . . .'

We follow him back into the bar. Nothing seems to have changed since we left, nothing further has happened. The blood has been cleaned up from behind the counter and the room no longer smells of cordite. As we walk in, Gene walks out, saying he's going to check on his rig again after the tornado. I join Will as he sits back down at the counter.

'Who's Sam, Will?' I ask.

He looks at me, caught by surprise. 'What?'

'Ben said I should ask you this question, so I'm asking. Who's Sam?'

'Did he now?'

I nod. 'He did, yeah. So who is she?'

Will's about to say something more, maybe give me an answer, when Christine calls him from the booth where she's sitting. She has her head in her hands, elbows resting on the table. 'Will, my head . . . my head's not feeling right.'

He looks at me and shakes his head. 'We'll have to do this later,' he says, and goes to tend to his wife and her suspiciously sudden change in condition. I can't say anything to stop him without alienating him and Christine, and instead I'm left to watch him conduct the pantomime of caring for his wife.

Perhaps I'm being paranoid. She's old and, after all, she did sustain a genuine blow to the head earlier. This could be real, merely a delayed effect of her injury.

Could be, but if so it's very convenient timing. Very convenient indeed.

Much like the timing of the developer's disappearance so soon after the death of Tracy MacBride fifteen years ago. A hit-and-run; in an area like this with almost no passing traffic, it's more than possible that it was one of the locals who was driving. If one of the locals also murdered the developer, that's two previous deaths someone round here has gotten away with in addition to the more recent three by the river.

There's got to be a connection somewhere, even with such a spread of time between the first two and the newest three. This isn't the Bronx; I can't believe there'd be a collection of unsolved killings here that weren't in some way related.

That's two sets of deaths, and at least two people keeping those secrets buried. If you kill someone and get away with it, the temptation to do it again only gets stronger. You know you can do it, and you know you might not get caught. PEOPLE ARE DEAD. OTHER PEOPLE COULD DIE.

The note also said: YOU HAVE TO KNOW WHAT I DID. So what did Sam do? Which of these clusters of murders was she talking about? The injuries the two adults by the Easy sustained looked too physically forceful to have been done by anything other than a man, and a big one at that. And what did the note mean by 'finding the crosses'? The three by the river didn't have a marker, but what about Tracy MacBride?

If this valley's seen so much hidden evil over the years, maybe the sickness runs all the way back to the building of the Foundations and the events that occurred back then. From the note, there's no way of knowing which of the deaths Sam was referring to.

'You said Peter, the guy who used to run this place, told you all about the Foundations,' I say to Isaac. 'He was around when they were dug, right? Ben said he was going to sell the bar back then.'

'Yeah, as far as I know. He certainly knew a lot about the Foundations.'

'How much did he tell you about the disappearance of the developer who was trying to build there?'

He shrugs. 'Nothing much.'

'He must have talked about it.'

'Just what I said earlier. The guy vanished with a bunch of cash that wasn't his and no one ever saw him again.'

'Nothing more?'

'No, sorry. I tell you what, though, Peter did leave a pile of his old crap in the cellar when he left. That might be some help to you if you want to know more about it.'

'What kind of things are we talking about?' I say as he reaches behind the bar for the keys to the basement.

'A couple of big boxes of old newspapers. One of the lines down there used to have a leaky connector. He kept paper down there to mop up whatever spilled. I had it fixed when I took over, but I never got round to clearing the papers out.'

'There's papers there from fifteen years ago?' I raise an eyebrow.

'Sure, maybe. They're big boxes, and what I remember of them is they're newer on top. And they ain't none of them *new*. He just filled them up as he finished reading, and he wasn't a great reader. Anyway, you got something better to do right now? Might as well have a look, if that's what you're interested in.'

I don't answer, just follow him out back to the low wooden door that leads downstairs. He unlocks it and flicks on the cellar light. Bare concrete steps down to an equally bare space with a bunch of different kegs stacked up against one wall, racks of bottles and a web of pipework and wiring. It reeks of the yeasty scent of beer mingled with the usual cold, damp smell of rooms underground. Scattered to the edges of the working section of the room are trash, old furniture, dusty boxes and a hundred other pieces of clutter just too much effort to bother cleaning out.

'You covered over those bodies by the river OK?' he asks now we're away from the main bar.

'Yeah. It was tricky, but we did it.'

'I wonder what the cops'll find out about them.'

'I don't know. They'd have more to go on if they had the woman's body to examine as well. They only died a year ago and the way the soil is, they're mostly intact.'

'Yeah?'

'But you don't remember anyone here going missing around then, right? Maybe they were passing through but they abandoned their car here. Maybe they stayed for a while and then just vanished one day.'

'Not really, no.' He pauses rooting around in the clutter and looks at me. 'To tell the truth, I don't pay much attention to the people who pass through. No one much ever comes back so I don't always remember them. It's just not worth it, y'know?'

'Sure.'

He grabs a couple of large cardboard boxes and tugs them clear into the middle of the room. 'These are the ones. Should be full of papers and whatever else old Peter used to soak up the mess. They're all yours.'

'Thanks.'

'Hope they've got what you need.' He shrugs. 'I'm going back upstairs. It's too cold to be hanging around down here. Just leave them there and turn the light out when you're done.'

'Sure,' I say.

I hear his footsteps cross the floor and echo faintly up the steps. Then the door closes and I'm alone in the basement with nothing but the hum of cooling units for company while I hunt around in the stacks of old newsprint.

Most of the papers in these boxes contain nothing of any interest that I can see on a quick skim. All local news, but what passes for 'news' round here would hardly set the world alight. Some of them seem to have been used at some point to soak up God knows what; that or there have been periodic leaks above the spot where the box was kept.

Half-way through the second box, I find a batch from the time period I'm interested in and a picture of what happened back then slowly begins to emerge.

31

The State Police looked into the disappearance of Moore Willis when neither his company nor its subcontractors had heard from him for over two days. With the financial situation at the construction site being what it was, people were anxious to trace him. When the black-and-whites found no sign of him at his home, and no indication that he'd packed to leave, two detectives were brought in to investigate the disappearance and the growing suggestions of massive corporate fraud in the company. The morning before his disappearance, he'd completed the withdrawal of a quarter of a million dollars in cash from the business's account. Just about the last money he could've taken from it; the banks had extended credit as far as they were going to.

The locals and the workers were all questioned, then the latter were sent home, leaving behind them an ugly lunar landscape of shaped mud and scattered concrete pipework, as well as a half-dozen bulldozers and mechanical diggers. The staff at the site certainly had reason to kill Willis; the company was so massively burdened with hidden debts that there was no chance of them being paid for their work. Both they and the locals denied any knowledge of Willis's whereabouts, and said they knew no particular reason why someone might want him dead. Aside from simple robbery and the disagreements over selling their land or resisting his advances, of course.

The cops also spoke to the MacBrides. The papers mention the death of Tracy MacBride not long before the disappearance. The family, as far as I can tell, mirrored the other locals in denying all knowledge of Willis's whereabouts. The detectives looked into the possibility of Willis being the driver in the hit and run that killed Tracy MacBride but found nothing to suggest that he was. He was questioned at the time it happened – she'd been trying to block his development, after all – but the officers looking into her death found his car undamaged and no sign that there was anything wrong with his story. They were also unable to figure out who Tracy might have been meeting when she died. None of the locals admitted that they'd been expecting a visit from her.

Nothing was ever found of Willis. Reading between the lines, the cops expected to catch him at an airport somewhere trying to get to the Caribbean on a forged passport, or to find his body in a ditch somewhere far away with all his money taken. He'd apparently intended to use the cash to convince his workforce that the project was still solvent and that they should keep at it, or, the alternate theory went, for a final attempt to buy the land he needed to persuade his investors that the more ambitious second phase of the development could proceed. If they'd been convinced, they might have pumped more funds into the project. If the development had been completed, his creditors could probably have been paid off and Willis's wrongdoing and constant dipping of his fingers into the honey pot would've stayed hidden.

While there's no way of knowing for certain if he was killed or not, it seems far and away the most likely outcome. Very few people who take the money and run succeed in vanishing like that. And this was two weeks after Tracy MacBride died . . . In such an isolated place, with just the tiniest handful of people living here, I can't help but see them as connected. I wonder what she was doing on the road like that and who it was she'd been going to see. And why they didn't come forward at the time and hadn't since.

The cellar is cold and damp and I can feel the air on the back of my neck. I slide the boxes back into place and go looking for more answers.

32

Christine is sitting by herself at the far end of the counter, apparently fully recovered from the sudden turn that afflicted her when I asked about Sam. She has a dog-eared magazine in front of her and is making a half-hearted effort to finish a crossword. Pure covering behaviour, trying to pretend what happened earlier this evening is all over. From her body language it's plain that her heart's not in it. It's just there to fill in the time, to give her something to think about beyond our immediate predicament and whatever trouble's been stirred up. She regards me with cautious, guarded eyes as I approach. Wary of me and my questions in a way I can't help but find suspicious.

'You and Will were living here when they built the Foundations, weren't you?' I say.

'I don't really feel up to too much conversation at present,' she says. Looks at her crossword and waggles her pen. 'I'm still not feeling well. You understand.'

'I won't keep you long.'

She shakes her head. 'It was all so long ago; I don't see the urgency. Can't we talk about it tomorrow?'

'With everything that's happened tonight?' I raise my eyebrows. 'You've got to be kidding me.'

'Very well. If you must.' Christine puts her pen down and looks at me fully. 'What is it that you want to know?'

'Tracy MacBride was hit by a car and killed on the highway near here fifteen years ago. Either she was walking down to the roadhouse to meet up with one of the handful of locals who lived here with you, or she was walking back from doing it. The police said she hadn't been meeting with anyone at the construction site.'

'And?'

'And I have no idea why she would have been here, for what purpose,' I say. 'If she was here, she was here to speak to someone. But I can't figure out who, and no one admitted it at the time. Was she especially friendly with anyone? Did she have any ordinary reason to be down here regularly? Anything like that?'

Christine's gaze falters for a moment and she drops her eyes to the magazine in front of her. 'It was a long time ago, Alex. How do you expect me to remember something like that? Fifteen years.'

I look down the bar to where Will's talking with Isaac. Neither of them are paying us any attention. I say, 'Come on, Christine. Fifteen years is a long time, but there's only half a dozen people who live in this valley at any one time, plus the MacBrides. There can't be that much that ever happens here. Tracy MacBride's death and what went on when they were digging the Foundations must have stuck in your mind. It's not like it's the sort of thing that happens every day here.'

'I don't know anything for sure,' she says, after a moment's hesitation. I wait for her to continue, but she stays silent. Delaying.

'But you know a possibility,' I say. 'You have a vague idea of what could've happened. What?'

'There was talk . . . I didn't really see her around, but Peter did. That's what he told me, anyway. He thought she may have been seeing someone down here. Keeping it quiet.'

'Seeing someone? As in having an affair?'

She nods. 'Yes.'

'Did he know who it was? Any idea at all?'

'No. And you must understand, that was only what he thought she was up to. He said he'd seen her around, never with her husband, coming and going at all sorts of strange times.' She sniffs. 'He might not have been telling the truth, of course. With Peter, you could never tell if he was spinning you a tale. I never saw her, so I don't know.'

I mull over her words. 'That's all he said? That was why he thought she was seeing someone?'

'That's what he told me at the time.'

'And he had no idea who?'

Christine shakes her head. 'No.' She pauses, then adds, 'It wasn't Will, if that's what you're thinking. I know that much.'

I don't know if I believe her or not, but I thank her anyway and allow her to go back to pretending to concentrate on the crossword. If Tracy MacBride really was having an affair, that makes her sudden death all the more interesting, and also all the more likely that it had nothing to do with the construction work.

Her husband could have found out that she was cheating on him and run her down in anger. It wouldn't be the first time such a sense of betrayal has led to murder by that method. Strange, though, that he didn't also vent some of his fury on the man she was seeing. Unless he couldn't work out who it was any more than Peter could. If that were the case, though, why would no one have mentioned the affair theory to the cops so they could look closely at her husband?

Alternatively, she might have been killed by the spouse or partner of whoever she was sleeping with. Another very traditional motive for revenge. I know the cops investigated the hit and run as well as they could. But having seen the state of most of the vehicles around here, and that they're almost all four-by-fours or pickups, less likely to pick up any damage from hitting a pedestrian, it would've been quite possible that the police would have missed a dent or a crack in the glass, and there's no reason to suppose the people they spoke to would have been able to convincingly deny any knowledge of her visits. No one much would have an alibi, since there's so few people here to spend time *with*.

Or she may have been killed by whoever she was

seeing. She broke off the relationship, said she wouldn't leave her husband, threatened to reveal all, whatever. Then: BAM. Again, it wouldn't be the first time. Same deal.

But if any of those were true, where the hell does the developer's disappearance or death fit in? The timing's far too convenient to be an accident. I wish I could talk to the cops who worked the case and find out more than the patchy records in the newspaper coverage. More than that, I wish I knew who Tracy MacBride was sleeping with. Peter seems an unlikely candidate since he apparently started the rumour, and if Christine is right about Will that would just leave the two brothers and Ashley's uncle. *If* Christine's right, of course. It could just be an old woman's wishful thinking, denying the truth of her husband's philandering to herself.

I'm still trying to picture the events of fifteen years ago when all the lights go out.

33

Silence broken only by the distant rain. Utter blackness except for a faint, ethereal shimmering. The few reflective surfaces capable of scattering what little ambient light is left floating in space, totally divorced from their usual form or context. The whole building seems to be holding its breath, waiting for the person responsible to step out of the shadows. Trying to figure out if this is it, time to die. Even I'm expecting to hear the creak of a door opening, the sound of knife blows, a gun. Screaming. The horror meted out on Craig and Spin.

The waiting stillness lasts a couple of seconds, then the fear sets in.

No one screams, but I hear what I think is Vince whimpering to himself, and a chorus of whispered questions and worries. *What happened? Who did that? Was it the storm? Get the light back!*

Some rattling around behind the bar, and Isaac snaps on a flashlight. Everyone freezes again, taking stock of the situation around them, checking for anything that's changed. He pans the beam around the room, making sure everyone's present and correct, and says, 'Well, that's just fucking great.'

The sentiment is echoed on every face picked out

in the sharp relief of the beam's glow. People are edgy, nervous, even more so than they were earlier.

A minute ago the bar was our refuge, our safe haven from whatever and whoever is lurking outside. A little beacon of light around which we could cluster until dawn, immune to the worst the world could throw at us. Losing power changes all that in an instant. It's why cops like to cut the electricity to buildings in hostage situations. For all our evolution, all our intelligence and rationalization, like the rest of humanity we're still scared of the dark, worried about what could be hiding in the shadows. Worried that whatever happened to Spin and Craig out there in the howling night could now happen to us. As if a few lightbulbs could have protected us before.

'Could this be just a blown fuse?' Christine says. Her tone says she'd like the answer to be yes. 'Could we fix it easily and get the lights back on?'

'Everything's died,' Isaac says. 'The lights are on a different circuit to everything else. I don't figure that for a fuse. Not unless the whole box has gone. Can anyone see if there's still power at the gas station?'

I move into position by the window. There's nothing but darkness and the storm out there now. Before, I could have seen the distant glimmers of the couple of working lights at Will and Christine's place. 'No. That's gone too. It's all dead.'

'Can you see anything in the parking lot?' Gene says. 'Anyone who might have done that?'

'No. There's no sign of anyone.'

'Someone killed the power,' Ashley murmurs. 'It's deliberate, it's got to be. Maybe we're next.'

'It's the damn MacBrides. They want us scared, that's all.'

'I'd say they've fucking got us scared, Will,' Isaac says. 'Maybe it was that Walker guy. He probably has reason to do this sort of thing if everything they said about him is right.'

'It could just be that the storm shorted out the mains for the whole valley,' I say, loud enough to shut the others up. 'A bolt of lightning in the right place . . .'

'Maybe,' Gene grunts. 'There must be a main power junction here somewhere, so maybe that got hit. Wouldn't be the first time, right?'

'What are our options here? Is there any backup power? Candles?'

Isaac shrugs. 'Maybe, maybe not. I've got some boxes of candles down in the basement. They're not brilliant, but they ought to do for now. Maybe you're right – maybe it's just a temporary problem and the power'll come back any time now.'

'With our luck tonight?' Ashley shakes her head. 'Forget it. Never going to work.'

'She's right.' Ben's voice growls from the shadows at the back. 'These things don't just happen. There's a reason for it all. This wasn't no accident and you all know it.'

Isaac shrugs. 'Let's check the box and find out. Maybe we can get the power working again. There might not be any need for this sort of talk.'

We follow him out into the night. The storm, waning before, seems to have strengthened again and the rain whips down in streamers. We can see maybe ten yards, no more than that, and once more we have to shout if we want to be heard. The back of the building is a flat apron of concrete with a couple of Dumpsters, both pinned back against the wall by the wind, shaking to and fro with every gust as though they're going to take off. Standing on its own is the rusting hulk of a steel enclosure almost as tall as I am. It's plastered with warning signs, but all I can make out are the 'danger of death' symbols.

Lightning ripples across the cloud ceiling and slams into the roof of Will's house with an ear-splitting crack. Isaac uses the flashlight beam to point at the torn metal of the junction box's access panel, once locked, now plainly forced open. Inside, the splintered remains of its circuit breakers are broken beyond all repair.

'It's fucked,' Isaac says. 'Well and truly fucked. Someone smashed this up good.'

34

Will stares at the wreckage, shaking his head. 'It's a miracle they didn't electrocute themselves doing it,' he says. 'So we've got no power to the entire valley now? Everything's shot?'

'It looks that way, yeah. We're gonna be on flashlights and candles till morning.'

'Who could've done this?' Christine says. 'I mean, what are those MacBride people playing at here? Why would they want us in the dark?'

'Let's do this indoors,' Isaac says. 'At least it's still dry in there. I'll go get the candles.'

We abandon the wrecked electrical machinery and move back into the bar. Candlelight doesn't do a great deal, but it's enough to see by and after a while my eyes adjust to the relative gloom and the flickering. It's not much, and it's certainly nowhere near as effective as the electric bulbs, but light's light.

'How many candles have you got, Isaac?' I ask.

'A couple of big boxes of the things. Should easily be enough to last us until morning so long as we don't cover the place in them.'

'How much longer until daybreak?'

'Maybe five hours until the sky gets light,' Will says.

I try to imagine another five hours cooped up in the bar. 'At least the candles might keep us warm,' I say. 'And we can toast marshmallows, so long as we do it one at a time. Be just like being in Boy Scouts.'

Isaac shakes his head. 'Ain't got no marshmallows, and potato chips don't toast in quite the same way. Sorry.'

'Well, that's just great,' I say. No one laughs.

'If it was one of the MacBrides,' Will says, changing the subject, 'or that Walker guy, what do we do about them? Do we go looking for him, or do we wait here until morning? What else could they do outside that could hurt us in here?'

I know what Ben's going to say before he opens his mouth. The bullish set of his features, the flat monotone certainty in his voice. I'm almost capable of mouthing the words he speaks in time with him. 'I reckon we should hunt the son of a bitch down. Split up, comb the area and grab him before he can do any more damage. Show him that we've all had enough.'

'All of us?' I say. 'Out there, looking for this guy?'

'Sure.'

'Even Christine? Should we get her out hunting too? Maybe we should unlock Vince and have him join the party?'

'You could. I'm not going to do anything now.'

I ignore him. 'Have everyone go out wandering

around the fields in the middle of a storm looking for a guy who may not exist? When God knows how many people have already died out there tonight?'

Ben just looks at me. His eyes are dead and grey. 'Yeah.'

'I don't think that's a good idea, Ben,' Isaac says. 'Not at all.'

The big man says nothing. Christine wraps her cardigan tighter around her chest and purses her lips. 'So what *do* we do if we're not going to try to find this person?'

'Get as comfortable as possible in here and hole up until daylight,' I say. 'If there's someone out there causing trouble, we should be able to avoid most of it just by staying indoors and out of harm's way. He's already cut the power; I don't see that there's much else he could try that could hurt us.'

My mind flashes with the image of a man, maybe the guy downstairs in the Banks house, throwing a lit Molotov cocktail through the big glass windows in the front of the bar. He has his axe in his other hand, ready to work on the running survivors. I try to ignore it.

'I think we've got most of what we need right here,' Isaac says.

Gene nods. 'So we, what, wait here until morning and then see the lie of the land, fetch the cops if we can?'

'That's about the shape of it,' I say. 'I don't see that we have a lot of other options right now.'

'What about getting some sleep?'

I shrug. 'Given everything that's happened tonight, I'd be surprised if anyone wanted any, or wanted to risk getting any. Not yet. But this place isn't so bad; there's plenty of bench seats. They wouldn't be so bad.'

Christine sighs and says, 'Well, if we're going to be staying together in here, I want to get Brandon and my long sweater.'

'He'll be OK on his own for now, Chris,' Will says.

'I don't care. I want him with me.'

I frown, confused. I know the name, but I can't remember from where. 'Who's Brandon?'

'Our golden retriever. She spoils him.'

'He needs looking after,' Christine protests. 'He's not a young dog any more. Besides, you know what he's like in storms. He's already been on his own for more than long enough. He'll be shaking like a leaf, poor thing, if he has to stay out there all night on his own without his mommy.'

'He'll be fine. You worry too much about him.'

'*Will.* I'm going to get him. It won't take a minute.'

'Last time you went out there some feller cracked you on the head,' he points out.

'I'm fine. And now we all know he's there. He's robbed the store, so he's got nothing left to bother me with. If he was going to do anything worse, he'd have done it before. So stop your fussing.'

The old man sighs. I guess this exchange – or at least this type of exchange – is nothing new to him. 'Fine. I'll walk you across the lot. It's your fault if I catch rheumatism from the rain. Yours and the mutt's.'

'Hush, you. You haven't caught it on all the other times you've gone off in the wet. I'll get your fleece from the closet while I'm there.'

Gene pulls on his cap again. 'I'll follow you. I want to check my truck to make sure the son of a bitch hasn't decided to wreck all the vehicles while he was killing the power.'

Will and Christine haul on their coats and grab Isaac's flashlight. The two of them follow Gene out the door together. None of them says a word.

I settle down for a few minutes and find myself almost nodding off, eyes feeling like lead. Days of fatigue catching up on me at the strangest time imaginable. The candlelight and relative warmth can't be helping. I drift in and out, trying to keep my head up. I can hear the dead girl whispering in my ears, catch the faintest of words passing her lifeless lips. When I finally snap out of my doze, Vince seems to be asleep against the radiator, Ashley's nursing a fresh cup of coffee and Ben's emerging from the restrooms flapping his hands dry. 'A couple of your candles in there have blown themselves out,' he says. 'Anyone got a match or something?'

Isaac nods and tosses him a box from behind the bar. He turns to Ashley and points at the coffee.

'How'd you make that? The machine's got no power running to it now.'

'I boiled the water on the stove upstairs. I'll make you some if you like.'

'Best ask Will and Chris as well. Where are they?'

'Not back yet, I guess.'

He frowns. 'How long does it take to fetch a sweater and a dog?'

'Maybe Brandon doesn't want to come out in the storm?' Ashley shrugs. 'Or Will's finally got that rheumatism he's always talking about.'

'Maybe. What about Gene?'

'Still checking his truck.'

'I swear I've never known a driver so obsessed with his damn rig before. You'd think that thing was his wife.'

'I guess it's his livelihood.'

'Even so. I mean, Christ, doesn't he have insurance? It's not as though he can do anything if the thing does get damaged.'

Ashley shakes her head and trots upstairs to put the stove on again. Isaac busies himself behind the bar, clearing and tidying, but I can see his gaze drifting towards the door more and more. Five minutes have gone by the time he looks at the four of us, the worry etched heavily on his face. 'We'd best go look for them, hadn't we?'

35

Will is hunkered down in the doorway to the small bedroom above the gas station's convenience store, crying silently. His entire body shakes with every sob, but even though his mouth is wide open in pain, nothing comes out, not even the sound of indrawn breath.

'Sweet Jesus,' I hear Ashley whisper.

Tony nods. 'Christine. Holy . . .'

Ben helps Will up from the floor and steers him away from the scene. He's still shuddering, tears streaming down his face, locked in a very personal hell. It's hard to imagine what's going through his mind after finding his wife dead in a state like that.

'Who'd . . . who could . . .' Isaac mumbles. I don't feel like answering that question, not now. The MacBrides from up the valley, if the stories are to be believed. One of us here in this room if they're not. Walker, maybe, as a long shot, if he's capable of such an act and had any kind of motive. None of these options paints a happy picture. I take a good, long look around the room, hoping the killer dropped something or left some clue as to his identity, but I can't see a damn thing.

'Shouldn't we, y'know, put a sheet over her or something?' Ashley asks.

'Why?' I say quietly, brain still trying to come to terms with the horror meted out on someone who would've been completely defenceless. In no shape to put up a fight even if she heard her attacker coming. 'I mean, no one's going to want to come back here. Will doesn't look like he's up to it and we're all staying over at the bar. This isn't like JC. We don't have to protect anyone from looking at it all the time.'

'But, she's dead, Alex.'

'She is,' I say, 'so it's not like a sheet's going to bring her back.'

Ashley gasps. 'Alex!'

'It's true, though. But more importantly, the cops won't want anything disturbed. At least, no more than they need to be. We don't have to touch a thing.'

On the way back to the bar Isaac spots Gene lying on the gravel of the parking lot, just visible as a darker shadow against the stones. Splayed out in front of his truck like it somehow came to life and knocked him down. When I check his body I find it's still warm, just like Christine, his wounds still fresh. What happened to him happened only a few minutes ago. He obviously put up more of a fight than Christine, but it didn't do him any good. Same time, same attacker.

I look down at his vacant, empty eyes, and I wonder why Gene never finished veterinary training, why he became a truck driver instead, and why the hell he was out here on a night like this. Whether there was some reason for him to die like this. What it was that drove him to walk out into the dark on his own.

'Do . . . do you think it was the same one that did this?' Tony murmurs. 'The same one as killed Christine?'

'Probably,' I hear Isaac reply behind me. 'Almost certainly, right? How could it be anyone else? Jesus.'

My gaze doesn't leave Gene's face. 'First one, then the other.'

'Yeah.'

He fought, and took the wounds that come from that, but he wasn't punished in the way Christine was. He can't have been the main target of the attack, just collateral damage. I murmur, 'I wonder if he saw.'

'What?' Tony says.

'Christine's killer. I wonder if he saw them or they thought he saw them, and that's why they killed him. What happened to him looks different to what happened to her.'

Lightning snaps overhead and in the afterglow I think I see Gene's dead features mouth the word 'Sam'.

'If it wasn't for this goddamn storm we might have heard something. Gene fought for a while. He must have made some noise. Maybe someone could've come out here, helped him. I don't know if he died before Christine or after, but we could've helped one of them if we'd known what was going on. Shit.'

'Alex . . .' Isaac says.

'I just wonder what was so important to him he'd risk leaving the bar in weather like this just to check on his damn truck.'

'It was a girl,' Isaac says, pointing up at the cab.

'What?'

'It was a little girl. He had a little girl out here.'

Standing in the doorway to the sleeper compartment, peering out at us with wide, dead eyes, there's a girl maybe eight or nine years old. She's stock still, eyes fixed on Gene's body. She doesn't seem to have registered us at all. I think I can see light from the bar glinting off a lone tear running down the side of her face.

'Jesus. Get the body covered with something,' I say. 'Make sure she can't see it.'

'Who do you think she is? I mean, keeping her locked in the truck like that . . .'

'I don't know. But I know looking at a cut-up corpse isn't going to do shit for her state of mind. Get Gene covered and bring her a blanket or something.'

Ashley scurries into the bar while Isaac covers Gene's head and chest with his jacket. The girl watches, still unmoving, until Ashley emerges again with a blanket wedged under her coat. 'What do we say to her?' she asks.

'I don't know.' Christ only knows what she just witnessed, what state her mind's in. I can only imagine.

'Me neither.'

'Tell her we're here to help her and keep her safe. Bundle her up and bring her inside, away from all this.' I rub my face with my hands. 'And if we can, we find out what she saw. She might have watched the whole thing.'

When we walk up to the sleeper doorway, sympathetic smiles beaming and blanket out ready to wrap around her shoulders, the girl just says in a small voice, 'Daddy?'

36

The way Will tells it, there was nothing strange about the short trip to the gas station. He and Christine leaned on each other as they walked across the gravel. The cold made the small of his back twinge, but it didn't hurt so bad because they weren't trying to hurry. They had to fight against the wind, pushing hard with every step.

'Then Chris laughed,' he says in a quiet, hollow voice. 'She was pointing at where our GAS sign used to be. The whole thing had blown clean away. I told her that my back was hurting and that she'd have to go up there to fix it tomorrow.'

Slow tears begin to seep into the lines around his eyes. Will doesn't seem to notice. 'She knew I was kidding. She always knew, Chris. She just smiled and gave me a dig in the ribs. It was funny, walking across the lot like that. We were using each other for support like a couple of drunken teenagers.'

'What did you do when you got to the station, Will?' I ask, soft and steady, coaxing the information out of him.

'I unlocked the front door and found a flashlight for Chris. It looked like everything was just as we left it earlier. You know how places feel different if someone's been there who shouldn't have? Well, it still smelled like home. That sounds so strange. Chris was always saying it, though. She told me to wait downstairs, that she'd only be a minute. I said I'd go with her but she said I was just being silly. All she had to do was grab her sweater and the dog and she didn't want me wearing myself out over nothing.'

He doesn't add anything, but I wonder if he wishes he'd gone up with her. Whether she'd still be alive. 'Brandon wasn't any trouble,' he continues. 'As soon as she opened the door at the bottom of the stairs, the damn dog came scooting out of there and wrapped itself around my legs. Dumb thing can't stand storms. I stayed there, trying to calm him down. He was whimpering and whining, looking this way and that at every gust of wind. The whole place was creaking and groaning.'

'How long did you wait for her?'

'I can't remember. Three or four minutes, I think. I didn't pay much attention when we went in. I called up the stairs to Chris, asking how long it took to find a sweater. She never answered me. I told the dog to stay by the counter, and I went to look for her. I . . . then I was in the bedroom doorway. I don't remember getting there. And there she was. I . . . I just wanted to die. I tried shouting for help, or I was just crying in the doorway, but it didn't matter and it's all the same and she's still dead.'

By the time Will's finished giving us the story of what happened, the tears seem to be slowing, but the hurt doesn't seem to have lessened at all. We leave him sitting slumped, ashen-faced in a booth near the bar, all alone with his grief. Ben keeps an eye on him from a distance, not talking, afraid perhaps of setting him off again. Ashley takes the little girl to a corner booth and does her best to get her talking. It doesn't look like an easy task; she's barely said a word since we found her. The rest of us huddle at the counter, leaving each of them with their misery for the time being. I try to see if anyone has blood on their clothes, any kind of indication that it might have been them that killed Gene and Christine – not much chance, since Christine wouldn't have been bleeding when she was cut and the blow that finally killed Gene could've been dealt from behind. I see nothing. Two people were killed practically under our noses and I'm no nearer knowing who did it.

Isaac pours himself a big glass of whisky and mutters, 'That was bad. That was TV-movie serial-killer bad.'

'No kidding,' Tony says.

'I mean, I've seen rough stuff before, but that was *bad*. Christine was an old woman, for Christ's sake.'

I think back to the scene in the bedroom. The whole place was furnished simply – lots of bare wood and furniture probably older than the couple them-selves, a couple of small prints of flowers on the walls – and most of the free area was taken up by a creaky-looking bed covered in small white feathers from a shredded pillow. Christine was sprawled on the floor at its foot. Her grey eyes were wide open, staring at a view forever hidden from this world. An angry red welt ran across her throat in a neat line the thickness of electrical cord – which was probably exactly what killed her.

But her killer didn't stop there.

Her mouth was open, stuffed roughly with a wad of feathers from the torn pillow, and an illegible mark of some sort had been hacked into her forehead. It could have been a name, it could be a symbol of some sort. The same knife which carved it had also been used to make wild gashes in her chest and neck. The ragged clothing, already soaked with red, and the savage nature of the cuts made it hard to tell exactly what the killer was doing, but they weren't controlled or considered. They were angry. There weren't any signs of arterial spray or bleeding from her wounds, so her heart can't have been beating when it happened. She must have been dead already by that point, which was something to be thankful for.

When I looked at Christine's body and the damage inflicted on it, I found myself thinking straight back to the dead guy buried out by the river and what happened to him.

Punishment.

Maybe. The guy was beaten senseless, while Christine was killed quickly and quietly. Still, someone hated her enough to think she'd done something to earn that kind of treatment. An old woman. Jesus.

I took one last look around the bedroom, hoping to spot something obviously missing or something left behind, some item that could point the way to the killer. But there was nothing there but personal oddments, a couple of family photos, some with a couple of kids in frame and some just a young woman. A dog-eared paperback by the side of the bed. Nothing taken, nothing added. Not that jumped out at me, anyway.

Will and Christine came in the front of the building. There was a back door at the top of the stairs leading to the kitchen at the back of the apartment. The guy who killed her may have come in that way. All assuming it was a guy that did it. The flight of steps ran up the rear of the building, out of sight of everything but the empty fields. The door didn't have a catch, and it opened when I tried it. There were damp marks on the mat inside the door, but nothing clear enough to tell me anything, not even the rough size of the killer's shoes. When I asked Ashley if this door would have been kept locked, if the killer would've needed a key to get in, she looked at me blankly.

'Lock it?' she said. 'Out here? Why?'

I conceded the point. Who'd lock up so far from civilization and the threat of passing burglary?

Gene's killing looked similar. Obviously not as premeditated; maybe the killer thought Gene might have seen him and decided to act. The gravel around him had been kicked and disturbed; he must have put up a fight before he dropped. The injuries he'd suffered bore that out. His hands and forearms had multiple slashes in them, typical defence wounds, and there was an indistinct muddy print over one knee where his attacker must have kicked him. Gene stayed up for a while before his assailant finished the job.

The blows that killed him were multiple and ugly. What I took at first to be a strand of hair stuck to the front of his face turned out to be a flap of skin slashed open by the knife. It was a clean cut, sharp and forceful, running from his forehead down his nose, and it wasn't pretty to look at. Smaller, quicker wounds laced the side of his throat, some deeper than others. I figured them for cuts inflicted while Gene was still fighting; his attacker lashing past his guard, without a clear sight of the necessary killing blow to his neck arteries or windpipe. There were three punctures to the front of Gene's chest and two to the back, angled up towards his kidneys. The wounds weren't stiletto-thin, but the blade certainly wasn't a massive one. A kitchen knife, maybe. Certainly deadly, regardless of size. The eventual killing blow passed just under Gene's breastbone and through his heart, to judge by the blood that had soaked his shirt.

I couldn't see any sign of the weapon used. It didn't seem to have been left at the scene. The keys to his truck were a couple of feet from the body. He probably still had them in his hands when the attacker struck.

Two people killed in a matter of minutes. One of them far from defenceless. It happened just yards from where we all sat, and none of us had a clue.

'We should go round up the MacBrides, get some payback,' Ben is saying.

No one has any response to that suggestion. I tell them, 'I think before you start throwing around accusations you're going to have to face the chance that it was someone in here who was responsible.'

'What?'

'One of us could well have killed Christine and Gene. Quite easily.'

They look at me. I look at them. Then Isaac says, 'How? Who had the chance?'

'Ashley and Ben had both just been out of the room when we finally decided to go looking for Will and Christine. I don't remember what you or Tony were up to, and I doubt any of you remember what I was doing either. And Will was out there with her. It could've been any one of us. Then there's Walker outside somewhere, and these MacBrides, if they really do the things you say.'

I'm expecting a storm of protest, particularly at the suggestion that Will could've killed his own wife, but I don't get it. None of them says a thing. They just look at one another, thinking. For all the talk of MacBrides and strangers in the dark before, perhaps now they're finally reassessing what they know about each other.

Ben shakes his head. 'I just went to take a shit. You

could interrogate the toilet bowl if you wanted.'

'I didn't go anywhere.'

'I was with you.'

Everything goes quiet again. 'Will said he didn't hear anything while Christine was killed,' I say. 'There was too much wind outside. Between that and the thunder he had no idea what was happening. But if Gene was killed while Will was downstairs, he must've been able to hear him being killed. He put up a real fight and I doubt he'd be silent while he was doing it.'

'You think he was lying? Seriously? Why would he do that?'

'No,' I say, shaking my head. 'That's not necessarily what I'm saying. The killer might have waited out the back of the gas station for Will to head upstairs looking for Christine before he tried to cross the parking lot. He probably didn't want to risk being seen. He might have spotted Gene like we did, half-way back, and attacked him then and there just to be sure he wouldn't identify him. Will looks like he's not been aware of anything much since he found Christine, so he wouldn't have known any of that. I imagine Gene could've been killed in the room next to him and he'd have been too wrapped up in his grief to realize. If it was one of us that did it, the killer would still have been back here well before we went looking for Will and Christine.'

'I can't believe this is happening,' Isaac says.

'Well, it is.'

Tony glances at the booth where Ashley is sitting next to the motionless girl. 'You think she's really his daughter?'

'Possibly.' I rub my face.

'Why leave her out in the truck like that?'

'He must've had his reasons. Tony, you come with me out to Gene's rig and see if we can find out who she is for sure. Maybe even a little about what was going on. Then I'll try talking to her.'

Checking the truck doesn't take long. In the glove compartment there's an unaddressed letter that says just 'Louisa' on the envelope. A sticker tucked in with it belongs to a remailing service.

'What does it say?' Tony asks, staring at the paper in my hand.

'"I guess you'll know by know that Penny is gone, and I guess if the cops talked to the people at the school you'll know it was me who took her."'

'Wow. So she is his kid.'

I nod, keep reading. 'Yeah, she is. Was. It sounds like it, anyway.'

And the little girl's mother doesn't seem to have been doing a great job, if Gene's message is to be believed. The girl, Penny, had told him she wasn't happy with her mother and some guy called Frank, who I guess was her boyfriend or second husband. Apparently, they ignored her for long stretches of time and spent most of their time out with Frank's friends, leaving her alone.

'"I'm not trying to criticize you or judge you, but

imagine how I feel knowing that when the court wouldn't give me custody because I was away too often on jobs."' I read out loud. 'He took his own daughter away from her mother because he thought she was being neglected. He had a better job lined up, one that didn't involve driving this truck.'

Tony shakes his head. 'Jesus.'

'Yeah. And now he's dead.' Gene apparently had some problems in his distant youth, minor misdemeanours that had affected his custody case years later. He knew he'd face a kidnapping charge when he took his daughter, but it seems he didn't care. Penny wanted to stay with him and he wanted to give them a decent life together, away from his ex-wife. The letter closes by telling her not to bother tracing it, and to say that once they were settled in, he'd get Penny to write to her as well.

We move on to check the sleeper cab. The tiny little space is full of neatly stowed toys and spare clothes for Penny, all brand-new, their price tags still attached. The bed where she'd been drawing in one of her exercise books from school. Pictures of trees and a river, and a man holding hands with a little girl. The teddy bear and crumpled covers where she'd presumably been curled up, trying to sleep despite the noise of the storm and the strangeness of her surroundings. Fake Canadian ID for the pair of them.

'At least we know why he kept coming out here all the time,' Tony says.

'That we do.'

'I don't know why he couldn't bring her in, though. We wouldn't have told anyone nothing.'

I shrug. 'Yeah, but he didn't know that. All he knew was that there was a bunch of strangers in here, some weird shit going on by the river, and he couldn't be sure the cops wouldn't show up at any moment. Someone asked questions, he'd be in serious shit.'

'Still, if he thought she was in danger from someone . . .'

'If he brought her inside, if we found out about her, he'd lose her for ever. Kidnapping case, prison, back to the mother who didn't care for her. She was at risk outside, but not much, so long as she stayed put. No one knew about her, so why would anyone find her, let alone kill her? The guy's a murderer, not a thief breaking into vehicles.'

'I guess. Still, it's a hell of a decision to have to make. Leaving your daughter out there alone in a storm like this.'

'Yeah, and it got him killed. And maybe there's a chance she saw the guy that did it,' I say. 'The killer didn't see her, or I guess he would have murdered her too. Maybe she saw the whole thing. Let's see if she can give us a description of the guy.'

37

Ashley's in the corner of the bar trying to persuade Penny to drink some hot chocolate, without much success. She looks up as I walk over with the exercise book in my hand. She shakes her head a little and says, as brightly as possible, still holding herself together, 'This is Alex. He's here to help look after you too.'

'Hi, Penny,' I say. When I get no reaction at all, I flick my eyes to Ashley. 'How's she doing?'

'I've made my best hot chocolate but she's being very naughty and not drinking it. She seems fairly snuggled in her blanket, though, so I don't think she's cold.'

'That's something.' I crouch down in front of Penny. 'A secret, just between you and me – I don't like her hot chocolate either. It smells like sweaty old socks.'

No response, but her gaze moves slowly towards me. The poor girl looks practically catatonic. Can't say as I blame her.

I hold the exercise book up so we can both look at it. 'This is a very pretty picture, Penny. Did you draw it all yourself?'

Still nothing. Her eyes move to the paper, then back to me.

'I'll bet you did. It's very good.' I point at the river. 'Is that the sea? I can't see any beaches.'

'River,' the reply comes after a few seconds' silence, time when I'm sure the trick hasn't worked. Her voice is tiny. 'It's a river, not the sea.'

'Oh, that's right. Very silly of me. And these, are these trees?'

'Yes.'

'They're growing next to the river?'

Penny nods. 'They're on the riverbank. They're big trees. You could put a rope swing on one of them and swing over the water in the summer.'

'That sounds like fun. I used to play on rope swings like that when I was your age. What are the riverbanks like, Penny? Are they steep, or can you climb down them?'

She thinks for a moment and points at the picture. 'They're steep, but there's places where you can get down to the water. It's not a fast river, and you can play in the water. There's fish and frogs you can catch where it's shallow.'

'Does it have pebbles that you can throw?'

'Yes. But not when people are on the swing or swimming.'

'Can you swim, Penny?'

She nods. 'Yes. I'm a good swimmer. I got badges for it. I can do breaststroke *and* front crawl. I can't do backstroke, though. Water gets in my nose and I sneeze.'

'Yeugh!' I exclaim with a grin. 'That's gross!'

She smiles briefly. 'Daddy told me if I did that in the river I'd have weeds and frogspawn coming out of my nose. He said everything would smell like fish for weeks if I did.'

'Your daddy was going to take you to the river?'

'It's next to our new house. He'll put up the rope swing for me and then I can play in the water all summer. We can have picnics in the trees. We never had picnics at home. Daddy's friend has a boat and he's going to show me how to row. When I'm older he might get me a boat of my own if I'm good.' She stops and bites her lip. Her eyes turn watery. 'But . . . he won't any more, will he? He can't. He's dead. Daddy's dead. He's not coming back, is he? He wasn't just lying down or hurt or anything. He's dead.'

She begins to cry. Sobs with every ragged intake of breath, but otherwise soundlessly. Mouthing words I can't understand, like a childish eulogy in some primal language of grief.

Comfort her, but try to keep her talking at the same time. 'Penny, did you see what happened? Did you see what happened to your daddy?'

She nods, keeps crying.

'What did you see?'

38

The wind rattles against the walls. The walls are funny, they look like plastic. It's like being in a giant ice-cream carton with a bed in it. Penny's favourite flavour of ice cream is Sweet Cream & Cookies. But the sleeper cabin doesn't smell like cookies and cream. It smells of oil and engines, even though Daddy's got one of those things like a tree that smell nice hanging up by the light.

The tree doesn't smell of ice cream either. Penny wonders if they make trees that do, and if Daddy could buy her one if they did.

The wind and the storm have been very noisy outside for a long time now. Sometimes the floor shakes and the walls make little hollow popping noises like when you squish a ping-pong ball or a drinks can. The thunder sounds are the loudest, and some of them seem very close indeed. Then Penny holds Mr Tumbleby tight and tells him not to be afraid. Mr Tumbleby doesn't like storms. He's a silly bear, being worried like that. She tells him it's all OK and there's nothing to be frightened of. The truck is huge and nothing's strong enough to blow it down, nothing at all. Sometimes she pretends that it's the Big Bad Wolf out there, huffing and puffing, but he can't do anything because the truck's bigger than him.

Daddy comes out to see her and make sure she's OK. He does it a few times. He knocks on the door so she knows to turn the light off in case anyone can see it outside. Then he opens it wide and crouches down so she can hug him, and then she doesn't mind that it's dark because he's there. He smells warm and dusty, like a big shaggy dog asleep in front of a fire.

She'd like a big shaggy dog, so she could cuddle him and stroke him and he'd be all fluffy.

Daddy tells her that everything's going to be all right, and that they can stay there until morning and then the storm will have gone and they can go again. They're going to Canada, where the river and the trees are that he's told her about. It sounds very nice and she's very excited, even though Mommy won't be coming. Mommy is very busy now and she has too much to do. Penny can't really say exactly how she feels about that. She's happy Daddy wants her to be with him, and sad that Mommy doesn't seem to want it, but she'll still miss her.

When she asks Daddy why the light has to be off when he has the door open, and who could see it, he tells her about the game they're all playing inside. Because no one can go anywhere because of the storm, they've all decided to play a game of hide-and-seek, and they've decided that Penny should hide because she's the smallest. Daddy isn't playing because he knows where she is, and so he can still make sure she's OK and come see her. If any of the others find her, then they'll win the game. But if Penny stays hidden in the truck until morning, if she doesn't let anyone see her and stays where she is, she'll win and Daddy will buy her a bike when they get to Canada.

She tells him she wants a big shaggy dog and he laughs and says he'll buy her one of those instead.

She tries to sleep after Daddy visits, because she's very tired and it's night. And she thinks it will make it easier to hide. But the noise outside is too much and even though she wants to sleep she keeps waking up, afraid of the storm. So instead she plays with Mr Tumbleby and Milly, her doll, and they tell each other ghost stories. Then they laugh because there's no such thing as ghosts and they're just being silly. When they run out of stories she sings songs because Mr Tumbleby and Milly like her singing. But she does it very quietly, just under her breath, because she doesn't want to lose the game. She sings the song they learned at school about a duck in the kitchen and then giggles to herself because it's so silly.

Daddy comes to see her again and he's looking tired like she is. She says he can sleep if he wants and maybe she'll be able to as well if he's there too, but he smiles and says if he did the others would come looking for him, and then they'd find Penny and win the game. So he'll stay tired so she can get her big shaggy dog, even though he really wants to sleep. It's very nice of him, and she does want the dog, even though she wants him to stay with her. She asks Daddy if he'll at least tell her and Mr Tumbleby and Milly a story, a happy story, before he goes again. He thinks for a moment, then he smiles and says of course he will. So she sits there and he reads her a storybook about a penguin going all the way to the North Pole to see a snowman.

Then Daddy sees something or hears something outside the truck. She doesn't know what it is. He tells Penny to shush and stay in the cabin while he has a look, and to shut the door behind him. She tells him she will, but she can't help holding it open a little way and peeking through the crack.

She wants to see who's looking for her and if they're going to win or if they'll miss her.

Daddy's somewhere at the end of the truck. She can't see him from where she is. But then she hears him shout — a rude word — and then he pushes someone out in front of the truck, like he's trying to keep him as far away from her as he can. The other man's big, bigger even than Daddy, who's very big. She can't see him very well because it's dark out there, even though she's trying very hard to see. The man is fighting Daddy, really fighting him, and she doesn't think he's playing hide-and-seek. Daddy's really strong and he's making lots of noise and shouting, and she can hear it even though it's still very noisy out there.

He grabs the man and sort of wrestles with him, but then she sees the man has a knife and suddenly she's very, very frightened. Daddy keeps trying to grab the man and grab his arms, and he's still shouting and trying to push him away from the truck. But the man's big, and he . . . he cuts at Daddy with the knife and Daddy has to let him go. And then the man is faster than Daddy and she can see that he's bleeding. He keeps fighting, though. He keeps fighting and stops the man getting close to Penny. He doesn't run . . . he doesn't run because he's very brave. He's very brave. And he doesn't want the man to get Penny. But then the man stabs him with the knife and Daddy falls over and Penny tries not to scream because the man might hear her. She holds her hand over her mouth and stops herself from sobbing. The man just walks away and disappears in the darkness, and Daddy still doesn't get up. She wishes and wishes and wishes with all her might that he's OK and he'll come back to her now the man's *gone, but he just lies there and she knows he's not just sleeping. And then the other people come and find Daddy, and they see her standing there.*

And she knows Daddy's dead and she wishes he wasn't, and she wouldn't care about not getting a big shaggy dog if Daddy could be all right again.

39

'That's all she could tell you?' Isaac asks, looking back at the little girl.

'Yeah. It's a miracle she told me that much – she's young, and that must all have been a hell of a shock. She's a brave kid, but I can't imagine what she's feeling right now.'

'She didn't get a better look at the guy?'

'No. Not from what she said. It was dark, and I imagine she was paying more attention to her dad than to the other guy.'

'Could it have been Walker?'

I wander over to Vince and nudge him awake with my foot. He looks at me blearily, his eyes taking a while to find their point of focus. Shock or blood loss. I wonder if we shouldn't have done more for him earlier, but I don't know enough about first aid to tell for sure. Gene might have known more, but he's gone.

'Huh? Yeah?'

'Vince, what does Walker look like?'

He blinks. 'Huh?'

'What does he look like? Short, tall, big, thin?'

'Maybe as tall as you. Same build, maybe a bit lighter. Same age as the others.' He blinks again. 'Can you unlock me from this radiator? I want to lay down properly. I'm all cramped.'

I look at him and I can't work out if he's putting on an act or not. 'Not yet, Vince. I'll get you a blanket, though. Make you more comfortable.'

I rejoin Isaac. He says, 'So? What'd he say?'

I shake my head. 'Walker's not bigger than Gene, not at all. He's more my size and Gene was a damn sight larger than me.'

'So?'

'If Vince and Penny are right, it wasn't Walker. Couldn't have been.'

'Wouldn't she see everyone as big, being that small?' He looks at me blankly. 'What's height to a kid?'

'To a kid, their dad is usually a giant. Massive. For her to think of someone else as being bigger than her dad, he must've been *really* big.'

'I suppose, yeah. Hey Ashley,' he calls out. 'You should take Penny upstairs, get her comfortable. She'll probably be better off up there, and maybe she should get some sleep if she can.'

'Are you sure? I don't want to leave her on her own.'

'We'll all be right downstairs. We can check in on her nice and regularly and she won't have to be surrounded by strangers all the time. Put her in my room. It should be warm and comfortable.' He lowers his voice to a hiss and she has to crane to hear. 'And if anything more happens tonight, it's better off she's not down here to see it or hear about it. She'll be fine up there.'

'While you're there, get a blanket and maybe a pillow for Vince, too,' I tell her. 'He doesn't look good.'

Ashley nods and leads the little girl by the hand towards the back stairs. As she goes, Penny stares at me with round, wordless eyes. Says nothing, her expression a totally blank slate. I can only imagine what's going on in her head right now. For her more than the rest of us, this all needs to stop, and soon.

I look back at the old man slumped in his booth. 'There's one more answer I need from Will,' I say. 'Something he can't avoid any more.'

He glances at me with dead, flat eyes as I walk over. His face is lined and hollow, sunken. Somehow older than he was earlier, all his years hitting him harder than ever before. Alone. Deeply and fundamentally alone.

'I'm sorry to do this, Will,' I say. 'But I need you to tell me about Sam.'

'I said . . .'

'You said you don't know anyone with that name. But Ben told me that you do. You know who she is and where she might be.' I emphasize the 'she', let him know that I'm not merely guessing; that this is certainty, not assumption.

He glares at me with pursed lips, his expression sour and bitter. Says, 'This isn't the time for this. My wife of thirty years just died. You got some nerve asking me about that now.'

'I do, but I've got to know.'

'I don't see why it's any of your business,' the old man growls. 'Let me have my peace.'

'A few days ago, I received a note through the mail,' I tell him. 'It said people were dead, that others could die, and I had to know what the writer had done, and that I had to "find the crosses". It was signed "Sam". Now we have three people dead for maybe a year out by the river, two that I know of going back fifteen years, and more people killed tonight, including Christine. Any or all of those things could be what the note was talking about. So I'm asking you right now to tell me who Sam is and where she is and then I'll know for sure what her role in all this is. Don't bullshit me, Will. I'm not in the mood for it any more and I don't think we can afford to waste time.'

He looks at me for a long time like he wants to snap my neck. The bar behind me has fallen completely silent, the whole place holding its collective breath. Then he stands up and says, 'All right, you son of a bitch. If it's so damned important for you to see Sam, I'll take you. Then you can go rot in hell for all I care. You don't talk to me about this again, you hear?'

Without another word or a backwards look, he leads me out into the parking lot, heading towards the gas station. Lightning ripples across the valley and the individual gusts and vortices shaped by the wind are given form for a second by the glare sparkling from the rain held within them. The truck stop and the empty countryside are woven and spun with a thousand curled spiderweb curtains hanging in the air.

At the back of the gas station there's a simple garden extending from the bottom of the steel steps which lead to Will and Christine's apartment above the store. The same steps her killer used to make his entrance. The garden runs for maybe thirty feet south before blending into the untamed plains beyond. Some flowers, trimmed grass, a couple of shrubs and a rockery. And at the far end, what looks to be a more recent addition. When I see it, I begin to understand.

Will leads me up to this cross carved out of granite, maybe three feet high. A half dozen varieties of tiny flowers grow at its base, somehow still standing despite the onslaught of the elements. I read the first line etched into its surface and know for certain just how far off the mark I've been: 'In loving memory of Samantha Middleton.'

'Our granddaughter killed herself six months ago,' Will says. 'She'd moved out, away from here, to go and work in Colorado. We couldn't get to her grave as often as we'd have liked, Chris and me, so we had this memorial erected here so we'd always have something to remember her by. I just hope you're happy now you've got an answer to your damned questions and you can leave an old man to grieve in peace now. For both of them.'

He turns to go. 'If you want to ask Sam how she

could've written that note of yours, or you want to interrogate her further, I'll leave you here to do so. Personally, I think you should ask for her forgiveness. Say you're sorry for forcing me to dredge all this up with a complete stranger not half an hour after her grandmother was killed.'

He's crying again as he walks off and leaves me standing in front of the dead girl's monument in the dark. I watch the rain bouncing off the stone and try to understand just how wrong I've been and how little I know about what's going on out here. To try once more to figure out the reason I came to this place, to reassess the nature of the message that led me here.

A cryptic note from a dead girl warning of death and murder. Three corpses no one claims to know, one of them vanished, taken almost as soon as I'd seen it. Two more killings fifteen years before, both unsolved. Some guy coming all the way out here because he'd helped someone cover the evidence of what happened to the dead family, his friends chasing after him to keep him quiet. Two people knifed to death when no more than half a dozen live for miles in any direction. Stories of lunatics living in the woods. Land steeped in old evil and me up to my neck in things which I don't understand but could, for all I know, get me killed.

Trapped out here, lost and alone, and everything I touch turns to dust.

40

Will ignores me when I walk back through the door, and I don't look at him. Ben and Isaac have both vanished. Tony's on his own by the window, looking worried. I get a beer from Ashley and go sit in a booth, alone with a cigarette. If Sam's dead, I can't figure out exactly what this means for me, for my being here. Unless the note took months to arrive and was written before her death, someone else must've sent it with her name at the bottom. Christ knows why, or what I'm expected to do now. I have no idea why someone would want to send me, of all people, a message purportedly coming from a dead girl telling me what I'd find here in the valley. Even if it was from the person who killed those people tonight, why me? Why now?

I'm in the middle of wrestling with these thoughts when Ashley sits down opposite me and says in a low voice, 'Hey.'

I look up from my ruminations and grunt.

'Are you still thinking about what happened to Gene and Christine?' she says. 'You look pretty down.'

'No. Will just . . . well, never mind that. I thought I'd had a message from his granddaughter and he just told me she's been dead for six months. After denying all knowledge of her for hours. He could've let me know about her ages ago, before Christine died. But now he's pretty pissed at me. Touchy subject, I guess, and especially right now.'

A confused look crosses her face, gone just as quickly as she dismisses whatever thought lay behind it. 'I remember when it happened,' she says. 'Isaac told me she was dead. They – Will and Christine, I mean – were really cut up about it. I never knew her name or anything, though. People don't talk about it much. I guess they don't want to.'

'You never met her?'

'No, she must have moved away from here before I came. Mind you, I've only been here nine months.' She sighs. 'I'm sorry he gave you a hard time, Alex. You couldn't have known if he didn't tell you already, and I suppose you had to ask. What did the note say?'

'Sam's note?'

She nods. 'Yeah.'

'It told me I had to know what she did, and that there was . . . bad shit that might happen if I didn't come and figure it all out. So here I am. And I don't understand it.'

'She threatened you?'

'Not as such.'

'But here you are. You said you used to be a cop.'

I laugh, despite myself. 'Yeah, that's right. Why do you bring it up?'

'I'm scared, Alex,' she says, knotting her fingers

together. 'Finding those people dead by the river, and what happened to … to Christine and Gene and everything, and it could be that it's someone I know that's doing it … Or someone that I thought I knew. But I can see you trying to do something about it all, so I want to trust you, whatever you are. Or whatever you're not. I just want to feel like I'm not alone.'

'You don't know me at all, Ashley. I could be some kind of psycho like Walker's crew. For all you know, I could be the most dangerous person here.'

'It's not like I don't know you a little,' she says. 'Besides, you could say you were all that and your eyes'd still call you a liar.'

'Would they now?'

'Eyes say a lot.'

'Yours are telling me you're looking for something I don't know I can provide, and you're so desperate for it you'll twist what you think you know to fit the ideal.'

She gives me a look like diamonds. 'You act like you know the law, and how it all works in the real world, and nothing seems to faze you for long. When the time came, you dealt with JC. You questioned Vince after you realized who he was. You've done all sorts.'

'And maybe I could've done some things differently. Like when we were at the house; I could've seen who came in, who they were, and maybe none of this would be happening now. We could've stopped it all right then and there.'

Another look. Then her eyes well up and she chokes back a sob. The whole response takes me completely off guard and I'm not sure what to say. She fiercely wipes away a couple of tears and says, 'I'm sorry, Alex. It's not your fault. It's just . . .'

'Yeah?'

Ashley falters, glances around her and says, 'Look, could we talk about this someplace else?'

The others seem to be paying us no attention at all, but I guess she's feeling vulnerable at the moment. Doesn't want to show this kind of fear in the open. I say, 'Sure.'

She leads me through to a stairway behind the bar and I follow her into the living quarters upstairs. They don't amount to much – a two-bedroom apartment which Isaac seems to keep pretty tidy, sparsely furnished and equipped. She leads me into a spare bedroom that looks like it's used for storing his junk and not much else. I know Penny is somewhere up here. Probably in the living room at the end of the hallway.

Ashley sits down on the bed and immediately begins to cry openly. She wraps an arm around me when I sit next to her.

'I'm sorry,' she says through the tears. 'I'm just *scared*. I'm really, really scared. Not just for me, but for . . . yeah, scared. I don't know how to deal with tonight. I'm scared and alone and I guess I'm just looking for something or someone I can rely on.'

I let her finish, then say, 'It's OK. I can understand that.'

'So tell me about when you were a cop. Where did you work?'

'I was in the FBI.'

'How long for?' she says.

'A fair while. It didn't work out. I haven't been in law enforcement in a lot of years.'

'So who do you work for now?'

'Myself.'

She nods like she knows what I'm talking about. 'Would you protect me if I needed it?'

'Like when?'

'Like if whoever killed Christine came after the rest of us. Or like if one of us snapped or something.'

'Sure. You think someone might?'

'I might.'

'I can't protect you from yourself.' I smile.

'The others can be dangerous, too. You don't know them like I do.' Her voice is bitter, empty.

'They seem OK, mostly.'

'Tony's strange and Ben frightens me. Isaac . . . I don't know about. Will is, sure. You can see it in him. A hardness.' She sounds lost, panicky. What she's saying could be nothing more than lashing out at those around her. Paranoia given a voice.

'I'll keep an eye on them,' I say.

'And what if the guy who killed the other two comes after the rest of us?'

'We might catch him before that happens.'

'Right.' She shakes her head.

265

'I aim to. I'm not planning on letting him do that sort of thing again if I can help it. We've already got an old man without a wife and a young girl without a father.'

'You've been aiming for a while now. Everyone else could be dead by the time you're done.'

'It'll make the job of identifying the killer easier,' I say.

'That's no way for a cop to talk.'

'I told you being a cop didn't work out.'

She reaches up and hauls me into a kiss.

41

There's a fierce intensity in Ashley's touch, need turned into pure force. Her lips taste of vanilla and salty tears. She holds the embrace for a moment, then pulls back and says, low and lonely, 'I just want to be held right now. I want to feel something else other than fear, want to feel like I'm not alone.'

'This feels like a bad idea,' I tell her. 'Like taking advantage.'

'If we survive the night, it's something I'm happy to give you.'

She kisses me again and this time I respond, holding her tight enough that I can feel her breathing against me. Her fear and desperation seem to spill out of her, dissolving all the remaining walls she's built around herself. She pulls at my clothes like fury given form and I follow suit, fighting to keep up with her as she twists and scrabbles, movement and energy building until we're completely adrift on a heaving ocean and all we can do is ride the waves. At their peak, her entire body shudders to its core, a faint sigh escapes her lips and then the sea falls calm again.

It may only be the eye of the storm, a temporary reprieve, but we lie there for a time, holding each other on flat water beneath the stars.

'When I was a kid,' she says after a while, 'I was never the one to be frightened of anything. I never had to deal with it.' Her voice is very small and quiet, muffled against my chest. Her hair is tickling my neck.

'Never the one?' I ask. 'You had brothers or sisters?'

'A brother. He was always the one to worry about stuff, and it would always be me who had to sort it out and calm him down.'

'Your parents weren't much help, huh?'

'It would usually be them that frightened him in the first place. Mostly his fault, I guess, but they had quick tempers. Never anything bad, y'know, I mean, they took care of us right and all. But he was usually the one they'd shout at. Sometimes he'd be mad at them for it, and sometimes he'd be afraid of what they'd do to punish him. Parents can be funny like that, I guess.'

'Yeah, I guess they can.' I think about Will's reaction to my questions about Samantha. Say to Ashley, 'So you said you never met Will's granddaughter.'

'No,' she murmurs. 'Never.'

'Does he ever talk about her much? I mean, the rest of the locals must've known her.'

'I don't know. Like I said, I remember when she died. Isaac told me what happened, that Will's granddaughter was dead and that I should be careful around him, and I'm pretty sure she'd moved away a while before. I don't think I've ever heard anyone else talk about her, though.' She raises her head and looks at me. 'Why?'

'Curiosity. Sometimes I just can't let things go.'

'Do you mind if I ask you a question?'

'Sure.'

'Were you ever married, anything like that?'

'No.' I shake my head. 'Came close once.'

'It didn't work out?'

'Like being a cop.'

'Story of your life, huh?'

'I guess.'

Her face, her eyes, tense up a little and I feel a faint tremor run through her body. I guess the break's over and we're going to have to deal with the real world again. She says, 'You really think you can figure all this out?'

'Maybe.'

'You think Will's granddaughter might be something to do with what happened to Gene or Christine or those people by the river?'

'Maybe. There's all sorts that could be linked. Gene I think was just unlucky; Christine's killer thought he might have spotted him. I don't think there was anything more to it than that. The others . . . I don't know.' I try to fit the entire picture in my head at once, but it just won't fit. With Sam suddenly gone from being a living suspect lurking out there in the dark to being a girl dead for six months, most of my thinking's fallen to pieces. 'Does he ever talk about the old days? Years ago, before all this trouble started with the MacBrides?'

'Will? No, he doesn't. None of them do, except

to tell ghost stories about the damn Foundations. It's something they just don't seem to want to dredge up. Same with my uncle David,' she says. 'Sometimes Will . . . well, he can be kinda strange. Especially about all that.'

'Strange?'

'Moody, y'know?'

'Sure. I saw some of that earlier.' Affairs. Disappearances. Hit-and-run murders. Silence settles again. I sit up and we separate. 'Sorry. I guess we'd better go.'

She smiles. 'It was nice while it lasted. Thanks.'

I chuckle, kiss her on the forehead. 'You're welcome.'

As we leave the bedroom, Isaac's just climbing to the head of the stairs. He sees Ashley and is about to speak to her when he catches sight of me in tow and his words falter for a second. 'Uh . . . Ashley,' he says, 'where's Penny?'

'In there.' She gestures at a doorway down the hall. 'She just wanted to curl up and go to sleep, so I figured that was best. She didn't want to talk about what happened, not to me, anyway. Poor thing probably wants to wake up and have her dad's death be just a bad dream. You want me to make sure she's OK?'

'Well, you did say you would,' he replies. There's a trace of admonishment in his voice, the faint edge of disapproval for what she's been doing for most of the past hour. Disapproval or jealousy.

If she notices it, she doesn't react, just creeps up to the door and gently pushes it open far enough to fit her head through the gap. Then wider, and she slips inside. I look at Isaac, then follow her. A sparse, slightly untidy bedroom, obviously Isaac's. Unmade bed, heavy curtains drawn in the window. As I turn the light on, Ashley ducks down to look beneath the bed, then starts yelling, 'Penny! Penny!'

'What's going on?' Isaac appears behind me in the doorway.

I feel a stab of panic in my chest. 'Penny's gone,' I say. 'She's gone.'

42

Isaac says, 'Gone? Gone how? Where would she go?'

'She's disappeared,' Ashley yells back. 'How the hell should I know?'

'Did she just wander off on her own, or did someone take her?'

She stares around the room, frantic and jerky. I feel strangely powerless, incapable of offering anything much by way of help. 'No, no,' she says. 'That bear. That bear of hers is gone too. If someone took her, they wouldn't have taken that too, would they? She must have run off.'

'How did she do it, walking out on her own without anyone spotting her?'

'She must have slipped out while . . .'

'Yeah.' Isaac glares at the two of us. I wonder if there was some noise, some sound, something we might have heard or acted upon but didn't. I wonder, if she didn't wander off but was taken, if we might not have heard a heavier footfall on the landing, a soft voice speaking to her. Something we could have responded to. Something that would have meant she was still with us.

But there wasn't and we didn't.

Isaac shakes his head. 'We'd best go see if she snuck into the bar somehow. Maybe she's hiding under a table or something. We can see if the others have seen her.'

'Why would she go like that?' Ashley murmurs as we head downstairs. 'Why would she do it?'

'Maybe she felt scared,' is the best I can say.

'Of what?'

'Us? This place? Maybe she wanted to go and find her dad. I don't know. But she's young, on her own with a bunch of strangers, and her dad was killed in front of her. She's probably not thinking straight.'

Down in the bar, Isaac explains the situation. Both the brothers and Will say they've not seen her at all since Ashley took her upstairs. But then none of them has been keeping an eye out for her. They thought she was with us. It's possible she slipped past them just like she slipped past us.

'Maybe she ran off,' Will says.

'MacBrides probably took her.'

Ashley shakes her head at Ben, says, 'If she came downstairs on her own, she might have taken the wrong door and headed out towards the storerooms and the back of the building. Not seeing anyone back there, thinking we'd left her, she might have been scared enough to run off to hide by herself. Or maybe she was just scared of us and wanted to get away from here.'

'Why would she be scared of us?'

She shrugs. 'We're strangers to her. That can be

enough to freak out a kid that young. Who knows? But it doesn't matter, does it? We've got to go and find her, and that's all there is to it.'

It doesn't seem likely that we'll find her, the way the night's going. But I've already seen one murdered child today and I certainly don't want to see another. And all this feels like it was our fault. 'Yeah,' I say. 'And quickly, too.'

Tony peers through the windows. 'She could've gone anywhere by now.'

'So we'd best look everywhere,' I say. 'Someone wake up Vince. See if he saw her leave. It's a long shot, but still . . . Best to cover every possibility.'

Our prisoner doesn't look in the best of health, even worse than he was earlier. He's still pale, still breathing shallowly. But he's alive after all this time, so I guess it can't be fatal. Ben prods him with a foot until his eyes snap open.

'Did you see the little girl, Vince?' he asks. No preamble.

'What?'

'Did you see where she went, or anything of what happened to her?'

'What? No, no. Been asleep. Fast asleep.' His head begins to loll again. Ben looks at us and lets it drop.

'Let's find her,' Will says. His voice is cracked, face unreadable. I can sense something boiling up inside him, something crackling in the air. The old man's just lost his wife in a truly brutal fashion, but some element to his character seems to be sparking him into life.

'There's six of us,' Isaac says. 'That's three pairs. Given what's gone on ...' He looks at Will for a second. '... I think it's best we stick like that for now. I'll go with Alex. We'll check the parking lot, the gas station and Will's place. Ashley, you and Will check the rest of this building, your place and maybe head up the road as far as the Banks house again. Tony and Ben can check everything else. Your house, the outbuildings, anywhere else that would make a good hidey-hole for her. She could have gotten into one of the old buildings and scooched herself down somewhere. If someone finds something, try shouting to alert the other groups.'

'That'll scare the shit out of Penny if she's hiding near by,' Ashley points out.

'Omelettes and eggs. Unless you know how to make us a couple of two-way radios out of tinfoil and beer mats, that's the only choice we've got.'

I follow Isaac out into the rain. He doesn't say it, but I guess his choice of split is deliberate. The two brothers are a natural choice to work together. Ashley's a softer presence to keep Will calm, and to steer him away from thoughts about the building where his wife lies dead. We can check the gas station without worrying about the old man's feelings. I keep pace with Isaac across the lot. Behind us, I can hear low, gruff chatter as the brothers fade away into the night, leaving us alone.

'You think we're going to find that little girl alive?' he says as we round the last of the parked cars and head for the gas pumps. The wind is whistling through the hoses beneath each nozzle, setting them swinging and clattering like flag lines. They're the only things I can see moving. The sound they make is discordant, jarring.

'Maybe, yeah. I certainly think she ran off on her own. No one took her.'

'Why's that?'

'Why snatch her? Why take that bear of hers? If it was whoever killed Christine, she'd be dead in that room. Christine never got a chance to call out for help, and Penny was asleep. She'd never have known what hit her. So I think she ran. She ran, she could be hiding, so it follows that she could easily be alive. We've got to look. It's that simple.'

As I say it, I realize there's another reason she might have been afraid of us. Maybe she recognized one face out of all those she saw. One of us strangers she'd seen before. Not recognizable enough to describe it to me when I asked, not enough maybe even to know for sure where she remembered it from, but on some level maybe she knew that *there* was the face of the man who killed her father, right there in the building with her.

43

Perhaps that same man saw her, realized he'd missed another potential witness, another person who might eventually identify him, and decided to act. Perhaps he felt that killing her in the bar was too risky, that it was better to get her away from any possible help first.

In her position, I'd have run as well. Found a deep, dark hiding place and stayed there until the police showed up.

I stop and glance up at the gas station, hoping to see some sign of life. Penny's face pressed up against one of the windows, candlelight in an upstairs room. Anything like that. I can't see a damn thing, and I feel a little drop of hope slip away.

'Where'd you want to check first? Inside? Outside?'

'Let's have a look around the building, see if there's any sign of her. Then we can switch to the inside. If there's no trace of her, we'll try the fields around.'

Long grass is pressed thickly against the sides of the building, a narrow strip where cutting would have been more difficult for the old couple. The growth masks a couple of small drainage gutters and one tiny, meshed-in basement window which I doubt even a cat could squeeze through. We check it all, but there's no sign of Penny, or anyone else for that matter. Isaac keeps up with his occasional comments, remarks I can only assume are meant to impress me or to make him feel better about himself. They could be nothing more than his fears expressing themselves; everyone must be dealing with what's happened in their own particular way. I remain noncommittal. As we complete our circuit of the building he says, 'So who do you think's doing this? Killed Christine and everything else?'

'I don't know. Maybe the same person as killed the three I found out by the river. Christine and Gene could just be the next in a line of murders like this.'

'My money's still on the MacBrides.'

'I don't buy it, not necessarily. I don't really see what they'd have to gain from all this death. Why do it?'

'Has anyone said anything about the people you found? Or seemed like they knew more than they should, if you see what I mean?'

'You got anyone in particular in mind?'

'No, no. Just wondering was all. Someone might know a little more than the rest of us, remember something happening, y'know.'

I bend down, shine a flashlight into the basement. It's relatively neat, and I can't see any sign of Penny. The window itself doesn't look like it's been opened in a long, long time. 'And you said you don't know anything about anyone going missing round here a year back, didn't you?' I say.

'I told you before. We all told you before.'

'Sure, sure. I was just wondering out loud.'

We move around the back of the building, check under the steps leading up to the kitchen. They smell of wet metal and peeling rust. I'm conscious of Isaac looming behind me while I scan the empty shadows by the wall, but I don't turn around.

'Have you ever killed anyone before tonight?' he asks. Softer than usual.

I stand, turn to look at him. 'Yeah. I have.'

For a moment, he looks as though he's thinking about asking more, prying further. Then he just nods, says, 'OK.' Like I've passed some kind of test or met some internal standard by which he's measuring me.

'Let's check inside, then the fields,' I tell him. 'She's not out here.'

At the front of the gas station, Isaac goes for the door through to the store but I stop him and point instead at the repair shop. It's darkened, closed and silent. But I want to check it all the same.

'She's not going to be there,' Isaac says. 'Hell, I don't want to go in there, and I'm a grown man. There's two corpses in there and they're not pretty. Why the hell would a kid like her want to hide somewhere like that?'

'Two reasons. First, if that guy killed her and

wanted to hide the body, this place would be ideal.'

'Seriously?'

'Ten years ago, maybe, there was this thing in Atlanta. This nightclub burned to the ground, killed a dozen people. But when they had all the remains laid out for identification, they found they suddenly had thirteen. Someone had tried to hide a murder victim in with all the others, maybe even starting the fire deliberately to provide them with the cover.'

'Jesus.'

'And the second reason's the main one. She was pretty comfortable upstairs. She can't have left because she wasn't settled in nice and snug.'

'So why would she go here?'

I open the door and look at Isaac. 'This is where her dad is.'

The smell of blood lies thickly in the sheltered air of the repair shop, sickly sweet, almost chewable. Isaac reels back, holding a hand up to his nose. 'Fucking hell,' he says. 'I'm not putting up with that, man. You want to dig around in there, you be my guest. I'll watch your back out here.'

I shrug. It's not pleasant, that's for sure. Cloying and disturbing on a subconscious level that tells us: humans are dead here. Stay away. 'Fair enough. It'll only take a moment.'

Isaac leans back against the wall while I duck inside. My flashlight beam sweeps across the room, cutting a line in the darkness just above the covered faces of the pair of corpses lying inside. Stark little hillocks picked out in deep shadow, and a haze in the air like mist or steam rising from them, so faint I'm not sure if it's just my imagination. Damp evaporating now they're out of the rain. The phantom breaths of the dead.

I walk slowly around the repair shop, playing the light all over. The place is silent and I can't see anything that seems to have been disturbed. Two bodies lying side by side under cloth. Thin trickles of congealing blood seeping from the wounds they suffered. No teddy bear. No child-sized footprints on the floor.

Gene is still hidden beneath a sheet spattered with old oil. I pull it aside and look down at his face. Cold, waxy flesh, eyes staring at nothing and no one. He doesn't look real any more. Like a mannequin, or a puppet with no controller; you can't quite believe it ever moved at all. It doesn't look as though Penny came out here to find him, and for her sake I'm glad. I cover him over again and stand.

I meet back up with Isaac and we search the rest of the gas station almost without speaking to one another. There's nothing there, nothing but dead air and fresh unhappiness. We make an effort to check the field beyond Samantha's memorial marker but don't do a particularly good job. The grass is too untidy, the night too dark, the flashlight too narrow. In daylight, we might be able to find her. Now, it's just not possible.

As we walk back past the marker I say to Isaac, 'Will's pretty pissed with me for asking him about their daughter.'

'Granddaughter,' he says on automatic. 'Sam was their granddaughter.'

'How come they were so close to her? I mean, I know grandparents can have that bond with kids, but not usually that strong.'

Isaac sighs and eyeballs the darkened gas station. 'Sam's parents died in an accident on US 106 when she was six years old, as far as I know, so Will and Chris took Sam and her sister in, raised them both. It's no wonder they're close.'

'Sam had a sister?'

'Jennifer, I think her name is. I've never met her and those two don't talk about her much. I don't think they get on. They argued or something.'

'What was she like, Samantha?' Isaac's face is guarded, suspicious, so I try a friendly smile. 'I have a hard time imagining a granddaughter of Will's that isn't just him in a dress. Telling people stories and all that.'

'She was nice. I guess. I never knew her parents, but she didn't take after Will much. She went off to college, came back, ended up working at the gas station for a while before she moved away again to Colorado. She was pretty nice.'

'Why'd she move away?'

'She got offered a job in Aspen. She didn't want to stick around here. I mean, who would at that age?

So she went. I don't blame her. There wasn't much for her here.'

'That was, what, a year ago? Just under?'

'Something like that, yeah. Went to work at a hotel for a friend of Will's.' He shakes his flashlight like he's worried about the batteries. A defensive tic, trying to dodge the subject.

'And she was happy out there?'

'I guess.'

'So what made her so miserable she killed herself?'

'Young people do it all the time. Maybe she was lonely or homesick or something. Kids get depressed about all sorts. You'd have to ask Will if you wanted to know more than that, but I guess if he's pissed with you he won't want to talk about it.'

The other four are already back at the bar by the time we return. They shake their heads. Penny is gone, possibly for good. And still the only things I have to work with are vague suggestions and some half-remembered local legends. Either it's the nutjobs in the hills, or it's someone here, and Christ knows which.

I've tried talking to one side. Let's talk to the other.

'I'm going to see the MacBrides,' I say.

Ashley looks at me like I'm insane. 'What?'

'It's the only way of finding out for certain if they're behind all this or not. I'm through playing hide-and-seek in the dark and I've got no other way of getting the answers I need.'

'You're crazy,' Ben says. 'They'll kill you, or worse. And the track up to their place crosses two of the streams that feed into the Easy. You won't be able to drive. You'll have to walk.'

Isaac nods. 'He's right. It's crazy. You've got no idea what they're like. You go up there, you might not come back.'

'Possibly.' I adjust my coat and light a cigarette. 'But it's got to be done.'

44

The air's cold and fresh. The rain and the lightning haven't let up, but they seem steadier, somehow less brutal than before. Maybe the worst of the storm really is over. It could be gone by morning. As I cross the road, I keep my eyes peeled for any movement in the darkness around me, any change in the shadows or the light dancing from the raindrops. Anything to suggest I'm not alone out here.

There's nothing. The fields are empty, and there's no sign of a human presence anywhere in the wind-tossed trees and grass, the handful of trailers and the scattered buildings.

A little-used dirt track now ankle-deep in mud takes me through a small stand of rustling trees and into a field full of thick chest-high grass, waving in the wind. I wade through the greenery with nothing but the occasional flicker overhead to light my way.

Then the ground drops away sharply as I reach the Foundations. Great gouges carved in the earth, roughly geometric slopes and mounds, sudden sharper outcrops marking old pipework or concrete shapers. All covered in grass, thorns and unkempt plant growth. I wait, paused on the edge of the trenchwork, for the next lightning fork to crash across the cloud above and light my way onward. When it bursts overhead, rippling along the roof of the valley, I have the briefest glimpse of the area picked out in light and shadow. It runs from where I stand maybe half a mile or more to the treeline to the north. I try to imprint the image on my mind, mark my route before I start out. Then darkness falls once more and I hop over the edge and into the maze of trenches and twisted land.

I quickly understand how those two kids in the story Isaac told became lost and separated here. The gashes in the earth are surprisingly deep, affording me little view of the ground outside the trench I'm in, and seem in the dark to follow no sane pattern at all. I have no idea what the design for this place actually was, but in my mind I have a picture of a sprawling Lovecraftian mansion where none of the angles quite make sense. Now, with fifteen years' worth of greenery covering it, all that remains is an old battlefield where madmen fought trench warfare. Twists and turns in the tunnels, sudden rises or holes in the earth. Within moments I'm no longer sure if I'm heading in the right direction at all, but the alternative is trying to cross the pockmarked surface, navigating over these gaps one by one and fighting my way through the straggling scrub that encrusts the top like barbed wire. The wind spins strange vortices in the maze of trenches, whistling and howling like an animal. Every flash of lightning sends shadows racing in all directions and makes me think there's movement all around.

Then I hear it. The sound of snapping twigs and a voice both very human and at the same time wholly alien. Keening softly for a few seconds, eerie and mournful, then breaking into jagged, splintered laughter.

It comes from close by, but with the storm and the strange acoustics here I can't tell from which direction. I clamp down on the stab of fear that runs through me and remind myself that they're only human and I'm here to speak to these people.

'My name's Alex Rourke,' I yell as another blast of lightning crackles through the air like bad fireworks. 'I need to speak to MacBride.'

Silence for a moment then another staccato burst of laughter, this time from what seems to be a different direction. I swallow hard and press on. Reaching the edge of one of the periodic sinkholes in the ground, circular shafts maybe six feet deep carved into the trenchwork like filled-in wells, I pause for a moment to consider how best to cross it given that I now seem to be being followed. Then what feels like a hand brushes against my shoulder and a voice says something too soft to catch.

45

I drop into the hole, scoot across to the other side and haul myself up as quickly as possible. Again I hear laughter like hyenas' echoing around the Foundations.

Another couple of switchbacks in the trench and a turn to the north sees me at the bottom of an open bowl with a wide, shallow ramp leading up to ground level. I can smell the woodland up ahead, wet tree bark and leaf mulch carried on the air. As I head for the ramp, I turn my head from side to side, keep a sharp watch around me for whoever's been dogging my footsteps in the dark. Hoping to see some sign of a human form lit up by the storm, known, identified and no longer nothing more than a shadow, a pure and unknown threat in the night. I'm disappointed, though. Once or twice I think I can see what *might* be figures – more than one of them – behind me, but they're so hard to tell apart from the terrain and the plant growth that I can't be sure they're there at all.

Past the human-engineered landscape of the Foundations, the land rises, low rocky ridgelines building like creases in the earth. Once over the cleft gouged by the Easy, they must rise into foothills and eventually the mountains bracketing the valley. The going's difficult underfoot, stones slimy with mud, sheets of broken scree and thicker and thicker plant growth as I enter the fringes of the woodland filling the upper reaches of the valley. The trees swish in the wind with a sound like I'm surrounded by a massive flock of birds. Twigs, leaves, fragments of bark and moss blow down from above, spattering off my coat along with the rain.

I can't see more than ten feet in front of me, and even that's strange and the shapes in the dark seem to make no sense. The lightning, which seems to be growing fainter and less frequent now, occasionally scares away the shadows and gives me some idea of where I'm heading, but I can't yet see any sign of light glimmering in the distance from the MacBrides' home. I'd use my flashlight, but all that'd do would be to blind me further to anything not picked out in its beam. Besides, it's not as though it'd help me spot their house until I was right in front of it.

And I'm not alone. Sooner or later, whoever's tracking every move I make is going to have to confront me in some way, to bring matters to a head. If they're just trying to scare me out of the woods, if I don't go for it, sooner or later they're going to have to try something more direct or give up entirely. Shit or get off the pot. If they're playing games, toying with me before beating me to death like the folks out by the river, then at some point they're going to have to make their move. And I aim to be ready for them.

I try not to dwell on the fact that I'm out here on

their territory and chances are they're a damn sight better at doing this sort of thing in the dark than I am. And that I'm outnumbered.

The distant sound of roaring water echoes from the east as I crest one of these folds in the land and start into the next. It could be the Easy or one of the streams feeding it; I know the road to the MacBrides' place crosses a couple of these, so it's a fair sign that I'm at least heading in the right direction. I pick up the pace and start up the next slope.

Then a chorus of high-pitched animal shrieks erupts from the ridgeline behind me, like baboons screaming at each other. I spin around to see one figure silhouetted against the lit sky beyond, just for a second. A big guy, tall and powerful, standing on the very top, baying in my direction. I can't see the others making the noise but I think for a moment I see a couple of much smaller shadows, like children, scuttling along the line of the ridge, fanning out behind me. A second cry echoes the chorus of the first, coming from somewhere up ahead of me. Ululating, whipped into strange notes by the wind.

'I'm here to talk to MacBride,' I shout again. 'Talk, that's all.'

Lightning flickers again and the figures are gone. I return to my course and keep going, ears straining for any sign of movement to either side. Brain trying not to think about a pack of children helping herd me onwards, nor about the person or people responsible for that second, answering cry.

A few minutes later I begin to see a faint orange glow up ahead and a little to the right. I'm aware that the group behind me are still somewhere in the darkness but I've not spotted anything yet of the ones in front of me. The light is flickering faintly. Firelight. It could be MacBride's home. I approach with a great deal of caution.

Closer. Closer. The fire's in the open and I can't see anything even remotely resembling a building near it. Something flat reflects the orange dully. Closer. It's the rusting shell of an old car, wheels long gone, nothing but rust. A bonfire has been lit in front of it. Hastily, guessing by the untidy nature of its construction, probably boosted with gasoline or lighter fluid.

It's a goddamn lure. A trap, and I don't know if I'm far enough away to avoid walking into it by the time the realization hits me.

Twigs crunch and splinter in the trees behind me and off to either side. My pursuers break into their strange whooping cries again, now tinged with victory. Elation. Hunger. At the same time, I see movement on the other side of the rusting car. The hunters, probably, lying in wait for me as the hounds drive me into them.

I reach down into the sodden leaf litter at my feet and grab a good thick branch and turn to face those coming after me. Then I leap to meet them. Cat and mouse is death to the mouse every time, and I'm not planning on fulfilling the role easily. I can hear nothing but howling animal noise around me and I can't tell if I'm yelling back. Then the big guy I saw on the ridge lunges out from behind a tree in front of me, hands outstretched. His eyes are too white, pupils too dark. Like he has no irises. Like he's not human. I snap the branch up into his chin. His teeth crack together and he drops to the floor, screaming and thrashing like a wounded beast.

Then something barges into the back of my knees and my footing vanishes from beneath me. I'm aware of hands, small but wiry hands, grappling with my limbs, trying to hold me down. *Children.* And there's still no noise but the animal hollering, nothing human at all. I manage to twist on to my back, ready to fight my way free, when another large figure looms out of the dark, probably one of the people who were hiding behind the car. I'm about to try shouting out again when he drives his knee on to my chest and raises his hand. I feel a sharp, stinging pain in my arm, see the needle, and wonder in the moments I have left whether this would've gone better if I'd pulled my gun and tried threats instead.

I try to call out. I try to break free. But it's as though all my strings have been cut and I no longer have any control. I watch as the guy pockets the syringe. He says something too far away for me to hear, and then he, and the rest of the world, vanish into the night.

46

I'm in a dark space, sitting on the floor, my back pressed against a wall of some sort. As though I'm in a cellar. At least, that's how it appears to begin with. I have no idea how I came to be here, no memory at all. Then I realize that I can see myself perfectly clearly, like daylight, and it's just that everything else – floor, wall, everything as far as I can see – is utterly black. Like space, not black paint. The complete absence of light.

And while I think I can feel something solid beneath and behind me, it seems to be without form or texture. Void.

Either this is something brought on by whatever the big guy injected me with, or this is what happens when you die. I don't like it.

'Where's the white light and the crowd of happy relatives?' I say to the blackness. My voice sounds strange. Probably my self-consciousness, feeling stupid just for talking at all.

I check my pockets. No cigarettes. Shit. That doesn't bode well. No gun.

A flash of something, like a flicker in the sky. Tiny hands grabbing at my clothing, spatters of blood on the air, the smell of smoke. A sound like cold metal.

No nothing of anything much, on me or around me.

I stand and will myself to wake up. To snap out of whatever this is. Nothing happens. So much for the power of positive thinking. 'There's no place like home,' I say and click my feet together. For all the good it does me. 'What, you never watched the movies?'

The blackness keeps its thoughts to itself.

'Talking to my damn self,' I say. 'I need to get out of here before I go nuts. Unless I'm dead. In which case, they lied to me in church when I was a kid. I'm pretty sure heaven was supposed to be more impressive than this.'

Another flicker in the void. The pinching pain, light on the hypodermic. Push the plunger, feel the warmth race around my body. The big man, laughing.

'Yeah. The drug. So this is my own head? I need to get out of my skull to wake up? There's a paradox for you.'

The blackness still says nothing. I wonder if this is the same kind of oblivion junkies run to whenever the real world becomes too much. If so, I don't see the attraction. But then, what do I have to run from that isn't in here with me?

Especially not now, unconscious and completely at the mercy of the people in the woods. For all I know, the stories the locals tell down at the roadhouse are true and the MacBrides are already skinning me and putting me over the fire.

Or delivering me to whoever the killer is back there.

One of the MacBride clan, lurking in the darkened parking lot. He watches Christine and Will cross the gravel and the old woman enter the gas station. He runs round the back and up the stairs. Sneaks into the bedroom after her. Grabs the electrical cord. Smiles as he whips it around her throat and cuts off her scream before it can even start.

I'm not sure why they would though.

Me, following Ashley up the stairs. Sneaking into the bedroom after her. I grab the electrical cord and whip it —

'Wait. That's not right.'

One of the MacBrides, following Ashley out into the parking lot where her daughter's hiding. She grabs a length of cord —

'Hey. That's not right either.'

Ashley takes Gene upstairs. They're mid-fuck when Walker comes in —

'What?' What the hell?

Where's that noise coming from?

Christine fucking Ashley. In her hand she has a bloody knife —

What the fuck is going on? 'I feel weird.' I feel weird. For a second I think I see the dead girl out on the edge of vision before everything gives one final twist and spins away from me.

Then something happens to the void and there's a noise like voices all around.

47

Ba-DUM. Ba-DUM. Ba-DUM.

My heart, pounding in my ears like the loudest drum in the world. And a taste in my mouth like old cardboard. They're the first things I notice. The first things that come back to me as the real world slowly returns. I feel as though I've landed with a bump. My stomach churns like someone's filled it with snakes and every muscle's made from stringy lead. There's a deep pressure at the front of my skull. Pain, maybe.

I'm sitting in a chair, and I can't seem to move my limbs. Perhaps I'm tied to it.

I crank open my eyes. The world's blurred and I find it difficult to bring it into focus. There's not much light in here, just the low orange of a fire in one corner of the room and a couple of dim, pale bulbs in the ceiling above us. Aged, solid wooden boards, dark and scuffed. Furniture to match. Real frontier chic. The place smells stale and earthy.

There's a guy sitting in an old oak chair by the fire, half-facing me. My height, but broader and weathered. You could probably sharpen knives on his skin. He must be well into his late fifties or early sixties, but his hair is still thick, if a little receded, and, like his beard, is a dusty orange swept with grey. He's wearing a well-used denim shirt, whittling a piece of wood with a knife, flicking the shavings expertly into the fire. It looks like he's carving a figurine of some sort. On a low, hand-hewn table next to the chair are my wallet and gun.

This must be MacBride. He's alone and there's no sign of the people who brought me here.

'You're awake,' he says. His voice is dry and firm. Matches his appearance. 'I've been waiting for a while. Thought you might be out all night.'

I'm on a wooden dining chair which, again, looks handmade. Neither my hands nor my legs seem to be bound at all; I just can't move them. For a second I wonder if I'm paralysed, if something's been done to my back, but then I remind myself that it could be an after-effect of the drug they gave me. Could be. Hopefully is. I want to be able to walk out of here if I survive.

Looking at MacBride, I don't say anything, just try to hide the fear coursing through me. Raw lines of adrenaline, like ice through the narcotic morass inside. I try not to think of the stories the others told, about the murders his family may have committed. I try not to think about dying out here in the woods. Woods no one else dares to visit for fear of the man in front of me and his family.

'I'm sorry it came to that. Misha thought he needed to have you unconscious, but he wasn't sure if the dose would be too big, or not enough. He's never

297

injected anyone with ketamine before. If I'd been there, if I'd known, I probably wouldn't have done it at all.'

My mouth is dry and heavy. 'My head feels weird.'

'You took a bang on the skull in that little scuffle you were in with the boys. It was bleeding a little, but it's stopped now.' His eyes stray towards the fire for a moment. 'It'll probably hurt once the sedative wears off properly but I don't think it's too badly damaged.'

'Ketamine?'

'Yeah.' He nods. 'We have some for the animals, just in case. A couple of times we've had to use it on people. Bet you had some real weird dreams.'

I just stare at him. Out of the corner of my eye, I can see my reflection in a window. I can't see any blood on my forehead but my hair's all matted at the back and I look badly strung out. Shell-shocked and lost.

'Funny,' MacBride says. 'A lot of people in places like this have had a go at trying K one time or another. Used to be a group of friends of mine hung out at this place by the crossroads near where I grew up who took turns snorting or eating that stuff. And they'd tell each other all the freaky shit they'd see.' He smiles, eyes sad. 'We're all dumb when we're young, I guess.'

'All I saw was a whole lot of black,' I say, taking time and effort to make the words come out clearly.

'A whole lot of black, and me alone in it with nothing to do but talk to myself.'

'Sounds kinda like you went through the "K-hole". Normally it's bright on the other side, though. Like heaven, they used to say.' He looks at the half-finished figurine and sighs, places it and the knife on the table.

If it's anywhere near like what I saw, you're not missing anything, I think. I don't say it, though. I just want to keep things calm, like they seem to be now, find out what he's planning on doing with me. Stay alive. Just stay alive. Try to stay unharmed. Don't end up like the family by the river.

'Name's Stuart,' he says, looks at me.

'Alex Rourke.' My throat's dry. My eyes feel like they're burning.

'So what were you doing on my family's land on a night like tonight, Mr Rourke?'

Don't sound like a threat. Don't make him think he's got to silence you. Don't say anything that'll stop him feeling safe and secure. Safe and secure, he'll leave you alive, awake and talking. 'I came out here to talk to you, Mr MacBride,' I say. 'That was all.'

'That's what Misha said you'd been shouting. He wasn't sure, but that's why he brought you back here rather than dumping you in the Foundations in the rain.'

'Misha was the big guy I saw with the syringe?'

MacBride nods, jabs the fire with a poker, sending sparks streaming up into the chimney. For a moment, the increased light allows me to see more of the room I'm in. It's a large open-plan living area with a kitchen at the far side. Almost all wooden, very few electrical items. I see a glint from what might be a TV further into the room, but I'm not sure. 'Misha's my eldest,' he says. Sounds sad, and proud at the same time. 'His mother's idea, calling him Hamish. A good Scottish name for a good Scottish surname, she said. But one way or another we all ended up calling him Misha. He's got kids of his own now, of course.'

'His mother was Tracy, your wife?'

He nods again, watches me with a slow, methodical eye. Long, dying thunder rolls somewhere outside. 'You heard about her, huh? Middleton shooting his mouth off, no doubt.'

'Middleton?' I think for a moment, blink sweat out of my eyes. 'Will?'

'Yeah.'

'He didn't say anything about her.'

'Is that so?'

'His wife did, a little. But most of it I picked up from the others and from some old newspapers in the roadhouse basement that talked about what happened to her.'

MacBride jabs the fire again. 'So you know she was killed?'

'Yeah.'

'Did they tell you why? Middleton's crowd or the papers?'

I choose my words carefully. The drug seems to

be wearing off and the wool coating my brain seems to be fading. I have some feeling, some movement in my limbs now. 'I know she died while you were fighting the building of the country club, while she was trying to organize some kind of legal action against the developer. And I know two weeks after she died, the developer himself vanished.'

'Uh-huh.'

I wonder whether this is a good idea. 'And I've heard a theory that she may have been seeing one of the locals. That that's why she was down on the highway when it happened.'

'Uh-huh.' MacBride doesn't flinch, doesn't even shift in his seat. No sign of anger or defensiveness. 'And why does all this interest you, Mr Rourke? So much so that you tried to walk up through the woods in the worst storm I've ever seen in these parts, with nothing but a list of questions and a gun, looking for people whose reputation you must've heard before you left.'

'I'm here because of what's been happening down the valley tonight.'

He looks at me and his eyes narrow, quicken. 'What d'you mean? What's been going on down there?'

'People have been killed, Mr MacBride. Someone's decided to start picking folk off while the valley's closed down.' He raises an eyebrow, so I add, 'Both bridges are flooded and the phones and radio are dead. There's no way out and no way of speaking to anyone outside.'

'People have been killed how?'

'A truck driver was stabbed out in the parking lot of the roadhouse, two guys ran off and met God knows what out by the road, someone throttled Christine in the gas station and a little girl's gone missing.' I rub some life back into my hands, watch MacBride to see if he reacts to me moving. He doesn't. Might as well be carved out of wood like his little figurine. 'And that's not the half of it. We had a bunch of crooks with guns show up trying to find a friend of theirs who helped someone in these parts conceal several murders a year or so ago. I'm guessing that person is the same one preying on people tonight.'

'Jesus.' I'm expecting him to sound shocked, but he doesn't. Not in the slightest.

'On top of that, I found the corpses buried by the banks of the Easy, the ones this crook, Walker, helped hide. Then someone took one of them clean out of the ground.'

'And they're saying we did it all, huh?' he says, looking at me with a dark twinkle in his eyes. 'Told you all sorts of stories about my family and said there was no one else who could've done such horrible things. No one but the monsters in the hills.'

I don't see any point in lying to him. 'Yeah.'

'Figures.'

'I'm not sure I believe all that, though. Stories are just stories.'

'Sometimes.'

'And then there's this talk about Moore Willis, the developer who built the Foundations, and your wife and everything that happened back then, and I'm wondering if it has some bearing on all this.'

He jabs the fire for a final time, then fixes his eyes on mine with the poker still gripped in his hand. 'What if you're wrong?' he says. 'What if we really *are* the only ones round here capable of such horrible things? We killed them all, we did it all, and now you've come walking in here and there's nowhere for you to turn to for help. You're a long way from safety out here, Mr Rourke.'

48

A chill steals over me. There's anger in his voice, a deep and abiding sense of bitterness, and for a moment I think I've made a mistake. That I *have* walked into the belly of the beast and that now I'm trapped.

Then MacBride shakes his head and leans back in his chair. 'Of course it's all horseshit. People always fear what they don't understand, and they sure as hell don't understand us. It might also interest you to know that you're not the first visitor we've had up here tonight.'

'Really?'

'My kids don't normally run around the woods in the dark like this, and the family's not usually awake in the middle of the night. You didn't think that was strange?'

'No stranger than anything else. And people do tell all those stories about you.'

He concedes the point with a nod. 'Not long after this storm blew in, my nephew heard someone yelling away down on the track. Him and his eldest went out there and found a feller screaming fit to burst by one of the streams that run down to the Easy. The guy cut down one of the trees on the banks, dropped it on the bridge and smashed it. Then he walked back off into the night. Never said a thing to them, like they weren't even there.'

I stare. 'Seriously?'

'Uh-huh. Now that wasn't one of my family who did that; someone from down the valley came up here in the rain with an axe and a screw loose and stopped us driving off our land. I got no clue why, but you can understand why we're all a little twitchy tonight.'

An axe. Jesus. The guy at the Banks house. 'Yeah, I can.'

'And now you come up here talking about that developer and what happened with Tracy, and thinking this might all be something to do with that, and I'm wondering if you're just trying to cause trouble or if you might not be on to something.'

When he mentions causing trouble, his eyes narrow. I hear a board creak outside the door and I wonder how many more of the MacBrides are waiting to pounce if the old man deems it necessary. If he thinks I'm a threat, or if he's got something serious to hide.

'I'm not here to cause trouble. I just want to figure all this out.'

'You know what day this is?' he asks, leaning forwards.

'No.'

'Fifteen years ago today, Tracy was killed out on that road. A lot of bad things came out of that day, things that've never really gone away. Seems to be a hell of a coincidence you mentioning her now,' he says. 'A hell of a coincidence. Now if I'm to decide what we're going to do with you, I want to know what your interest in these events is. Why do you need to know? You're not one of them and you've got no stake in this land.'

'I came out here following a note from a girl I'd never met who turned out to have been dead for six months. Will's granddaughter Samantha. The note said people had died here and suggested that more might follow. At the time, I wanted to see if it was right about all that, and if I could find the other things it talked about. Now a bunch of people really are dead and we're stuck here. The bridges are out and no help is coming. I just want to stay alive, stop anyone else getting killed and go home.'

'And where is home, Alex?'

I think for a moment and realize I'm not certain of the answer. 'I don't know, Mr MacBride, not these days. Not any more. Boston, I suppose, but I only live there.'

'Call me Stuart,' he says, rising from his seat. 'If you're feeling up for it, come for a walk with me and I'll try to make you understand what we had at stake when that guy was trying to build his country playground. Maybe then you'll understand why what happened happened.'

My knees tremble as I try to force some weight into them and for a moment I think I'm going to collapse. I lean on the back of the chair, do just enough to stand upright, and I feel my muscles creaking stiffly into some sort of working order. It's as though they haven't been used in hours. I can see a little more of the room. There is a TV in the corner, must be ten years old, with a handful of equally aged furniture around it. Enough seating for a good eight people. There are stairs leading up to a second storey, doors leading further into the building, which must be pretty big. All made from the same solid wood. It smells of smoke and the herbs hanging in bunches in the kitchen area. Like something out of a western, preserved for use in the modern day.

MacBride grabs a heavy canvas coat from a hook by the door and heads out into the night. I think about taking my gun and my wallet, but the threat he represented has faded and, for whatever reason, he doesn't seem to consider me a danger to him, armed or otherwise. I might as well let them remain there as a matter of trust. I follow him outside.

The door leads out into an uneven open compound flanked by another four or five structures built in a similar style to the main house. Light gleams from the windows of a couple of them, spilling out into the rain. I can see the edges of the treeline surrounding the clearing, broken in a couple of places by quick gaps plunging into shadow. I guess one such break is the track leading down to the highway. The other, no idea. There's no sign of whoever was waiting outside the door just now, listening in on our conversation.

The wind's dropped from its peak but it's still strong enough to set the tops of the trees lurching against one another.

'It's not just me and my kids live here, Alex. That there,' he says, pointing at one of the buildings, all dark, 'is my nephew Logan's place. Him and his wife moved to join us with their children after my brother died. That one over there is my daughter Fiona's. And Misha and his family live over there.' He gestures at the last of the houses. 'All told there's fifteen of us up here. More now than there used to be back when the trouble started, but it was always more than just me and Tracy. Always.'

'So selling your land would've meant a real upheaval for your whole family.' The cloud above rumbles fitfully but there's no flash, the last throes of the storm wearing themselves out.

MacBride shrugs. 'It would, yeah, to say the least. But that's not all.'

A kid maybe fifteen or sixteen years old emerges from one of the houses and looks at MacBride. Calls out, 'Everything all right, Uncle?'

'Yeah,' the old man shouts back. 'Just showing our visitor around. Do me a favour and go back to the house, get a pot of tea going, will you, Del?'

The kid nods, glances at me, then scurries in the direction of the building we came from. I wonder if he was one of the ones out there in the woods. I wonder what he thinks of me being here now, an interloper in their lives. If he overheard the reasons for my visit and what's going on down the valley. What he thinks of it all, and whether he cares what happens to the people he's been brought up to see as the enemy.

MacBride leads me around the compound to a pair of smaller, rougher structures. Each has a small fenced corral peppered with the tracks and smells of animals even under several inches of fresh rainwater. MacBride leans on one of the fences and gestures at the shed. 'We've got sheep and goats. Half a dozen of each. We graze them down by the Foundations, and have done since before they were built. There's chickens down the slope. Even got a couple of donkeys to help us with the workload round here.'

He gestures at the swaying treeline. 'Most of the forest up here is replanted or managed in some way. Some we can use for wood, a lot of it is fruit, there's useful plants we've put out in the undergrowth, things that don't need too much light. Further up the valley we have a couple of open fields to grow veg and grain. We take water from the springs feeding the Easy and treat it ourselves. We have a couple of hydro turbines in the Easy and even a few solar cells to provide us with power.'

'You're completely self-sufficient?'

'More or less. We have enough extra power that we can sell some back to the grid. The cash we make from that covers gas for the truck, clothes, anything else we need.'

'I heard everything built in the valley fails,' I say. 'The land dooms it all to fail.'

He nods. 'Old rumour, but it's not entirely true. The roadhouse has been there for years, and Middleton manages to keep the gas station going. The stories don't ever seem to mention that, do they? No sense in letting the facts get in the way of a good theory, after all. The reputation's helpful to us, though; it keeps people from wanting to move out here and cluttering the place up. But don't put too much stock in rumours, Alex. They don't hold much water.'

'What about the one that says people are either born here or come here to pay for sins they've committed elsewhere?'

MacBride's dark eyes glitter at me. 'That one's got a little more value to it, if you ask me.'

49

'The land's good and there's no curse on what people do with it,' he continues. 'But it doesn't mean the worst of human nature, the worst people, don't get drawn out here because they've got nowhere better to go. So much bad blood and bad thoughts have collected here down so many years. It leaves a mark, but on the soul, not the land.'

'You seem to be doing OK, though. Got it pretty good here.'

He steers me back in the direction of his house. Says, 'It's not easy, don't go thinking that. It takes a lot of work to make it worthwhile, and it took a lot of work in the first place to make it happen at all. I've been living here for nigh on twenty-five years now. It didn't just spring up overnight. Whether I could do it again now, from scratch, at my age . . . I don't know.'

'Why'd you get the idea for this kind of life in the first place?' I ask.

'My dad fought in World War Two. My granddad, he fought in World War One and then lost everything in the Depression. I grew up with Vietnam all over the TV and lectures on how to survive nuclear fallout in school.' We walk back into his house, out of the dying storm and the tattered night. There's an iron pan on the fire half-filled with a creamy brown liquid. The air's full of the scent of spices and herbs. 'We make it from some of the things we grow,' he says, gesturing at the pot. 'The climate's not right for tea or coffee, so we have to buy in. But this is just as good this time of night.'

'It smells nice.' It seems like the expected thing to say. After an evening of Isaac's coffee, it does too.

'Like chai, or so they tell me. Made with goat's milk. Pass me two of those cups on the side there, would you?'

I do so and he ladles out a helping each and passes one over. He drops into his chair and waves at me to pull the other one closer, which I do. I say, 'So you grew up in the middle of the Cold War.'

'Yeah, that's right. I missed out on getting drafted for Vietnam, but not by much. A lot of people went crazy back then. Made themselves bunkers up in the hills, stockpiled food, bought a truckload of guns to repel looters or overthrow the government or whatever the hell it was they thought sounded good at the time, and they waited for the end.' He slurps his drink and nods. 'I wasn't one of them. I was just tired of living in that world. Of being a part of something so dark that it seemed like it'd never have an end. I wasn't paranoid or afraid; I just wanted to get away from all that rot, seeing as by that time I was married to Trace and all ready to start a family. We talked it over and I convinced her we could make it work, so we looked around for a lot of cheap land somewhere quiet. This valley had jack in it except for a beat-up roadhouse and a gas station no one much used. The land wasn't good enough for most people to pay for the privilege of farming and wasn't pretty enough for some government agency to make it a park, so it was next to worthless.

'And now, all these years later, here we are. Most of the craziness that went on back then is gone, but the same darkness is still here, just in a different form. Fear and suspicion don't go away, they just change shape. I don't regret the decision we made for a minute. In fact, it's been good enough for us that a lot of the rest of the family wanted to come out here too. We've grown quite a bit since those first days.'

I breathe in the steam rising from my cup before taking a sip, let the silence grow for long enough to be certain he's finished. Eventually, I say, 'Why tell me all this? You don't know me from Adam.'

'So you'll understand what all this means to me and my family, and what kind of people we are, Alex. We're not mutant freaks out of some horror movie, despite what folk might tell you. Despite what we're happy for them to believe. We're decent, normal people. We just don't want to be a part of the world you're from, the world of Will Middleton and the rest of them down the valley, or the world of that goddamn property guy.'

I nod. 'So your family does its best to scare people out of coming here? Watch for anyone walking into the woods or into the Foundations and do your best to freak them out so much they never come back?'

'Just about, yeah. At least, that's what we've done since all the troubles started. We don't want people up here, intruding on our world. Messing up our way of life. Hell, even finding out the kind of life we have. You think Will or the others have a clue what we've built here? My kids can sit here in the houses *we* built, eating food *we've* grown and still access the internet using electricity *we* generate. At least when the phone lines are working. And there's no outside corporation or government or whatever that makes it happen for us. It's just us. So, sure, we want to protect it.'

I shake my head. 'They don't have a clue. None at all.'

'There's only been a couple of times we've had to go as far as drugging someone like we did with you, though. I don't like the idea of things turning nasty. I'd rather give someone a scare, have them run off and never come back than do anything bad to them. Let their own mind keep them from prying into our lives. Let them build up their own stories to add to the legend. The kids treat it as a kind of game. Just a bit of harmless fun, like Halloween.'

'You said you convinced your wife that this was the life for her too. She wasn't as immediately keen on it as you were, Stuart?'

He shakes his head, stares at the fire with an expression of overwhelming fatigue. He's an old man, and every once in a while his composure slips enough to show it. 'Not entirely, no,' he says. 'She liked the life in a lot of ways, but being so isolated up here . . . it was hard on her. If it hadn't been for the kids, I don't know if she could have stood it. I figure that's why she started seeing someone else when the construction thing started. She was feeling lonely, cut off. It gave her a way to reconnect.' He must see my expression because he goes on. 'Yes, I knew. And it hurt, but what was I going to do? Have it out with her and drive her away? My wife loved me, Alex. She really, truly did. She just needed to feel there was something beyond these woods and what we had out here, just for a while. When that Willis guy bought the half a square mile plot of land next to ours, where the Foundations are now, we both wanted to stop him building if we could, or stop him buying up the rest of the valley if we couldn't. We figured he'd never be able to make a business work out here with just the building complex he was going to put up first. He'd need the rest of the valley to do it. So Trace started talking to some of the others – the Middletons and Peter from the roadhouse wanted to sell up and move away, but the two brothers and the other guy, David, didn't want to part with their land, nor see that monstrosity built on their doorstep. And I guess being involved in something like that together made them real close.'

Keep my face calm, but my mind's turning at double speed. MacBride's wife was seeing one of the two brothers. That must have been it. I picture Tony with his odd, dismissive nature and suppressed fear. I picture Ben with his strange moods and his overbearing nature. Did Tracy begin an illicit affair with one of them, both keeping it a secret from their families? Did the other brother find out and, afraid of having the only family he had taken from him, decide to do away with her once and for all?

'You don't know who it was, though.'

MacBride shakes his head. 'I could've asked, but I guess I didn't want to know for sure, and to have that argument with her. I knew she wasn't trying to hurt me. She was just lonely, and I guess I wasn't the easiest guy to get along with sometimes. So I never let on that I knew, because I loved her, and then one day she never came home. Someone ran her down on the highway when she was walking back up here.'

'She never drove?'

'We've only ever had the one truck. Either she didn't want to risk me finding out what she was doing by taking it, or she thought I needed it. Either way, she was killed because of it. It wouldn't, couldn't have happened if she'd been driving.' MacBride shakes his head and seems to shrink in his chair. He clasps his mug like it's about to break. 'I don't know who killed her and the cops never figured it out either, but I know for damn sure it was someone down the valley that did it.'

'How do you know?' I say.

'About a week later I found a parcel waiting for me on the track leading up here. It had a note in it that said, "Play nice or you're next." They wanted me to drop the fight we'd been putting up over the development.'

Or she died for some other reason and they just wanted it to appear that way. 'Did you show the police the note?'

He sighs and I can see the emotion, the grief and the anger, that the subject still carries for him even after all these years. The words are flowing more and more easily. 'No, no I didn't. By then I was tired of seeing them, of having to think about what happened to Tracy and why. For years we'd been making our own life, our own world and our own rules up here, and now the woman I loved was dead and I had to deal with them and their ways? You've got to understand, Alex. Losing Trace like that ... I was just demolished. I can't tell you what it felt like, the loss. And the anger, that someone had done that to her ... Rage, rage and grief. And I had no way of finding out who'd done it for what? Money? A pile of cash for a few acres of land and some lousy country retreat for rich idiots from the city? Jesus. I just lost it completely.'

I start to see where this is heading, what the result of her death was. Say, 'So you did something to Willis, didn't you? Because you couldn't get back at whoever had done it directly, you decided to stop them profiting from it.'

'Yeah,' he says. 'I did. I sure did.'

The fire crackles away in the grate. I sip my drink, watch the old man staring at the flames. 'You killed him.'

50

He stays still for a long time, thinking back fifteen years or wondering whether or not to finish his confession. Then he nods. 'My brother Ivan helped me, along with a couple of the older kids. They understood why I wanted to do it. Once our minds were set, we watched the site and waited for Willis to be alone down there. He used to stay late in that office of his sometimes, going over plans or doing his paperwork or whatever the hell it was he needed to do. Cheating on his accounts, from what I heard later. And when he was all alone, in we went. He acted like we must've come to see him to sell up at last, or that what was going to happen was something he could negotiate. He had a whole pile of cash with him. I don't know if he was stealing it for himself, or if it was supposed to be used to buy us off or pay his workers like the papers said afterwards. We brought him up here trussed like a chicken and we put him in the goat shed, buried under a load of straw. Took his car, too, so they wouldn't know something had happened to him.

'The cops came asking a couple of quick questions and, as far as they were concerned, we didn't know a damn thing. They never came back. Once we were sure the coast was clear, must've been a few days later, I took a shotgun and I ended that man's life. It didn't give me any pleasure to do it, but it still felt right. It felt like I'd done something for Trace, and I owed her that. The first thing we did with some of the money Willis had was hire a couple of good lawyers to fight the development and try to kill off that whole goddamn project. I don't know if we could've done it without that. The rest has gone in bits and pieces over the years, but it's helped give my family a better life and I think that's something Trace would've liked even if she didn't agree with how we got it.'

He lapses into silence again and I let what he's just told me sink in. Those two deaths in quick succession go a long way to explaining the bitterness between the different families in the valley even now, fifteen years later. Will and Christine must have felt like they'd missed out on a fortune because of it.

'What did you do with his body?' I ask.

'We buried it up in the woods here, well away from anywhere anyone would come across it. We did the same with his car – took it to pieces and hid or destroyed anything that could be identified. We were careful.'

I nod, then ask the difficult question, one that'll ram home what he's just done. 'How come you're happy telling me all this? You don't know anything at all about me.'

'I don't, Alex, you're right.' He stirs in his seat a little and for a second I wonder if he's regretting confessing all and revealing the truth, whether I'm going to end up buried in the woods like Moore Willis. Then he gets comfortable again and finishes his drink. 'But that's kind of the point. You came up here tonight because some bad things have been going on at the roadhouse down the valley, and because you knew something of what happened here fifteen years ago. I don't doubt Middleton and the others would be happy to lay the blame for the whole damn lot here with me. So since you seem to be the one asking the questions down there, I need you to understand the true state of things and the kind of people you're really dealing with. Because it's not been me or mine running around killing people, so it's someone else, one of them. And finding them will be easier if you're sure it's not us.

'And the reason I'm happy telling you is because who could you pass it on to? And what could you give them? It all happened so long ago there's not going to be any way to tie it to me or to us even if you did want to. All I'd have to do is deny everything. Willis won't ever be found. Trying to turn me in won't bring him back. He was a crook and a cheat and he probably didn't deserve what he got, but he's long gone and that's that. We've got kids to raise here and a life to give them. Seems to me that should matter more now than a bunch of old anger. I killed a guy fifteen years ago and I have to live with that, but I'm no killer. I never did it before or since and I don't plan on starting. We keep people away from our land

and we'll scare the hell out of them to do it if we need to, but we're not bad people, Alex.'

I let that one stew for a while too. His isolationism might border on paranoia and the hardening of his attitude towards Will and the others might only have made things worse as far as the build-up of resentment over the years is concerned, but I don't know if I can argue with MacBride. What he did was wrong, but by now, there'd be nothing gained from trying to expose it. He's right – I don't know what it'd do to the families living here or the life they've chosen for themselves. Probably destroy them. My own moral compass has taken quite a battering and these days I don't know if I can really sit in judgement on anyone else.

Besides, allowing for his family stalking me through the woods and having me forcibly drugged, I find myself liking the guy.

'Fair enough,' I say. 'Is there anything you know about what happened tonight, or about anything that might have gone on down the valley maybe a year ago?'

'What do you mean?'

'The three bodies I found by the river have been dead for about that length of time. Not long after they were killed, Will's granddaughter Samantha moved away from the valley. She ended up killing herself a few months later. I don't know if the two events are connected, but the note I got from someone signing her name mentioned that people had died.

I'm just wondering if you or your family know of anything strange that happened then, Stuart.'

'Can't say I do, no,' he says after thinking for a while. 'I don't pay much attention to what they get up to down there, but I wouldn't put it past any of them to turn to murder. Someone killed Trace and got away with it; I don't see any good reason they wouldn't figure they could get away with it again if they wanted. Over money, probably. And after what happened earlier tonight, I'm damn sure that at least one of them down there has flipped completely.'

'You mean the guy who came up here and demolished the bridge?'

Stuart nods. 'Yeah. I didn't see him myself, but the way I heard, it was as though something in his head had broken, and broken good. Guess he could easily have gone for murder too. Feller walks around in the dark with an axe like that ... What else was in this note of yours, Alex?'

'What do you mean?'

'You told me earlier it said people had died here and that you were looking for them and for the "other things" it talked about. What were they?'

'Crosses. It said I had to find the crosses, whatever and wherever they are.' I shrug. 'I heard that one time you scared a couple of kids out of the Foundations and left a kind of wooden crucifix on one of them as a warning a few years back. For a while, I thought it might have referred to that. Was that a regular thing?'

MacBride shakes his head. 'I don't think we've even done it once. Certainly not enough to be crosses plural, anyway. That sounds like plain old rumour to me. And there's no crosses in the valley I know about. Only one I can think of is the one where Trace is buried, but that's just the one.'

And Samantha's makes two, I think, but say nothing.

'Was it spelt like a proper name?' he says, the question coming out of the blue.

'Crosses?'

'Yeah. Was it written like it could've been a name?'

'The note was all capitals,' I say. 'I've got no way of telling. Why?'

'There was a family whose surname was Cross. They stayed briefly in these parts a year or so ago, so around the time you were interested in. Travelling types, I think; I only ever saw their RV, with the father driving. People like that come through occasionally, looking for work or a place to stay a while. From what I heard in Fairlight, they moved on after a couple of months. Maybe they're the Crosses you're supposed to find.'

I feel my heart miss a beat. 'They were a family?'

'A couple and a kid, I think. The guy tried to take a look at the Foundations at one point, but the kids freaked him out enough that he never came back.'

The bodies by the river.

51

Misha and a couple of the kids escort me back through the woods. MacBride stays inside, waving goodbye from the doorway. He shook my hand and we parted without any threats or warnings, but I have the feeling that just because we've talked doesn't mean I'm welcome to return. I asked him to tell his family that if they come across a little girl wandering around the countryside tonight, they're to take her in, look after her, and then hand her over to the authorities when the bridges are back up and the cops get here. I trust him to do it. Whatever else he is, whatever else he's done, Stuart seems to be a man who understands what family means. Misha's a tall, rangy guy built like a woodpile, somewhere in his mid-twenties. I'm amazed at the ease with which he and the two younger ones find their way through the trees. When we come in sight of the Foundations they leave me to continue on my own. Misha apologizes for drugging me. I ask if the guy I hit with the tree branch is OK and he shrugs, says he'll have a bruise for a while but it could've been worse.

Could've been worse. I guess that sums up the truth about the family in the woods when compared to the image that's painted of them down the valley.

Painted by people with a past just as brutal and murderous as the stories they tell about others.

A year ago, Will's granddaughter Samantha apparently had something to do with the deaths of the entire Cross family. I don't yet know if she actually had a hand in murdering them herself, but certainly she was involved or knew about it. Either the knowledge led to her suicide, or it wasn't the depression that finished her but someone wanting to make sure she stayed silent about what had happened. It was someone at the bar who killed Gene and Christine. I know that now. Not a MacBride and not Walker. And I know that when Evan Walker showed up in the valley and started all this trouble, he was here to blackmail a friend, a friend who'd killed the Cross family over what looked like something personal and who'd then asked him to help hide their vehicle. Years before, someone killed Tracy MacBride, who was having an affair with one of the locals. Her death was fifteen years ago tonight. It's all tied together. It's got to be.

I need to find out more about Samantha. I need to find out who Tracy was seeing. I need to figure out who killed who before there's none of us left.

The gas station is dark and feels empty. No damp footprints on the floor save for the muddy scuff marks left by the groups of people who've come and gone this evening. I head for the stairs without using my flashlight in case it can be seen from the bar. Nothing here's been moved or disturbed since I was here with

Isaac, not as far as I can tell. Besides, the killer doesn't seem like the type to return to the scene if there's nothing worth going back for. What's done is done.

Christine's body is still on the bedroom floor, exactly as we left it. Her blood's soaked through the carpet in dark brown blotches. I think about the way her and Will seemed so easy with each other. Such an old, established relationship. I think about the killer's need to punish her for something, just like the Cross guy was punished, and I wonder what could've lain buried behind their cosiness to warrant such a death. And if she'd done something to earn it, I can't believe Will isn't up to his neck in it as well.

Unless he killed her himself, of course.

I keep my flashlight low as I search the room, making sure the beam doesn't glance across any of the windows. As I saw when Christine was killed, there's everything here I'd expect from an old couple's home, including framed family photos on the dresser. One of them shows Will and Christine with the two girls, Jennifer and Samantha, between them. They're both slim and cheerful, wearing brightly coloured, happy clothes. One has dark hair falling loose around her head, the other wears hers up in a ponytail. A second shows one of them, I guess Samantha, by herself, now a young woman, standing in front of the gas station. The third and final one was obviously taken some time between the two and shows her as a teenager, probably around sixteen years old. There are no more of Jennifer.

As I bend down to check the drawers I catch sight of a dark smudge on the frame of the second picture. It's a thumbprint in dried blood, hard to see against the grain of the wood. Looking closer, there's a faint mark on the glass, spattered and dribbled. It looks like someone's spat at the photo. Could be semen, of course, but I doubt it.

The guy sneaks in through the kitchen, throttles Christine, cuts open a pillow and stuffs her mouth with feathers, then hacks her body up. But before he leaves the scene, he sees Samantha's photo and can't resist showing his contempt for her.

I guess that ties in with the damage done to her grandmother's body, and it suggests that whatever she was punished for, Sam had a share in it.

The top couple of drawers are full of clothes, neatly folded and arranged. The bottom one is different though, packed with assorted personal trinkets and memorabilia gathered from down the years. Photo albums, postcards, well-worn old notebooks. And in a bundle held together with an elastic band, a small stack of letters addressed to 'Gran' and 'Gramps'.

They seem to come from two distinct time periods. The first is from a few years ago – Samantha's college days and the year or so immediately afterwards while she struggled to make a living for herself. From the dates, Samantha would have been about twenty-three or twenty-four by the time she died. On a quick skim, it seems as though she moved back here to work for her grandparents, pay off her loans and get some money in the bank before having another crack at the job market. It can't have been easy; I don't imagine the gas station made enough to provide her with a great deal of money. The second period begins nine or ten months ago. As soon as I see the date on the first of these letters, I stop skimming and start reading properly.

52

Dear Gran and Gramps,

I hope that everything is OK with you and that everyone in the valley is the same as ever. I've just finished shopping for a proper winter wardrobe and all the little things that a new house needs. It's already getting chilly now – I can't imagine what it'll be like by the middle of winter. Aspen's very nice, but very different from back home. Lots of rich people from LA and places like that, but if they weren't here I wouldn't have a job, I suppose. The people at work seem nice and they've helped me settle in quite quickly. I'm so glad for that. I don't know if I could've taken it if they'd made it difficult.

I'm sure you're right about Michael as well, Gramps – he'll probably be a great guy to work for. He says he's happy to have me even though you still owe him a hundred bucks from the Army.

I'm rambling. I guess it's just so nice to get away from it all and start again someplace else. I can't say how glad I am for the chance. It's all so new and fresh out here and I've been sleeping so much better since I arrived.

All my love,
Sam

Most of the letters follow a similar tone. She seems to have written about once a fortnight after moving to Aspen, and most of what she says is regular day-in-the-life stuff. She was working in some kind of managerial role at a hotel owned by an old friend of Will's, but it's hard to tell if she was happy there. A lot of the cheeriness, the easy banter between family members, seems somehow forced, artificial. A deeper depression, maybe, buried just below the surface. There are very few allusions to whatever it was back here she wanted, or needed, to get away from, and they're mostly cloaked in the same kind of language as in the first letter. Whatever it was that happened left her with painful memories and regular night-mares, at least until she moved away and her environ-ment no longer gave her constant reminders of the original event. One letter about three months into her stay in Aspen catches my eye, though.

I'm sorry I couldn't come and visit like you asked. Work's been busy, and Graham asked me out to a movie and I was nervous. I know I've told you a little about him. He's a nice guy. Real funny and very nice, not at all pushy. Very polite, like a real Southern Gentleman. But . . . well, I just felt kinda funny and I thought I needed to get my head straight about that here instead of coming back to you guys. You can understand, I guess. Every time I think, like, 'what if it goes further than just a film?' I start feeling all nervous. I wouldn't want the nightmares to come back.

Anyway, I think I've dealt with it now. I'll try to come and visit in a few months, when the season's over. I hope you understand.

While this seems to fill in a fair number of blanks, it could still mean all sorts of things. From what she says, I guess either she was assaulted somehow and it was the memory of this attack that she was happy to get away from, or that she spurned someone who wanted to go further than she did and things turned sour between them, or that they were in a relationship where he'd belittle and abuse her which eventually turned properly ugly. I've seen all three before, and I've known them all have similar outcomes.

And at around the same time as that original incident happened, someone killed the Cross family.

Did Mr Cross try to rape her, and did someone else exact revenge for it? If so, why kill the wife and child as well? And if that was what happened, why did someone also want to punish Christine twelve months later?

Or did Sam reject someone, one of the locals, who blamed her family for keeping him away from her ever since? Maybe the three by the river simply ran afoul of his anger back then and he's been biding his time ever since. Or maybe the Crosses had nothing to do with this and the note lied. Maybe what happened to them was a different crime entirely.

The one person who'd know for sure is Will. Getting Sam's identity out of him was a real struggle.

It'll only be harder to extract the details of what happened to her. Maybe it'll be easier now I'm better armed with the facts. He can't keep all the secrets of the valley hidden for ever.

I replace the letters and close the drawer. Out in the kitchen, I take a good look through the windows, scanning for any sign that someone knows I'm here, that someone's out looking for me. For a moment, I think I see a light, dim and distant, out in one of the fields, but it's so brief and so indistinct that I can't be sure it's not a figment of my imagination. I walk back out into the night.

The wind's gusting on-again off-again, cutting in and out. The rain has slowed to sporadic bursts. Only a couple of hours to dawn and the storm at last seems to be properly dying for good. I cut around the bar and head for the brothers' house. They were the only other locals who were here when Tracy MacBride was killed and who are still here now, and they seem to be the two most likely to have been seeing her in secret. Exactly how that ties in to Samantha and what's been happening tonight I don't know, but I can't believe it's wholly unrelated.

The trees snap and chatter in the wind, rubbing against each other like they're huddling for warmth. The brother's tumbledown home lurks between them, dark and uninviting.

And locked securely, I quickly discover. I'm surprised, to say the least; no one seems to bother locking their doors in an empty stretch of land like this. I wonder why they're so cautious. I don't remember whether they were closed tight when we all came to find them after the shootout with Walker's friends. The windows are dark and I can see next to nothing through them. The faint and ghostly shapes of furniture mere glimmers in the night. Everything's shut down tight and there's no way I could get in without breaking in, and if it turned out Ben and Tony were innocent . . . It'd be hard to explain away.

It's still tempting, sorely tempting, but without being sure . . .

I back away into the trees again and head instead for Ashley's trailer. She lives on the north side of the road and her place is reasonably sizeable, plenty of space for a woman living alone. Its shell is in decent shape except around the wheels, where it seems to have been patched many times by many different hands. I guess it dates from her uncle's days. There are a couple of outhouse-type structures built either by Ashley or by her uncle, I guess for tools and the like. One smaller than the other and both looking more or less unused. The whole place is dead.

It's unlocked, though. I climb in out of the rain and shut the door behind me. The trailer smells of burned dust from the heater and stale coffee from the tiny kitchen. Ashley isn't especially tidy, but then no one gets the chance to clean up before their evening goes the way tonight has. Her front room is cramped, filled as it is by a couch, TV, clothes rack and some rough shelving holding a handful of CDs and DVDs, along with a few old magazines. There are a few items of discarded clothing lying where they were tossed on to the furniture, and it's all hers. No obvious sign of anyone else's presence.

I look through the kitchen cupboards, but there's nothing unusual in any of them. The sink contains a dirty plate, a frying pan and a cup waiting to be washed. There's not much in the trash. I move on. The bottles in the tiny cabinet in Ashley's equally tiny bathroom are nothing especially exciting. Tylenol, stuff like that, and a half-empty pot of non-prescription sleeping tablets. Everything I'd expect, nothing I wouldn't.

Ashley's bedroom is dominated by a double bed that extends out of the back wall. There are a couple of small closets, some unoccupied floor space. The bed hasn't been made. The clothes in here are all hers just like in the front room. Her closets contain clothes, old shoes, some photos from a fair few years ago and a different place to this one. A record of a past life.

On the top shelf of the closet, almost out of sight, I find a couple of old shoeboxes covered in dust and bring them out. More photos, probably a few years old. There's a guy in the pictures, sometimes with Ashley, sometimes on his own. I'm guessing he was her husband. A couple of them have the name Kevin scribbled on the back. I wonder why she kept them if he really was the kind of asshole she described to me.

In the second box, old paperwork. Forms and

records, the sort of thing that everyone keeps, everyone needs from time to time. Birth certificate, licence records, social security number, things like that. A couple more old photographs, this time showing her as a child with her family.

I'm reading the name, her maiden name, on her birth certificate when I hear the trailer door swing open in the front room and a man's voice hiss, 'Ash?'

I turn around with my gun in my hand as he steps into the bedroom, his own pistol out but lowered. A young guy, probably a year or two younger than Ashley. A couple of inches shorter than me in a rain-slicked leather jacket, looking pale and nervous, mousy. Couple of piercings and a scar on his right cheek. He double-takes when he sees me, then clamps his jaw shut and a hardness comes over his gaze. The lean, predatory look of a wounded lion backed into a corner. I glance at his gun and shake my head, wave my own a little to make sure he realizes who's got the upper hand here, say, 'You must be Evan Walker. Your sister's not home right now.'

53

'Who're you?' he asks. He hasn't moved and his expression hasn't changed. Wary, untrusting. From what Vince told me, he has good reason to be. He's involved in a lot of ugly business and a lot of people would be happy to see him dead.

'My name's Alex Rourke.'

'Do I know you?'

'No,' I say. 'But I'm nothing to do with the people who came here to silence you, and I'm nothing to do with the people you know here. I'm not a cop and I'm not a crook. But we need to talk, you and I. Right here and now.'

He still doesn't move. 'What about?'

'About what happened to a family of three buried out near the Easy River a year ago. About you helping their killer hide the evidence. About who that killer is and what exactly happened back then. About what you know about what's gone on here in the valley tonight and in the past. So put your gun down and let's talk.'

'Fuck you, pal.'

I shake my head. 'This isn't a game. People have died tonight and more could still be killed, including your sister, if we don't figure out why it's happening and who's doing it.'

'I can protect her.'

'You can protect her by hiding out here in her trailer? Great plan.'

'It's worked so far.'

'And when the guy killing people runs out of other places to look, it'll protect her then as well? That's bullshit and you know it.'

Walker stares at me for a good long time. Then he shakes his head and tosses his gun on the bed. Sniffs and rubs his nose like a naughty schoolkid, but his eyes are afraid, and not of me.

'What do you need to know?' he says.

'What happened to the three people, the Cross family, by the river. Who killed them?'

He sits down on the edge of the bed, rubs at his fingers like he's trying to restore some warmth to them. 'I know the story. I heard it all.'

'The story you were going to use for blackmail, right? What your friend told you about what he'd done.'

'Kinda.' He looks up again, says, 'Look, if I tell you, you've got to help me get out of here. And you've got to look after Ash. Promise me that.'

'Look after her?'

'Me, her, you, we're all fucked if this doesn't stop. I'll tell you what you need to know if it means we're safe. If you're not going to do shit for us then I got nothing to gain by talking to you.'

'Ashley's been sheltering you?' I say. 'Ashley?'

'Just for tonight, yeah.'

Ashley was the one Evan came out here to see, to hide out with and to go start a new life with. The person he'd share his retirement fund with. She sheltered him, stayed quiet, and never gave a hint that she knew him even after Vince told us what he'd done. She sheltered a killer and she kept silent. And I trusted her. Christ. 'And you're on the run, right? Your friend Vince said something about a murder down south.'

He shrugs. 'I'll take my chances with that. But I want to get out of here. I want to get both of us out of here.'

I think for a while, weigh up the choices. On the one hand, he's a killer and – through his friends – he had us all at gunpoint earlier on. On the other, none of that matters for shit if none of us survives the night. I nod. 'OK. I won't turn the cops on you or Ashley, if you tell me what you know, and if it's good enough. And I'm aiming to stop *anyone* else dying tonight. So what happened?'

54

A year ago. It's not yet fall but the nights are already growing colder. The wind's howling outside the roadhouse but the sky is clear. Isaac locks the doors once the others have all arrived. Only Christine and Will have any idea what's going on, and the mood inside the bar's no more settled than the weather outside.

'What the hell's so all-fired important I had to leave my goddamn dinner going dry on the stove?' Ben says, shrugging out of his coat.

The rest of the group stays quiet, waiting for an explanation from Christine, who's wringing her hands at the centre of their little semicircle. Eventually she says, 'Something's happened with Cross.'

'Son of a bitch,' Will says. His face is set like granite and his eyes are pin-sharp with fury. 'Goddamn son of a bitch.'

Tony sighs. 'Cross? What's that asshole done now?'

Christine squeezes her husband's hand and lowers her eyes. She hasn't spoken much, but there's something about her that suggests she's as angry as Will. It's understandable. Billy Cross and his brood have been nothing but trouble since their battered RV arrived in the valley three months ago. Every single one of the locals has had something stolen or broken, land trespassed on, or seen Billy nosing around up to no good. Nothing provable, of course, but everyone knows it's them. No trouble round here until they showed up. Frank from the sheriff's department has said he can't do a damn thing to deal with them or move them on, not yet.

'Billy Cross attacked Samantha,' Christine says with a glance at Will.

'Fucking hell. Is she OK?'

'She's upstairs now,' Isaac says. 'She's all shook up, of course, but Christine gave her something to help her sleep. We'll all do everything we can to make sure she's properly looked after.'

'What about Cross?'

'That's the problem.' Christine looks at her husband again.

'I was going to teach him a lesson,' the old man says in a voice like winter. 'Good and proper. Make him pay for what he did to my little girl. I ain't going to rely on the cops or the good Lord to give me justice.'

Christine nods. 'I stopped him before it went too far. I said he should speak to all of you. I can't . . . I can't lose Will, not over someone like Billy Cross. It was just . . . He was only doing what any father would. But the cops never see it that way.'

'I caught up with Cross and beat the living shit out of him with a tyre iron,' Will says. 'He's a real mess. A real goddamn mess. He's out cold and he's in a real bad way, but he's still breathing.'

'Holy shit,' Tony says.

'We've shut him in the auto-repair shop until we figure out what to do,' Christine says. 'Sam said she didn't want us to go to the police. She just wanted him scared away, but I don't know if we can just do that now.'

'That bitch wife of his or their kid might go to the cops. If he don't come home, or he comes home all beaten up, it's not like she won't notice. She'll have the cops down here and all hell's going to break loose. Cops won't care what he did, just what happened to him. If you don't want to risk it . . .' Ben doesn't finish his sentence.

'Cross is nothing but a sack of shit,' Isaac says. 'He deserves to be punished good and proper if that's what he did. No one who does that kind of thing to a girl like Sam should get away with it.'

'How, uh, how about . . .' Tony says. 'Why don't we do what Sam wants? We wait for Cross to wake up again, give him back to the rest of the family and tell them to get the hell away from here. Forget all about this place if they don't want the same thing happening to all of them. Scare them. Run them off.'

'I ain't letting that son of a bitch get away with this,' Will says. 'To think of him out there, walking around, breathing free air, after what he did . . . That ain't going to happen.'

Ben thinks about Cross's wife, Rhonda. A ratty, shrill woman. Always screeching at that evil little brat of theirs. Or at the locals whenever they dare to criticize her family. A real mess. Probably as much of a wino as her husband. If they're even properly married.

'Let's see how bad Cross is,' he says. 'Then we can decide.'

The repair shop's cold and smells of old oil. Billy Cross is lying in a semi-foetal position in the middle of the floor, unmoving. Like Will said, he's a *real* goddamn mess. Both arms look funny, bending in places they shouldn't. He's got blood here and there all over his head and down the front of his jeans, and his skin's pale as marble. He's breathing, but only just, and his chest doesn't move like it should. Billy was a ragged, greasy bag of skin and bones at the best of times, but now he looks completely broken.

Will doesn't seem to feel any pity, leans down to him and yells, 'Goddamn sack of shit. Bet you regret what you did to my granddaughter now, huh?'

'You did this, Will?' Ben says.

'Yeah. Ain't no more than he deserves. It's a whole lot less, though.'

'If he doesn't get to a hospital fast, he's going to die, you know that?'

Will looks down at the body in front of them and shrugs.

'You're going to let him die?'

'Well, we can't . . . I mean, surely this is enough?' Tony asks. 'I mean, Jesus, look at the guy.'

'The cops'll look at the guy too, and then what?'

Christine says nothing, just purses her lips and brings her hand up to her face. Looks at Will with fear on her face.

There's a piercing shriek and Rhonda Cross runs through the doorway to the repair shop, arms outstretched in the direction of her husband. The noise, the volume, the sheer horror in that cry is terrifying. Then Ben whips a wrench down on the back of her head and she crashes to the floor.

55

'Holy fuck,' Isaac yells. 'Sweet holy fuck.' There's a thin moan from Cross, or seems to be, but his wife is completely silent and still. If she's alive, it's only barely and won't be for long.

No one else says a word. Ben looks at Will and Christine, one eyebrow raised as if challenging them. 'You think she would've gone quietly?' he says. 'You think she wouldn't have told the cops? What else could we have done?'

Everyone stays quiet, occupied with their own thoughts. Considering what Ben's just done. What Will did before him. How things seem to be spiralling out of control, how they're now in some way accessories to all this. And wondering whether, if any one of them was to object now, to say they wanted no part in this, everyone else would turn on them. Silence them in the way Ben just silenced Rhonda and they'd join her lying on the floor. Wondering whether they themselves would be willing to help silence someone else if they objected. Wondering if there's any way of changing the path they now seem to be locked on to and whether any of them would still take it if they could. Or if it's too late and their actions, their fates, are all irrevocably tied together.

'Finish him, Will,' Ben says. 'The son of a bitch has earned it. It won't make no difference either way now.'

No one else says anything. Will vanishes briefly into the gas station and returns with his shotgun. He presses the barrel to the side of Billy's face. Will's expression is blank and empty. Everyone holds their breath for a moment. Just by standing here, saying and doing nothing, they've already crossed a line they can never uncross.

BOOM.

Billy's face streaks across the repair-shop floor. The amount of blood and flesh and bone is incredible. Ben's never seen anything like it. There are spatters everywhere. They've ended a human life.

All of them.

Then Christine says, 'Do we do the same to their child too?'

56

A heavy, terrible quiet falls over the group. After a moment's pause as everyone digests the meaning of the question, Tony says, 'What?'

'If it's the only way we have to silence him, we have no choice. I'm not losing Will to jail. I couldn't. And now we're all in this together. We've killed two people. He'll know what we did.'

'But it's a child.'

Ben shakes his head. 'It's the way it's got to be. It was them or us, and it was all or nothing as soon as Will beat the hell out of Cross. Anyone who thought otherwise was fooling themselves. That boy of theirs is only ever going to end up just like his dad. Coming from where he does, with those two for parents, he's got no choice. He's a brat now. Give him another ten years and he'll be stealing cars and pushing drugs, you can count on it. He's got nothing to look forward to. We don't have to like it, but we've got to do it.'

'Couldn't we take him in, take care of him?' Isaac asks. Even as he does it, they all know the answer.

'No. The sheriff's office or Child Services will realize something funny's going on sooner or later and then the questions will start and then we're all heading for jail.'

'Which is where we'll be if they find three bodies.'

'We can blame the MacBrides. So long as we don't leave anything pointing to us, the cops can't possibly know for sure. A live child is different. Especially one that's old enough to know exactly who his daddy is and not fall for whatever story we tell him. We can't keep him.'

Christine nods, and the inevitability of what's coming is now obvious to them all. Tony won't stand up to his brother any longer and the old couple are in this together. Isaac can't make it seem like he's not one of them, like it or not.

Ben still hasn't put down the wrench he hit Rhonda with.

'We've got to strip these bodies,' Will says. 'Burn the clothes and everything else. Wash down the floor. We can bury them all together later.'

Ben nods and Will looks for a second like he's about to say sorry. He doesn't though, and the locals get to work stripping Billy and Rhonda of their things.

When they're done, the group troops down the road to where the Cross family RV is parked up by the trees. Isaac's trying not to think of the mess that was left of Billy's groin when he stripped the body and is desperately rubbing at his gloves, hoping to get the blood out of them. It's not shifting.

The lights are on in the RV and they can hear a television playing inside. Canned laughter and muffled dialogue. Christine and Will lead the group up to the door and motion the others to be quiet. Neither of them seems to be reacting at all to the horror of what they're about to do, to the reality of child murder. Like a dream. Like someone else's hallucination in which they are merely illusions.

They troop into the RV as quietly as they can. It smells stale. Old cooking and sweat. Young Eddie Cross is asleep on the couch. Christine sits down next to him with Will watching over them. She looks down at him with sadness, maybe even regret. But she still holds the pillow over his face and keeps it there until he stops struggling. Isaac watches the silent tears run down her cheeks without saying a thing.

When she takes it away again, Christine smoothes his hair away from his brow and murmurs, 'I'm sorry.'

'It had to be done,' Will says. 'No other way. At least he went quiet, probably didn't know anything much about what happened to him.'

Ben mutters, 'Kid was a goddamn little shit anyway.'

They bury the bodies that night, out in the field overlooking the river. Land owned by no one and thus with no clear ties back to any of them. Ben insists they won't be found, though. After all, who would ever go there? Their clothes and personal effects are burned, while the non-flammable items like jewellery are smashed up and thrown in the Easy.

It's done and can't be undone. They've gotten away with murder, but it doesn't feel like it. It never feels like it. The knowledge is always there, squatting inside them like a cancer.

57

'Then Ben asked me to help him get rid of the RV,' Walker says. 'Everything else he said they knew how to deal with. But something that size needed to disappear properly a long way away and he didn't know how to make it happen.'

'Ben was the one?' I ask. I picture the big man. That guarded nature of his, eyes wary and suspicious. And I wonder what set him off tonight, why he killed Christine and Gene. Whether he was the one who made Spin and Craig vanish, and whether he did the same to Penny. I think about what Stuart told me about the strange events at the bridge near their homes, the lunatic with the axe.

'Yeah. Him.'

'How did he know you?'

'He was friends with my uncle David. Had been for years, going way back. He knew from him that I'd been in trouble with the law. When I was younger, he used to drive into Fairlight and I'd meet up with him, sell him pot or set him on his way to whatever it was he wanted on the, ah, other side of things, right?'

'I think I get the picture. Drugs?'

He shrugs. 'Drugs, hookers. Whatever. Nothing

big in a town like that, but he needed help and I got a cut for sorting him out.'

'Nice.'

'Anyway, a year ago I was back home for a while, where my folks used to live, and he called me up out of the blue; I hadn't spoken to him in years. He asked if I could help him ditch a vehicle. He only told me what had happened when he realized just what kind of shit I'd been up to.' He shrugs. 'I guess he figured it made us the same, what he'd done and what he knew I did.'

'But it didn't?'

He shakes his head, snorts. 'We're a long way apart, him and me. And it's always gonna be like that.'

'In what way?'

'I ain't fuckin' crazy,' Walker says. 'He's batshit. You can trust me on that. Two states we drove in that RV. Found a nice bad neighbourhood in a nice big city, wiped it down and dumped it. Thing would've been torn to shreds for parts in hours. Anyway, that was a long old drive for him to be talking on. He told me what happened to them people, and he made it sound . . . not like he'd enjoyed it, but like he might just as well have been squashing bugs. And he talked about other stuff, things he thought or he'd heard or shit, and trust me, he is one fucked-up guy. He's always been kinda strange, but that . . .'

I realize I've still got the pistol in my hand and put it away. Walker's no threat to me, not now, not any more. 'You were going to blackmail him with what you knew?' I say. 'You were willing to take that risk with someone that odd? And besides, he doesn't strike me as the kind of guy to have a lot of cash.'

'Don't you believe it. Him and that weird-ass brother of his have a load stashed away that they don't talk about. They don't ever do anything with it, y'see. But I *know* he's got it, because I saw it back when I was helping him score drugs.' He shrugs. 'I don't know exactly how loaded he is, but I know he's got enough to get me and Ash away from here. Gonna go to Alaska, far as you can go from anything without leaving the country, and we're gonna start over.'

'That was the plan,' I say. I emphasize the 'was'; I can't see it working out now.

'Yeah, it was. I called Ben a couple of days ago, said we needed to talk. Said we had things to go over. I don't know if he knew what was coming or not, but he told me I'd have to come out here to meet him tonight. Time and place. Ash didn't want anyone knowing I was here, so she picked me up in town and said I could hide out until we had our meeting. I'd get the cash and then we'd fly away before people came looking for me.'

'Did you meet him yet, or is that still to come?'

'Yeah, I saw him. Saw him earlier this evening.' A wide, haunted look comes over Walker's face and he stares at the floor again. 'He said he'd have to find the money for me, but first I had to help him with something. He's fucked in the head, man. I'm telling you.'

'What did he want help with?'

'One of the bodies. He wanted me to help him dig up one of the bodies by the river. He dug it up, and he . . . well, he did something, and then we threw it in the river. He said we had to so no one would know what he'd done.'

Jesus Christ. 'What do you mean "did something"?'

'He cut it open.' Walker's voice is so low I can barely hear it over the wind thrumming against the trailer. 'The woman. He cut the woman open and he took a chunk out of her. It was so fucking gross, man. I don't know what he did with it afterwards.'

'And you went along with this?' I say.

'I didn't know that's what he was going to do, I swear. And when we got there . . . that's when I realized that he just wasn't right in the head. Not any more. Something'd gone real wrong in there, and I didn't want to risk having him turning on me. I was afraid. I really was.' Walker sniffs. 'Then he said we could go back to his place and sort out our business. The way he said it . . . the look in his eyes . . . Yeah, I ran when I got the chance. I don't know if he tried chasing me, but I ran like shit.'

'And you've been hiding here since?'

'Pretty much. I've been out a couple of times.'

'Why?'

He shrugs. 'Sometimes I think I've heard someone outside, someone creeping around. And . . . well, there's a feeling. Like this place isn't safe. So I go out, have a look around, make sure no one's on to me.'

'You didn't see me coming.'

'I didn't say I was perfect, just that it made me feel better. Less like a rabbit being hunted.'

'Did you see a little girl on any of these trips?'

'What?'

'One of the people killed tonight had his daughter with him. We were looking after her, but either she slipped out and ran off when we weren't looking, or someone took her. Did you see her?'

He shakes his head, and I can't see any sign of a lie in his eyes. 'No, sorry. So what're you going to do now?'

'*We* are going to go over to the roadhouse, and we're going to stop Ben.'

'Woah, woah. Me? I ain't doing shit. He'll kill me.'

'You want to protect your sister, this is the way to do it. Two of us. If I go in there with nothing but accusations, he could kill me. Especially if Tony's watching his back.'

I think about the younger brother. What I've seen of him and the way Walker described the Cross murders and his attitude to them. Maybe he wouldn't want things to turn ugly, but how it would be if Ben was threatened . . . I don't know.

Walker looks at me, picks up his gun and says, 'Fuck.'

I take that for agreement.

58

It's still dark outside and drizzle continues to blow down from the cloud roof, but everything out here feels like morning. There's a freshness to the atmosphere, air yet to be breathed and burned and dirtied by the day. A promise that change is on its way, just a couple of hours over the horizon. It might be night for now, but the end's in sight at long last.

It feels good.

It doesn't feel close enough.

When we cross the highway, I'm brought up short by the sight of Isaac sitting with his back against the door of his car, staring out across the deserted parking lot with a thoughtful look on his face. When he sees us, he breaks into a gruff smile.

'So you made it back? The MacBrides talked to you?' he says, voice quiet and steady. He doesn't look at me for long before dropping his eyes again.

'Yeah, they did.'

'Didn't think they would. I wonder how much they knew. Probably a whole lot.'

'Isaac . . .'

'Who's this?' he says, glancing up at the man next to me.

'This is Walker. That guy those people were after.

He's Ashley's brother, and she was helping him hide here. Isaac, what the hell happened?'

'Storm looks like it's over. Maybe things are changing. Take it as a sign.' He sighs. 'It's sure as shit been one hell of a night, huh? This place used to be real quiet. Nice that way, y'know? No trouble, nothing to bother a man. I used to like that.'

'I can imagine. We all want someplace quiet.'

'I guess we do. Never would've thought so when I was younger, though. I was such a dumb punk.'

The front of his coat is drenched in blood and punctured in a good three or four places. His skin's pale, lips smacking dryly as his body loses vital fluids, and his eyes aren't focused on anything much, lolling here and there as his brain tries to retain a grip on the world around it. The ground beneath him is dark with blood already.

He's dying and I know there's nothing I can do to stop it.

59

'What the hell happened?' I repeat the question, kneeling down next to the dying man.

'I don't know,' he says. 'I didn't see anything. I just came out here because Ben wanted a word with me in private, away from the others. I was waiting for him. Then someone was behind me. They grabbed me, pulled me back, and there was this pain in my chest. Took my breath away. Just paralysed me, y'know? I could see something moving, the knife, I guess, but my memory's all hazy now. All slipping away. I just kind of sat, started going cold. Hoped you'd find me, or the others'd come looking.'

'You didn't see the guy?' I light a cigarette. Isaac twitches his mouth like he wants one, so I oblige. Try the old joke, 'These things'll kill you.'

He smirks sleepily. 'I didn't see shit. I'm pretty sure it was a guy, but I don't remember it too clearly. Might've been Ben, might've been Will. I know either of them could do it. I always wondered that, whether you'd know what hit you when it hit you. Always wondered. Guess you don't.'

'I'll get help. Maybe we can patch you up.'

'Right.' He half snorts, half laughs. Then something crosses his face and he grabs my arm. His grip's firm, but doesn't last. 'There's . . . things I've got to tell. Before it's too late and I can't do it. And you're the only ones here. Don't you leave me. *Don't you leave me.* Not until you know.'

'I already know about the Cross family. I know what you all did.'

He nods slowly. 'It was never gonna last, that. As soon as you found them, I knew it.'

'If I get help we might be able to keep you alive.'

'Bullshit. I'm a dead man. Can't feel anything much already, 'cept the cold. Don't you leave me. *Don't you leave me.*' He sighs, makes an effort to draw air through the cigarette, but it just hangs limply from his lips. 'Don't wanna be . . . alone. Girl. Dead girl comin' and I don't wanna be alone.'

'Sure.' I picture the dead girl in my mind. Glance quickly around the parking lot half expecting to see her.

'We should never have done it. Didn't want it, but I couldn't . . . couldn't . . .' He blinks once or twice, leans in a little towards me, sharing a secret. He sounds sad, sorry for his own words and the thoughts behind them. 'Cross didn't deserve to get . . . get away with it. Shouldn't have done. Like in Iowa, years ago.'

I don't know if he means Cross or himself. 'Iowa? You knew Cross before all this?'

'No, no.' He shakes his head, sagging a little, muscles fading. Coughs, laughing, I think. 'Iowa. Asshole of the country. Place called Walnut. Cops . . . they asked a whole bunchastuff . . .' The words come out as one in a single exhale. His voice is becoming quieter and quieter. '. . . Asked everyone. What they'd seen and shit. I . . . I was worried. Scared. An' I couldn' stay. Couldn'. With all that . . . that there with me. So I came here. Getaway. Din' . . . din' wanna feel it any more.'

I flick my cigarette away into the darkness, say, 'So that's what you did.'

Isaac's breathing is coming slower and slower and his voice is dying. His eyes are closed now. Words come and go like a radio periodically losing reception and I find myself trying to fill in the blanks myself. Without much success. 'Samantha . . . Samantha. I thoughtabout Iowa . . . an . . . an thass why I wenalong with it. I . . . I wanted . . . see them pay, 'cause I hadn'. They . . . poor Samantha . . . she was . . . was nice . . . we . . . killed, killed . . .'

There's a thin hiss, the last of the air leaving his lungs, and Isaac says no more. He's a self-confessed accessory to murder, so I can't find much sympathy for him. And his death, out here in the open like this, makes me wonder how much has changed inside. If Ben's lost it completely and abandoned all caution, killing as he pleases.

Walker looks at me, about to say something, when a gunshot splits the air from the direction of the bar.

60

I burst through the front door, pistol already snug in my hand, Walker in tow. The atmosphere inside is rich with the ozone smell of gunfire and everything seems momentarily frozen in place. Will's standing stock still, staring at Ben. He's holding Isaac's shotgun. Ben has a revolver in his hands and a mechanical, dead look on his face. Smoke rises from the gun's barrel and I can see a bullet hole in the wall by the old man's head. A simple miss or a deliberate warning shot, I don't know. The front of Ben's jacket has blood on it. It doesn't look like his, so I'm guessing it's Isaac's. Ashley and Tony are staring at the two men, looking frightened and confused.

Ben glances at the two of us and shakes his head. 'Stop right there,' he says, voice sounding anything but sane. He sees Walker behind me and his eyes narrow sharply. 'You little shit. What're you doing here?'

'What's going on, Ben?' I say.

'What's necessary, that's all.'

'Payback?'

'Punishment. Atonement that's been long overdue.' His eyes are blank and his face is set. He looks almost sad. There's not an inch of give, not an ounce of hesitation in his body language. He means to kill us all and he's made his peace with that.

'For what you all did to the Crosses, or for what one of you did to Tracy MacBride?'

He says, 'Stuart talk to you, did he?'

'Yeah, he did. He's not the only person I found interesting things out from, though. It was either you or Tony having an affair with Tracy; seems pretty obvious now that it was you, this being the anniversary of her death, and you being the nut with the gun.'

'You've freaked out big-time, man,' Walker says, moving to stand next to me. Ashley glances at him, at me, and her eyes drop. Ashamed that her secret is out. That I know she was the one hiding this guy, even after everything he'd done, and that she'd kept that fact from me all night. That I know she's a liar. 'What the fuck did you need to do with that woman's body?' he continues. 'Why'd you *do* that?'

Ben licks his lips, eyes twitchy and nervous. 'Tony needed protecting. He's my brother and he didn't want us killing those people. They do all kinds of things with DNA and bullshit like that these days, and he didn't deserve bein' dragged into this when he didn't want it to happen.'

I turn towards the younger brother. His face has fallen, again, almost with shame. 'Me and Rhonda . . .' he begins, then his voice breaks and he lets the words trail away.

'I couldn't let them find out that kid would've been

yours. I shouldn't have done . . . what I did when we did, not if you didn't want me to. Not like that. Not when she was . . . only a couple of months, but still . . .' Tears begin to roll down the big man's face. 'I'm sorry, Tony. I'm so sorry. I'm so sorry.'

Walker spits on the floor. 'Some fuckin' brother you are. You killed her when she was gonna have your brother's baby? You're fucked up. I'm gonna enjoy knowing –'

The *crack* is near-deafening in the closed atmosphere of the bar. Walker's face erupts in a gout of red and pink and he drops like a sack of bricks. Ashley screams, a horrifying, skin-crawling sound tearing up from her guts, and runs over to him. With Ben's rage and attention focused on his former confidant, I see Will bring up the shotgun, about to make full use of his advantage over his cousin.

Then Tony runs forward and grapples with the old man. He's shouting something but, like his brother, he's crying, and the words are nothing more than babble. The two of them are trying to shake each other's grip loose on the gun, yelling incoherently into one another's face, when one of them pulls the trigger and Tony's throat vanishes into red mist.

61

When his brother dies, Ben whimpers like a spanked child. All the colour leaves his face and whatever bizarre emotions motivated him before, there's nothing left behind now but grief and fury. He turns the pistol on Will as the old man levels the shotgun at him. Will's eyes are pinched and cold, and I remember that Ben killed his wife only a few hours ago. Ashley's still crying next to Walker.

'Put the guns down, guys,' I say. 'This has gone far enough.'

'No. We deserve this,' Ben says. '*He* deserves this.'

'We could sort this out, Ben. We always did before.' The old man's voice is taut, controlled.

'You mean kill these other two and we'll tell the cops any story we want?'

Will nods slowly. I don't think he believes it. Says, 'It'd be a damn sight smarter.'

'Just like always, huh? This is your fault. If you hadn't beaten that guy so bad in the first place . . .'

'You didn't have to do what you did to his wife. We could still have worked something out.'

'You and Christine were the ones who didn't want any trouble coming back to you for what you did,'

Ben says. His face is like poured concrete. 'There wasn't any other way and you know it. I don't remember you having any trouble pulling the trigger when you had to either. You didn't blink when you did it.'

'That was different. You know what that man did to Sam. Jesus Christ, Ben. I couldn't let that son of a bitch get away with what he did to my little girl.'

'And he didn't, and neither did his family. You should be happy.'

Will shakes his head, voice choking as he says, 'I did that to protect her. I'd have done anything to see her OK, not to see her suffer. She deserved a better life. But I had to live with that. You killed my wife in cold blood when there was no reason to.'

'There was every reason to. We did wrong. All of us, including you. Both of you. She had blood on her hands the same as everyone else,' he says. 'And you and her were the ones got us into that mess. She didn't have no problem with what you done, nor with getting the rest of us involved. Making us all guilty. You and her were both happy with killing, so long as it suited you. So don't act like she didn't have it coming. Like right now, you killed Tony. Why'd you do that? Why'd you have to pull that trigger? He never hurt no one.'

'Ben, Christine wasn't the only one you killed tonight,' I say, keeping my voice quiet, conciliatory. 'You killed those two guys, Craig and Spin, who ran off after the shootout . . .'

'I knew they were no good. They deserved what they got when they ran into me. Chickenshit scum were already scared half to death when they met me. I gave them what they had coming. They earned that pain. And it was quicker than it might have been.'

'. . . and you killed Gene.'

'The trucker?'

'The trucker. You stabbed him in front of his little girl. *He* didn't deserve that, and neither did she. He didn't do anything to the Crosses, but his child had to watch you stab her father to death. Neither of them had earned something like that.'

The big man shakes his head a little, a sad, solemn movement. 'He saw me. Or I thought he saw me. Coming out of Christine's, y'know? I didn't realize he was there when I went inside; I was sure he'd seen me coming out. I'd just been trying to avoid Will. I didn't know about him.'

'Did you take care of his little girl the same way for the same reason once you knew she'd seen you kill her father, you sick son of a bitch? What exactly did she do to earn that?' My voice is laced with contempt for the big man's feeble justifications. 'Did she need to die so you could protect your dirt-farming existence here? Or were you not planning on leaving anyone to survive the night?'

Ben says nothing, but what sounds like a thin growl escapes his throat. I don't know which way to take that, but I guess I've hit close to the mark.

'And you, Will,' I say. 'You shot Billy Cross in the

face after you'd done beating on him when other people in that situation might have realized what they were doing, the path they were going down, and stopped. Don't pretend to yourself that you've never done evil. All of you back then killed those folks. Man, woman and child. An entire family. Just to protect your good names.'

Will shakes his head. His face sets like granite. 'You weren't there. You don't understand.'

'I understand you wanted revenge for the rape of your granddaughter, so you beat the living shit out of the guy responsible. Maybe I can even sympathize a little. But then your actions made everyone else join in, have yourselves a good ol' fashioned lynching. Ben killed Rhonda Cross and then because you were all murderers, you decided to finish off the rest of the family to make sure you wouldn't get in any trouble. You even killed their little boy. A fucking *child*. Even apart from anything else, you deserve to rot for that. All of it because you didn't have the goddamn balls to accept responsibility for your own actions.' I feel like spitting on the old man. 'You both deserve whatever's coming to you.'

'Deserve it?' Will says. His voice is scratchy, face stern, angry. 'I'll tell you who deserved what they got – Billy Cross. That sorry son of a bitch earned everything he got and more, after what he did to my Samantha. That man tore our lives apart.' There are tears in Will's eyes. 'My little girl had to live with what he did for the rest of her life, and there was nothing

367

anyone could do that could ever make her forget it, make her what she was before. Death was too good for him. You have any idea how difficult things were for her after that happened? How hard it was for us? And we all had to figure out how to make sure she knew how much we loved her without making her afraid.

'Of course she wanted to get away from here,' he continues. 'And who could blame her? I got her a job way out west and I never saw her again. We'd talk on the phone, and she'd write, but she wouldn't come back, not with the memory of what that man did to her. She had nightmares for weeks, months afterwards. You know that? Couldn't sleep. It's like she had to learn how to live all over again. And in the end, it killed her.'

'That doesn't justify what you did, and you know it.'

'I would've done anything for those two girls. It was bad enough that Jennifer wouldn't talk to us ...' he says, then stops himself. 'Won't talk to me, not at all, not for years. I couldn't see Sam destroyed like that. I just wanted both of them to have the lives they deserved. Not like him.' He gestures at Ben. 'He's just a psycho. He's snapped.'

The big man shakes his head. 'I wanted a life once, too. It never happened and I learned to watch out for what was mine. So fuck all of you.'

When he says that, the final piece clicks into place. The sheer promise and commitment in Will's voice when he talks about giving his two grandkids a better life, and the bitterness in Ben's as he talks about the one taken from him.

'You killed Tracy MacBride,' I say to Will.

62

'Ben was having an affair with her, and you ran her down on the road. Fifteen years ago today. That's right, isn't it, Ben? This is why you picked tonight? Walker coming here to blackmail you was just the final straw.'

The two men glare at one another. The old man's gaze frosted with guilt and long bitterness, Ben's with rage and a sense of old suspicions confirmed. I laugh once, shake my head.

'All this,' I say, 'everything, it all started with that bullshit property development, didn't it? You and Christine wanted to sell to Willis and use the money to move away to somewhere better for the kids. But the two brothers and the MacBrides were happy here and wanted to fight.'

'You don't know anything,' Will says through gritted teeth.

'Tracy MacBride was the one who was trying to organize everyone and get them working together to stop the construction in its tracks. She was holding all your plans up and you couldn't take it. You didn't want your grandkids' lives to be nothing more than a flea-pit gas station in the middle of nowhere and half a dozen people who only live in a place like this because nowhere better would take them. You couldn't let her put an end to your dream, could you? So you waited until she was on her way back up the valley and you ran her down in your truck. It's not as personal as shooting her, but it was just as deadly.'

Ben's hands flex on his gun and I can see the murder burning in his eyes. 'And you, Ben, you'd gotten it into your head that Tracy might move down the valley and stay with you. Leave her husband and her family behind. You'd never settled down with anyone before, and here was a woman who seemed interested in you. But it would never have happened. She wanted to feel something outside of her day-to-day life up the valley, just to remind herself of the outside world. She would've had enough sooner or later and this dream of yours would've died.'

'Shut the fuck up.'

'I've talked to Stuart. He knew his wife probably better than she realized, and I've got no reason to doubt him. She loved him and he knew she'd never leave. Maybe one of you was deluding themselves, but I guess that doesn't matter – she died and everything changed. You lost it. You stopped caring about anything or anyone else. And look where it led, especially for your brother.'

'No . . .'

'Yes. And Will never got what he wanted from killing Tracy because MacBride was so devastated by what happened that he was willing to kill to exact revenge. He didn't know who'd done it, but he knew why – the money. So he grabbed the developer, Willis, and killed your dreams of selling for a better life instead. And this valley's been nothing but resentment, bitterness and anger ever since.' Disgust courses through every word I spit. 'All of you, locked in a cycle of greed and self-interest. I don't know if anyone else suffered for it in the time between, but it certainly came round again fifteen years later. You were all happy so long as you came out on top, with your money or your revenge, and it didn't matter whose blood or how much of it you had to wade through to get it. You both make me sick to my stomach.'

Silence falls over the bar for a second. Then Ben takes in a great, shuddering breath and says to Will, 'You killed Trace. You killed her. Why did you kill her?'

Before the old man can respond, Ashley stands up with Walker's gun in her hands. She's shaking badly, tears streaked down her face, as she levels it at Ben. She says in a thick voice, 'And you shot my brother. You shot my kid fucking brother.'

63

The two men look at her, at one another, each trying to figure out their moves. Each wondering if they can cover both the others safely.

'Brother?' Will says. He looks baffled.

'Evan Walker was Ashley's brother,' I tell him. 'She still uses her married name. I guess her uncle was her mom's brother. Walker helped Ben hide the Cross's RV after the killings. He came back out here to blackmail Ben, clean him out of cash, so he could take him and Ashley away to start a new life somewhere else. That was the plan, but it went screwy real quickly.'

She sniffs hard, chokes back a sob. 'He was my baby brother. You killed him, you son of a bitch.'

'Your brother was a murderer and a thug, Ashley. I know he was family, but he knew what he was getting into when he did the things he did. Life just caught up with him. Don't put yourself in his corner now; he's dead, he doesn't need you looking out for him.'

'I wasn't involved in any of what he did, Alex. You've got to know that. We just wanted to start again.'

'But you *were* involved, Ashley,' I tell her. 'The

moment you agreed to go away with him on the back of money that wasn't his, that he earned through helping these two hide their crimes . . . The moment you sheltered him, you became involved. You're not stupid, you knew that was what it meant.'

'What was I supposed to do? Tell him I wasn't going to help him? He was family.'

'You know what he did. You knew what he was going to do.'

She shakes her head. 'He never told me and I never asked. He was my brother and I loved him. You think I should've had him go to jail instead? My own fucking brother?'

'He made his choices and he should've faced the consequences. Don't join him by acting this way.' I can feel a tugging in my chest. A yearning for her to see what she's doing, to see the error in it, and pull back from the brink.

'Evan and me . . . well, it wasn't always easy growing up. Especially out here in the sticks. Mom and Dad did what they could, but it wasn't like we had much money and there wasn't much to do when we were young. He wasn't a bad guy,' Ashley says. 'He'd get into trouble and stuff, but that was just because he was bored and frustrated, and getting into trouble for it just made him feel worse. He'd break stuff and do dumb things just because he could, like he couldn't see any point either way. Just stupid juvenile shit, but, still, it was his thing.'

'Ashley,' I say. 'Don't try to defend him here. I

374

talked to him, and I know what he was. What I'm trying to say is that you don't have to do this. Let this go, please. Walk away from it.'

'He wasn't a bad guy. He just got into all sorts of drugs and shit down south and it messed him up. That and the people he was with. So yeah, he did some bad things, I know, but he wasn't a bad guy underneath. It's just, well, like a habit. He does things like they're a habit. But he didn't deserve to die. He could've changed once we were away from here. I know he could.'

The other two men have stayed still and silent through most of this exchange, probably trying to figure out whether she's really dangerous or not, and which one of them has the most to fear from her. 'You,' she says to Ben, 'you killed my brother. I loved him; it didn't matter what he'd done. How dare you? How dare you?'

'Ashley,' I soften my voice. 'Let this go.'

'I can't.' The tears begin falling again.

'You can. Don't follow the same path these two have. Please.' I lower my gun, put it away, and hold out my hand to her. 'Revenge, even if you take it and survive, will only take you to the same place that Will and Ben are at now. And there's nothing there. It's not worth it. And right now, you've not started on that road.'

'I'm so sorry, Alex.'

'You don't have to fall into the same pattern as everyone else who comes to this place, Ashley. There's years of bad blood here, but you have the choice. You can break the pattern. You can come away, now, with me. Choose something else and let the past stay where it is. Both these men are going to get what's coming to them, one way or another. You can walk away right now.'

If I could grab her, haul her away by force, pull her back from the edge, I would. But if I touch her, if I break the spell, I'm afraid she'll act, shoot me, shoot Ben. Do something that will taint her for ever and end all this in blood.

'Please, Ashley,' I say.

She's crying freely now, like she knows where this is heading. 'He was my brother, Alex.'

Ben glances at her, at Will. The revolver wobbles between the two of them. 'Put that gun down, Ben,' the old man says. 'Put it down right now. Both of you. This has got to end.'

'The hell with the pair of you.' Ben's fist tightens on the grip.

All three of them covering each other. Guns drawn, hands twitching, sweat prickling on their brows.

64

'Whatever happens here,' I say, 'you two haven't got any place to go. The cops will show up and you're going to have to work real hard to explain all this without the truth coming out. Neither of you is going to have anyone here to help you lie this time, and you can't hide these deaths.'

'I'm an old man with a dead wife. Cops'll believe whatever I want them to believe.'

Ben shakes his head. 'They'll believe you killed her. And they'll believe I stopped you killing me too.'

'Ashley,' I try one last time, 'you're the only one who can still walk away from this. You sheltered your brother, but you haven't done anything to put you with these two. You can leave if you want, with me. Right now. You want a different life, you could come with me, see what happens.'

She just shakes her head, eyes still on Ben. My heart sinks.

The room falls silent for a moment. Even the air seems still, locked in place. The dim light from the candles, competing now with the deep blue glow from outside, is steady and fixed. Nothing moves.

'Will, Ben, you two are just as bad as each other,' I say. 'Both of you. And you know what? I don't give a damn about what the pair of you do or don't do. The shit you've done, that you were willing to do. For what?' I pull up the collar on my coat and light a cigarette, trying to keep my hands from shaking. 'Those who are dead will still be dead, no matter what you do or what I do. And you've both fucked up your lives by allowing yourselves to be filled by revenge and greed. It's cost you both everyone you've ever loved. Fuck the pair of you.'

I turn to Ashley. 'If you change your mind, if you want another chance, you can come with me. Catch up with me on the road, look me up when all this is over. You've got that choice, Ashley. You don't have to do this,' I say again.

As I move slowly towards the door, Will yells behind me, 'Don't you go anywhere, Alex. You walk out and I'll shoot you myself. You can't leave.'

'Maybe you will,' I say. 'And a shit lot of good it'll do you. Both of you. Any of you. It's time you learned that.'

I push open the door and wedge my hands deep in my pockets as I step out on to the gravel. No bullets. No gunfire. Nothing. It swings shut behind me again and I'm alone in the inky morning twilight. The cloud above is black and heavy still, but ragged, losing its consistency as it begins to shred.

The breeze is fresh and cold as I walk across the parking lot. I wonder if the river's dropped back to normal, if I can swim or wade across. How far I'll have to walk until I reach the nearest town.

I'm a couple of hundred yards down the highway when two sharp crackling gunshots split the air, echoing in the emptiness. I could turn around, go back and see. But I don't want to know, not for sure. Not that way. If Ashley makes it out and she wants to, she'll come after me. Sometimes it's better not to know for certain. And after everything that's happened out here, everything they've done, I never want to see either of the other two again.

Two crows wheel overhead and swoop away to the north. My eyes turn to follow them and as they do I think I see two small figures walking away into the grass. Penny, hand in hand with the Cross boy. Stepping with tottering child strides from one tuft to the next, free and uncaring, laughing in each other's company as they vanish into the green horizon.

I smile. The new day is here and I walk right into it.

65

It doesn't take me long to find Jennifer Middleton, the one remaining person who could possibly have written the note that took me out to the valley. When I find out she's working in a Detroit hotel – the same one which played host to the job I took shortly before receiving the note from Sam – I at last understand why I was chosen, how she knew where to send the message.

When she sees me waiting for her at the end of her shift, she doesn't act surprised. I don't know if word has reached the outside world yet of what happened in the valley, if she knows what's become of the rest of her family. She had apparently already done her best to cut them out of her life, so maybe not. We go to a diner near by and talk over cholesterol and coffee.

'Did you find them?' she says. Jennifer looks only a little like her sister, or at least like the photo of her taken outside Will's gas station. Her hair's shorter, carved into spikes and swirls. An angry, aggressive style very different to what anyone would expect with her family and background. The noise of the diner around us sounds wrong, all wrong, after the valley.

'The Crosses?' I say. 'Yeah, I did. You sent me the note?'

She nods. 'I ... I didn't want it hidden any more.'

'Why? Why so long after it happened? And why not just tell me everything you knew straight out?'

'Because you'd ask questions, and you'd ask the same ones of my granddad. And if you did that then he might know they came from me, that I'd told you everything, and I'd be in danger.'

'Really?'

'I ... yeah.'

'Danger, from Will?'

She looks down. 'What he's capable of ... I mean, especially because he idolized Sam. I don't think he ever liked me.'

'Why not just go to the cops?'

'They'd never have believed me, and what did I have to tell them? That a family called the Crosses were killed in that valley before my sister moved away and that I had no idea what happened to them or where exactly they were buried? Would you pay much attention to a story like that?'

I shrug, let the point go. 'So why'd you wait so long? Your sister had been dead several months by the time you contacted me.'

'She was.' Jennifer plays with her coffee cup. 'You've gotta understand, I had to think about it. About everything. Knowing what had happened, and what she'd done . . . I had to try to figure out what was the right thing to do.'

'You didn't know if you should get your grandparents in trouble?'

'No. No, not that. I've known . . .'

She trails off. I wait a moment for her to finish, then say, 'Known what?'

'I knew my granddad had killed someone once. Years ago, when I was a kid. I was playing outside and I saw blood on the bull bar of his pickup. He washed it, of course, but I still saw it. And then they said a woman had been killed on the highway in a hit and run.'

'Tracy MacBride.'

She nods. 'I knew it was him. And at the same time I didn't know if you understand me. I couldn't be sure, y'know? But I wanted to get away from there as soon as that happened. I wanted out.'

'That's why you don't talk to them any more?'

'Yes,' Jennifer says. 'I didn't want anything to do with my granddad, and I couldn't believe Gran didn't know. If I did, she must've done.'

'Actually, I don't think she did,' I say. 'She seemed completely in the dark about what happened back then. All she knew was that it wasn't Will having an affair with Tracy.'

'Oh.'

I finish my coffee. 'So when Sam moved out to Colorado, she ended up telling you what had happened?'

'She did. She was so cut up about it. I mean, really, really shattered by it emotionally, and she just needed to talk. I didn't know she was feeling so bad that she'd end up killing herself. If I had . . .'

'It wasn't her fault,' I say. 'What Billy Cross did wasn't anything to do with her.'

Jennifer shakes her head and won't, can't meet my eyes. 'I thought maybe you knew,' she said. 'I don't know how, but I hoped you did. Billy Cross never raped my sister, Mr Rourke. It was all a lie.'

66

The news hits me like a punch to the kidneys. 'She *lied*? Cross never raped her? What the hell happened?'

'What Sam told me,' Jennifer says, trying to choke back tears, trying to hold back a wave of transplanted guilt, 'is that he did everything short of that. She thought he might. He was always pawing at her, waiting for her after work . . . stalking her, I guess. And she hated him. She said he made her skin crawl. And he just wouldn't leave her alone, no matter what she told him. For weeks. Months.'

'Did she tell your grandparents?'

Jennifer nods. 'They tried to keep an eye on him, hoping he'd go away. But it didn't do any good. And then one day he came by while they were away and she said he was worse than ever. And she was so afraid that next time would be the last time . . .'

'So she told Will he'd raped her and begged him not to go to the cops.'

'She wanted him to run Cross out of the valley, to scare him away.' Jennifer wipes away the tears that are running down her cheeks freely, silently. 'She thought he'd send him and his family packing, threaten them so they'd never come back.'

I shake my head. 'Jesus.'

'And that's what they told her they'd done. That he'd run off with his family and she'd never see them again.'

'How did she find out the truth?'

'The guy who runs the bar – I don't remember his name – he got drunk one night and she said it just came pouring out of him. What they'd done, killing all three of them to stop anyone being able to tell what they'd done. To stop her granddad going to jail for beating on Billy Cross. How she was safe from him now, and how no one would miss a guy like him.' Jennifer's face is covered by her hands now and I'm having a hard time making out her words through the sobs. 'And she knew what she'd done. She tried to leave, to make a new start, but she couldn't stop feeling . . . And then it all got too much and . . .'

'And she killed herself. The only way she could escape her sense of guilt.'

'I couldn't let her do that and have everyone else get away with it, I just couldn't. I wanted to find someone who could uncover what they'd done and stop them doing anything like that again. And then there was that thing at the hotel, and you were there, and I asked the manager who you were . . .'

The words tumble out of her without pause now. Then the tears overcome her and she folds her head into her arms and bawls like a child. And this is where my life has led me. Everything I once had gone. Chasing other people's secrets until they're finally all used up and I'm sitting in a shabby diner with a woman I don't know who's crying and sobbing in front of me, feeling a dozen eyes I can't see watching us with a mixture of pity and disgust. And knowing how futile and wretched it all is. How easy it is to destroy everything we claim to love.

Jennifer begins to quieten and I say, 'You sent me that note and it got a lot of people killed.'

'It runs in the family,' she says.

JOHN RICKARDS

WINTER'S END

They have the body of a slaughtered woman.

They have a half-naked man standing over her.

They have no idea how to make him talk.

And so they call in ex-FBI interrogator Alex Rourke to the traumatized Maine town of Winter's End. The Boston Private Investigator knows the place well – it's where he grew up. But as Rourke probes the mind of the enigmatic 'Nicholas', he is forced to re-examine his hometown and his own past – and what he finds is a place built on secrets.

Strange things have been happening in Winter's End. The question is why. And if the man in custody does hold the answers to crimes both present and past, then Alex will have to get to them – and quickly. Because it soon becomes clear that what Nicholas has been waiting for from the beginning – is Alex Rourke.

'A clever, gripping and original thriller' *Time Out*

'Grips you from its chilling opening scene to its stunning conclusion. A fine debut' Peter Robinson

JOHN RICKARDS

THE TOUCH OF GHOSTS

Boston private investigator Alex Rourke is looking forward to the weekend. He's heading to Vermont to visit his girlfriend, and also plans to do some checking on his latest missing-person case: a young man named Adam Webb who made the same journey, and never came back.

But the truth about Adam Webb isn't the only secret buried in the Green Mountain woods. Hikers have gone missing, a prostitute has been murdered, and something sinister is happening in the ghost-town of North Bleakwater. It soon becomes clear that in the mountains, who you trust can mean the difference between life and death. And Alex will have to make decisions with his heart as well as his head.

Because a single bullet is about to blow his world to pieces.

'Compelling psychological thriller which marks Rickards out as a key new voice in crime thriller fiction' *Crime Time*

JOHN RICKARDS

THE DARKNESS INSIDE

Seven years ago, Cody Williams was the FBI's prime suspect in a series of horrific New England abductions.

Seven years ago Alex Rourke put Cody Williams behind bars.

Now Cody Williams is dying. He wants to set the record straight.

And he'll only talk to Alex …

Former FBI agent Rourke has successfully re-invented himself as a private detective, but he's still haunted by the Williams case. And facing the monster again will mean squaring up to some demons from the past. For Cody has nothing left to lose – and a big final hand to play.

For when it appears that one of Cody's victims, Holly Tynon, might still be alive but still held hostage, Alex is left to make a terrible choice that, either way, will mean the end of at least one life …

He just wanted a decent book to read ...

Not too much to ask, is it? It was in 1935 when Allen Lane, Managing Director of Bodley Head Publishers, stood on a platform at Exeter railway station looking for something good to read on his journey back to London. His choice was limited to popular magazines and poor-quality paperbacks – the same choice faced every day by the vast majority of readers, few of whom could afford hardbacks. Lane's disappointment and subsequent anger at the range of books generally available led him to found a company – and change the world.

'We believed in the existence in this country of a vast reading public for intelligent books at a low price, and staked everything on it'
Sir Allen Lane, 1902–1970, founder of Penguin Books

The quality paperback had arrived – and not just in bookshops. Lane was adamant that his Penguins should appear in chain stores and tobacconists, and should cost no more than a packet of cigarettes.

Reading habits (and cigarette prices) have changed since 1935, but Penguin still believes in publishing the best books for everybody to enjoy. We still believe that good design costs no more than bad design, and we still believe that quality books published passionately and responsibly make the world a better place.

So wherever you see the little bird – whether it's on a piece of prize-winning literary fiction or a celebrity autobiography, political tour de force or historical masterpiece, a serial-killer thriller, reference book, world classic or a piece of pure escapism – you can bet that it represents the very best that the genre has to offer.

Whatever you like to read – trust Penguin.